# Tom Sawyer's
# Civil War Chronicles

# Tom Sawyer's Civil War Chronicles

John Bradley Jones

*Foreword by David L. Johnson*

RESOURCE *Publications* · Eugene, Oregon

TOM SAWYER'S CIVIL WAR CHRONICLES

Resource Publications
An Imprint of Wipf and Stock Publishers
199 W. 8th Ave., Suite 3
Eugene, OR 97401

www.wipfandstock.com

PAPERBACK ISBN: 978-1-7252-9188-1
HARDCOVER ISBN: 978-1-7252-9189-8
EBOOK ISBN: 978-1-7252-9190-4

03/05/21

This book is dedicated to my wife of fifty years
for her steadfast love of an imperfect man.
To God for his infinite mercy
To my wife who sacrificed much on my behalf
To Mr. Samuel Clemens for his imagination and inspiration

"My oft expressed desire is that all citizens, white or black, native or foreign born, may be left free, in all parts of our common country to vote, speak and act, in obedience to law, without intimidation or ostracism on account of his views, color or nativity."

HIRAM ULYSSES GRANT, JULY 28, 1872

# Contents

# Foreword

In the concluding chapter of his famous first novel, *The Adventures of Tom Sawyer,* Mark Twain informs the reader that most of the book's characters were, in fact, drawn from real people who were then (at the time the book was published, in 1876) still living. "Some day it may seem worth while to take up the story of the younger ones again and see what sort of men and women they turned out to be; therefore, it will be wisest not to reveal any of that part of their lives at present."

Nearly 150 years later, John Bradley Jones has risen to Twain's challenge—and produced a remarkable novel that faithfully carries forward those characters of Tom Sawyer and Rebecca Thatcher. Tom and Rebecca are, indeed, fully grown up, and now, from the opening shots of the Battle of Bull Run, thrust into a world of fear and war far distant from the seemingly carefree days of their earlier years. Tom's sense of risk and adventure (and Becky's basic common sense) are all still recognizably present. But the world of Civil War America, in some ways so much like the world in which we find ourselves today, brought a spotlight to deep and passionate division. Seemingly well understood and widely shared concepts of integrity, patriotism and loyalty could suddenly trigger controversy, conflict and loss. Yet such times could (and can) also lead to genuine love and hope, in the hearts of the right characters. And in the hands of the right author to tell their story.

John Jones is the perfect guide to take Tom Sawyer's story forward, and to show all of what Tom, indeed, could turn out to be. An avid reader of fiction, an eager student of Civil War history, and a shrewd observer of human foibles (and grace), John also has a deep faith in God and in the possibility of human redemption. His is a faith that shines through in this work. I have known John, as a family friend and fellow Civil War fan, for nearly thirty years. His own constant values of dedication, family, friendship—and fun—are all abundantly present in the pages that follow. He ably recounts moments, battles, leaders and personalities of a transformative time. John also shows how seemingly average (if fictionally famous) "main street" Americans can come to play such a consequential role in preserving a nation, and moving it forward.

There are good and important lessons here for all of us. And like everything that has forever been connected with Tom Sawyer, there is also a great adventure ahead.

**David L. Johnson**
Author, *Learning from My Father:*
*Lessons in Life and Faith*
Indianapolis, November 2020

# Preface

I have always been a fan of Mr. Samuel Clemens and his writings. As I was re-reading The Adventures of Tom Sawyer, one paragraph contains Judge Thatcher's wish to see Tom as a great lawyer or a great soldier. I took this as a sign that God was affirming an idea for my novel. I thought about the notion of Tom Sawyer growing into manhood and what this life might be like. The Civil War seemed the perfect setting for his next big adventure. Thus my wife's wish for something to keep me occupied during retirement was at least partially fulfilled.

My fascination with the Civil War started long before I retired. It was hard to imagine so brutal a contest on American soil. I was curious to see if any members of my family fought in the War. I did find some ancestral links to the war and was proud of their service. I knew I needed to increase my knowledge of the Civil War if I was to have any chance of writing a credible novel. I went to the library, bargain book stores, and online purchases to get research material. There came a point where I felt sufficiently knowledgeable to begin the book. I began blending the historical account of the war with Mr. Clemens' fictional characters. During subsequent drafts, I found the characters taking on a life of their own. The writing became a labor of love.

It took me three years of patiently reading, writing, and fact-checking using both the internet and written texts to complete the first draft. When the first draft was completed, I wanted to visit some of the locations in the novel. My wife agreed to take a Civil War vacation. Visiting some of the locations helped me gain a better frame of reference for some scenes in the book. After the trip, I made significant changes to the novel. Six drafts later, I had converted additional narrative into dialog for clarity. I had some help from a local writer's group to accomplish this task. This novel satisfied my burning desire to create a story that would entertain, raise the importance of faith, the injustice of slavery, and provide interest in the events surrounding the Civil War. The Civil War took over 600,000 American lives. Faithful on both sides believed in God and the cause they were fighting for.

# Introduction

I am Tom Sawyer. This is a story about my adventures during the Civil War. I don't mean it complete or boastful, but it seemed relevant enough for me to chronical my experience. I will leave the judgment part up to you. I was lucky that my experiences as a youth didn't leave me dead long ago. But as I grew, I found my sense of adventure still needed to be fulfilled. Thanks to a small sum of money and a lot of study I became a lawyer. Judge Thatcher took me to task until such time as I was able to practice on my own. He taught me that God should be the most important thing in my life, and putting God first made me whole. I took this to heart and became a leader in the community of faith. He seemed to know that my adventurous spirit would not stand for me lawyering for long. He used his political connections with an Illinois congressman to secure me an appointment to West Point. I took to fretting over my acceptance as it meant lots of discipline. Seeing my free nature bottled up like this took considerable thought but in the end, I relented. That's where I met Sam Grant. You will discover in the chronicles that having Sam as a friend was a real blessing. It was also where I got into the biggest adventures of my life.

I hope you will gain some bits of knowledge about the war from this writing. It was a terrible time in our history. These chronicles are meant to point to some things I learned about God, love, faith, and, manhood during my years in the army. I wrote it to let you know that no matter how dark things seem, having faith in God will always help. Yes, I did some stupid thing during the course of my army time, and for that, I ask the readers forgiveness. I consider it a part of recognizing I am human and will make mistakes. Reading The Adventures of Tom Sawyer by Mark Twain, may refresh your memory about my childhood.

The Chronicles begin on July 21, 1861, at a place called Manassas in Prince William County, Virginia. It is my first regimental command as a Major of the 79th New York infantry. During the fight, I am seriously wounded, and spend some time in a field hospital. I make friends with a man named Silas who cares after me. I had no idea that this friendship would change my life. As part of my duties in the Army I am given the choice to become a spy for the union army or resign my commission. It all makes for some harrowing experiences and is the reason I wrote these events down for you.

# 1

## The Young Rebel

A butterfly flitted amongst the clover. It's funny how a simple thing can trigger memories. It all came flooding back; the river, the sunshine, the joy of playing pirates with Huck Finn and Joe Harper. But this—this was not child's play. This was war. My Lieutenant's gruff voice snapped me back to the business at hand.

"Major Sawyer, the troops have been supplied and are ready, sir. The brigade officers are on their way to meet with you."

"Thank you, Lieutenant. And Lieutenant, make damn sure everyone has sixty rounds of ammunition."

"Yes sir, sixty rounds." he saluted and spun his horse around.

Soon I was surrounded by the brigade officers. Most were innocent young faces, thirsting for battle, with no idea of the horror that awaited them.

"Men, I am Major Thomas Sawyer, just assigned to your brigade. For many of you, this will be your first taste of war. While I haven't had the opportunity to be with you long, I've fought in Mexico and know the realities of war. You must bolster your courage, for this will truly be a test for us all. Have your companies form in line of battle on the far-right of the 79th. Do not advance until you hear the command. Dismissed."

As the battle raged on our right flank, Colonel Cameron shouted, "79th New York, forward!" The regimental bugler sounded the charge.

I saw the line stretching before me, a sea of men in blue, colorful insignias, flags waving in the breeze. Were it not for the horror that awaited it was a grand sight. I pulled my horse to the front of our line and was greeted with cannon fire bursting nearby. Fear grasped me hard as I resolutely pointed my sword forward, and we began to move. Cannon fire ripped apart the earth and men crumpled to the ground. A few cowards dropped their weapons fleeing the ranks only to be rounded up by reserves. A few men froze when the firing began and had to be forced forward. The line moved with fits and jerks as if it were a snake without a head. The first volley of fire from the Confederate infantry drove us back.

"Lieutenant, reform, shift right, shift right! Fill in the lines with reserves and get them to the front double-quick!" I clenched my teeth.

As I rode ahead, walls of minié balls came zipping past like swarms of bees. A cannonball split the line a few feet from me, and several men who had been there just seconds earlier disappeared in an eruption of earth.

"Fill in your ranks, fire! fire!"

"Major—Rebels on the left flank, sir."

"Shift the line left, double quick. Bring up the reserves!"

"Yes, sir."

The maneuver was too slow. Sulfurous smoke filled the air, and my view of the men faded in and out as the smoke grew thicker. The front line halted. I turned to them, waving my sword.

"Rally round me men, rally round me, on to Richmond!"

A noise rose above the sounds of war and pierced the cannon and musket fire. It was like no noise I ever heard before. It was the Rebels, delivering a high-pitched scream as they counter charged. It sounded like a thousand eagles, all screaming at once.

"Hold your position! Fire! Fire!" I screamed.

I lay on my horse's neck as the next volley came, and the horse was shot dead beneath me. We tumbled forward, landing in a ravine beside a large tree. The second line of the 79th and reserves streamed past me now, in full retreat. I drew my pistol, aimed at the smoke-shrouded line of men in gray heading toward me, and fired.

Emerging down the ravine I was in were more Rebels. I reloaded my pistol and looked up. There, standing just feet apart from me, a young Rebel soldier. He was just a boy of maybe 15 years. He had a strange look on his face, a look of fear mingled with pain. Blood ran down his cheek from a wound on his forehead. We both stood transfixed for just a second or two. He pointed his musket at me, and I pointed my pistol at him. I fired, striking him in the chest. At that same instant, he fired his musket at me. His shot hit a tree limb next to me and ricocheted off. Pain hit my left shoulder, and it felt as though it had been ripped from my body. The impact spun me around, and I landed face to the ground, pinning my right arm beneath me. Overrun by the Rebels, I lay motionless. The smell of grass, dirt, and gunpowder filled my nose. Gradually, the sound of the battle faded.

I spit the dirt from my mouth. "Hello, please help me."

I heard only musket fire and the distant groans of other wounded echoing the same cry across the field. I resolved not to die in this field, under these circumstances, with this young lifeless body lying just feet from me.

"Help me!"

It was only later that I recalled what occurred after I lost consciousness.

> *The blackness overcame me, and I thought, I'm here God—Right here. I tried lighting a lantern, but the matches were wet. Strike one, strike two. My hands shook. The matches fell to the ground. I knew God was there, but the only way to see was to get that lantern lit. Everything was wet, cold, and foreboding. This must be the road to heaven, I thought. Peace overcame me. I saw myself lying there in that ravine with the dead and dying all around. I went up and up, away from the horror of war, away from the acrid smoke, away from the guns and the violence. A bright light surrounded me, and I felt as if joy was mine. My spirit was afresh, and there was no more weakness, no more sorrow, and no more pain. I felt safe, warm, and secure. "Tom. Tom, you need to go back." "No!"*

My eyes opened. My forehead felt like a hundred ants were marching into my eyes. I realized the ants were beads of stinging sweat. I wanted to go back where I had been, but reality and the pain wouldn't let me. I could see nothing but a watery world and kept blinking to clear away the sweat.

"Help me!" Distant rumbles of cannon answered.

"Help me!"

"Oh, oh, I am dying," exclaimed a voice from a few yards away.

I prayed, *"God, if you're with me right now, help me get the hell out of here."* I used my right arm to push myself up. My hand felt something warm and soft. I turned my head slightly and saw my hand inside the torso of what was left of Private Lars Winston. He was cut in two, and only his upper half remained. He stared into the distance with the glassy fixed gaze of a man frozen in time. I pulled my blood-covered hand back and used my elbow to prop myself up. I remember thinking what a waste it would be should I die here. My law degree, my service in the army, all of it was a big waste. The next thing I remember, a voice.

"Major . . . Major!"

I felt my head being shaken softly from side to side as a hand lightly tapped my face.

"Is you still with us, Major? The doctor says that ball got to come out, Major. You lucky we was able to get you out."

My eyes gradually fixed on a blurred vision of white canvas, slowly lifting with the wind. I had survived. I saw a huge dark figure hovering over me, and whoever he was, this vision wasn't reassuring. I tried to speak but could only manage a few raspy, incoherent expressions. I felt my self being lifted and carried. Pain shot through my shoulder. I longed for the peace of that bright light.

"Major, I am Captain Hargrove. We have some chloroform here, and you will soon feel no pain. I believe we can save your shoulder as it is a clean wound. Stay with us, Major."

My head pitched, and my body began to shake. I could smell the chloroform, and my vision began to blur again. When I awoke, the mysterious black figure was hovering again.

"Say there, Major, I is Silas. I has some water here if you want it."

"Silas," I whispered, "What is the news of the battle?"

"You don't worry yourself none 'bout that, Major. You just get better now, you hear. Silas is goin' to take good care of you. I sure is glad to see you is awake, Major. Most don't make it."

"Well, Silas, you gave me a fright for a while. Do me a favor, will you? Get word to Judge Thatcher in Galena, Illinois, and tell him I have been wounded but am alive."

"I will try, Major, but they tells me the telegraph lines is down right now. Your loved ones is just going to have to wait a bit."

I realized I was in a field hospital with soldiers in various degrees of pain and suffering. Drenched in sweat from head to toe, the pain in my shoulder felt like someone was drilling me with a hot iron poker. I rolled to the right and tried to retch, but there was nothing in my stomach. I thought of my childhood in St. Petersburg, of being lost in the dark cave with Rebecca. Whenever I closed my eyes, that fear of being lost in that cave came over me. This is silly, I thought. You are a grown man, so don't be afraid of the dark. Silas returned to re-bandage my shoulder.

"Major, the doctor, he says you stand a good chance. But I knowed you does cause I got a message from God that told me you was blessed. I prayed for you an' God told me you is going to heal. You believe me, Major?"

In some strange way, I did believe him, but I couldn't bring myself to answer. This man with gentile hands appeared to have some spiritual connection. As the days progressed, a kind orderly consented to help me write a letter to my darling Rebecca.

*To Miss Rebecca Thatcher*
*305 Elk Street*
*Galena, Illinois*
*Dearest Rebecca:*

*Please do not be angry with me that I didn't see you before departing. As you know, I tend to be a bit reckless. When I received my three-year commission as a Major, I was excited to join the fight. Rather than wait for the formation of a company in Galena, I rushed to Virginia. I was given service by the Union army as part of the 79th New York under Colonel Cameron. Before we marched to Manassas Junction, most of the talk from the men in this regiment was about how easy it would be. A single battle to drive the Rebels out of the area around Washington, and then it was on to Richmond.*

*I was as brave as I could be but was wounded by a single Rebel in close quarters. Do not worry yourself, my love, as I am healing, and the doctors say my chance of recovery is good. I hope this letter finds you as beautiful as the day I left you. I love you and miss you so. I believe keeping this Union whole will be at much cost. The alternative seems unthinkable, and I do not want to consider it. I try to keep up a strong front for the men, but my thoughts often turn to home and to you. I still carry the Bible you gave me, and I won't lose it. I keep it close to my heart. I have done a good deal of soul searching since our childhood days, and if I knew then what I know now, I would have treated you much differently. Your family has been a great benefactor to me, and there is no way I can repay the debt.*

*I am enclosing a letter to Reverend Gideon Blackburn of Blackburn Theological Seminary. Word reached him that I am a leader in the Galena community of faith and might be interested in attending Seminary. While the possibility intrigues me, I will decline the offer. This war is now predominant in my thinking. I do not have the address of the Seminary so please pass this along.*

*Promise me that if the fighting gets close, you and your parents will leave the house and seek protection on your cousin's farm. It is but a few miles travel, and I hope your horse is still sound afoot. I have already lost many friends from my regiment, and I can't bear the thought of losing you. Jason Arde, who enlisted with me, has disappeared. I lost track of him early on and don't know where he is. There is sickness amongst some of the men, and those afflicted are not in any condition to carry a canteen into battle, let alone a musket. Most of them haven't seen the face of war as I have. Fighting in Mexico was not the same, and I am concerned that the troops will continue to be weak. I received a letter from my friend Grant, and he is now with the Illinois Volunteers. I wished him well in his new command.*

*Meanwhile, please pray for me and these brave men. It is almost daybreak, and the army is preparing to engage the enemy again. Did I mention that I love you and miss you? I am sure I have.*

*Thomas*

Sights of blood and gore, smells of rotting flesh and vomit, occasional cries of anguish, oppressive heat, and dusty air were all a part of my life for the next two weeks. I felt more fortunate than most for other survivors lost arms and legs.

"Hello, Major, I am Captain Hargrove, company surgeon. I performed the surgery on your shoulder. You were probably in no condition to remember me when you came in. How are you getting along?"

"Better now, sir, I have Silas here to take care of me. Thank you for saving my life."

"We best get you well. We need good officers. God awful business this war, I would much rather be in my practice in Philadelphia. Good thing it will be a short war as I don't think I could stand much more of this." He turned to see more wounded being carried into the surgery tent.

"You will excuse me, Major. It seems I have more work to do."

The surgery tent was across from mine, and I saw the flow of wounded continue to increase. Captain Hargrove would occasionally exit the tent to take a break. He would be covered in blood and had an expression of both exhaustion and resolve on his face. Then back into the tent, he would go as if diving into a swimming hole. I could overhear him at times.

"Chest wound, soldier, I am sorry, but there is nothing I can do for you. I am afraid your wound is mortal. Sergeant, take him to the field behind the tent and bring me the next man."

The wounded man spoke up. "Can I get a message home to my wife before I die? Can someone help me . . . please?"

"The sergeant here can take down any last request you have. God be with you."

Night fell, and it was a relief when the tent flaps were pulled down, and I could no longer see the surgery. The low moans of the wounded and dying were like an eerie spirit haunting the entire grounds. I was trying to think of happier thoughts when the tent was illuminated by two privates toting lanterns. A Confederate was carried in on a blanket and placed on a cot near me. Blood was oozing from the bandaged stump that used to hold his right arm. He couldn't have been more than twenty years, thin, with long blond hair and a ruddy complexion. He had on a major's uniform, with the exception of his right sleeve having been cut off in the surgery. He suddenly sat up, eyes wide, and his gaze darted from place to place around the room. He stared straight ahead for a moment then turned his head to look at me.

"Y'all wouldn't have got me sept that cannonball hit an' took my arm. I gave my right arm for the cause. What did you give? Yank!"

There was a tense silence in the tent.

"Yank . . . damn Yank, you got a name?"

"Yes," I responded. It's Tom."

"Well, Tom, let me tell you somethin'. General Jackson whipped you Yanks an' you doesn't stand a chance. Y'all may have the numbers, but we got . . . we got—"

He flopped back on the cot and passed out. The next morning found the Confederate still unconscious. It was probably a good thing as Silas returned to the tent.

"Say there, Major, how is you a doin' this morning? The doctor says you is going to Washington by ambulance today."

The Rebel awakened, sat halfway up, and stared at Silas.

"Don't you touch me," he shouted, "don't you touch me! I ain't havin' no slave do nothin' to me. What you doin' in here anyway? You ain't fit for nothin' 'cept plowing the fields an' pickin' cotton. Why don't you go find a rope an' do us all a favor?"

His body began to shake, and with his left hand, he made a fist as if to fight Silas with one hand if he came near. Silas turned to him with a focused gaze. I guessed that Silas was around twenty years, over six feet six inches tall, muscular build, and weighed about 250 pounds. He could have easily killed this Confederate with one blow from a huge hand. Instead, no anger or hatred came to the fore as he spoke.

"I ain't here to fight you. If you want, I'll leave you alone. Just know that shoulder ain't going to heal on its own. You got to choose if you want to die here or let me change that bandage. I ain't beholden to you none, so the choice is yours."

Silas and the Rebel kept eye contact, and I saw the Rebel's hand slowly unclench. He hesitantly lay back on his cot.

"Silas," I whispered and motioned for him to come close. "It's a good thing you didn't let your anger loose on this man."

"Major, some people only see what they want to, not what God wants them to. That Rebel, he ain't see'n God right now, only anger and pain, but I see God in him."

I gained a new respect for this big negro man. He seemed to have a way about him that was indeed extraordinary. The Confederate gave Silas angry glances as he changed his dressing.

My breakfast consisted of a bit of pork, hominy, stewed peaches, and coffee. Soon the heat began to build. My tent became like an oven as there was no breeze. Those who felt strong enough left their cots and sought the shade of trees outside. I fought back the pain to join them under a large pine tree. By the tent entrance, a short, burly sergeant who was both picket and nurse to us during the night lay in repose. He was sitting against some barrels and sleeping very soundly. I believe we could have been overrun by the Confederate army, and he wouldn't have moved. I soon fell asleep in the shade of my tree only to be awoken by a loud banging and howls of laughter. I quickly discerned that several conspirators tied a rope from a nearby tree to the top of the tent. From that rope, they tied another rope hanging down just above the sleeping sergeant's head. A bucket of water was attached to the rope. When the banging startled the sleeping sergeant, he was soon doused with water. Covered in wet clothes and looking much disgusted, he stomped off to howls of laughter.

"You men ought to be placed on report for this action," I said. "But since you are not under my command, I will report this incident to the officer in charge. You men go and apologize to the sergeant." The conspirators left, seemingly embarrassed by what they had done. I was in no condition to do anything about the incident so I let it go.

Moments later, there was a commotion in camp. General McDowell, with some of his staff, entered the far end of camp. He dismounted, talked briefly with some on guard duty, and began visiting with some of the wounded. He projected a striking figure in his blue uniform with a polished sword pommel. The sun flicked like fireflies from his buttons and the silver on his sword scabbard as he walked. His hair, mustache, and goatee were slightly graying. He climbed onto an ammunition limber and spoke.

"Officers, soldiers, and friends of the Union . . . we have stopped the Confederate advance, and this area is now safe. This battle has clearly been a setback to our forces, but it is just that, a setback. I express my gratitude to you men for your unwavering gallantry in the face of such devastating enemy fire. You didn't come away unscathed, but you have my respect as fellow countrymen of this great Union. It is my belief we will indeed succeed in this war. I have received a telegram from Secretary Stanton expressing his gratitude to all of you who were a part of this battle. I must leave you now as I have been recalled to Washington. My prayers and the spirit of God go with you all."

With that, he turned, jumped to the ground, mounted his horse, gave the command to move out, and they were gone. It seemed as if the general was a bit disingenuous. I knew we were badly beaten, and so did the rest of the wounded. A breeze kicked up, which I suspected was making the tent more bearable, so I went in to lie down. The Rebel major, still lying next to me, reached out with his left hand, grabbed a bowl from the stand beside his cot, and flung it to the opposite side of the tent. He began to laugh hideously.

"To hell, that's where you're a-goin'," he said. "You and that two-bit general, he ain't got sense enough to tell a mule to turn right or left."

He fell back into his cot with a thud. The next few minutes passed with silence in the tent. The Rebel again turned to me, and his expression changed.

"You know Yank, you ain't so bad a-lookin'. Have you got any children to speak of?"

"No," I said. "I am not wed."

"Well, I got young 'uns, plenty of em. I got three boys an' three girls waitin' for me and a wife that expects me to come straight home after we whip y'all. Course I won't be of much use on the plantation with one arm, but I reckon that's why I got them young 'uns . . . hu—say Yank, what you fight'n this war for anyway?"

"To preserve the Union and end slavery," I responded.

"Well, I'm a fight'n to protect my family an' my freedom to do as I please without any interfearin' from Washington. We got Southern pride an' that will go a long way toward winnin' this war." Blood began oozing from his wound.

Thankfully, they came to move him to another tent. I couldn't take much more of his jabbering. Besides, I don't know why they put him with us in the first place. He was, after all, the enemy.

Lunch was served. Boiled beef, potatoes, and half an apple seemed like a delicacy compared to the field rations. After lunch, I began to feel sick and was sweating profusely. I was not sure if it was caused by the heat of the day or something else. Silas came by and placed a wet cloth on my forehead.

"Well, Major, seems we got ourselves a fever here," he said. "We're going to keep you cool as we can. Let's get that shirt off. I got a pan of cool water here."

Night fell, and the promised transport to Washington didn't materialize. It was not unusual for this new army to have plans derailed, and the word of what I assumed was an ex-slave was not exactly like a telegraph message from headquarters. I recalled dreaming an awful dream.

*"Well, counselor Sawyer, what have you to say for your client in summation?" "My client is innocent, your honor. It is not his fault he was a slaveholder; he did not beat his slaves as the prosecution suggests. The scars on this slave were from self-inflicted wounds to make it look as if he were beaten. My client is a decent, upstanding citizen of the southern aristocracy. He could not possibly be involved in any illegal activity."*

*"Very well, jury, what say you?"*

*"We, the jury, find the defendant not guilty, your honor."*

*"Case dismissed."*

*"Go for those guns, I said, fire. Fire, you fools!"*

*"We got him, sir. That plantation owner won't bother any slaves again. Sorry, counselor, but you won't be getting paid for this case."*

*"The courthouse is burning, sir, and we must get out. You dive into this stream, quickly now before it's too late."*

*"I am drowning . . . help me!"*

Two days passed, and I was in and out of consciousness. I wasn't able to separate what was real from what was a dream. I only know that as much as I wanted to, I had no control over what my body would do. I was fed soup and water by several sets of hands. I tried to control my thoughts when awake by focusing on simple things: sometimes a number, sometimes a flower, and keeping hold of it in my mind for as long as possible. I also recited the 23rd psalm from the Bible. This was a great comfort to me as I went thought this time of darkness. It was my hold on reality and protection against the raging fever. I kept thinking of Jesus talking to the women who touched his garment and his saying: "Daughter, thy faith hath made thee whole: go in peace . . ." I prayed for God's comfort, and then I slept for what seemed an eternity. I awoke with really bad chills and shivering, and I couldn't stop the shaking. I was in an unfamiliar place, and the new attendant standing before me was a sergeant I later learned was from a company out of Michigan.

"Well, Major," he said. "I see we are finely awake. You have been out for two days now, and we thought you might not make it. By the way, welcome to Washington."

"I thank you for your care, Sergeant. Where am I?"

"Douglas Hospital, sir. It ain't much of a hospital, but it's the best we got. We will try and take good care of you."

The sergeant was kindly to some patients and, at the same time, short with others. I managed to get on his good side by telling him funny stories of life in Galena. It was different here, cleaner, beds with fresh linens, and better care. Gradually, I began to heal, and after two weeks, I applied for a six-month leave to go home to Galena. I assumed the war would be over by then, and my services would no longer be needed. To my joy, the leave was granted. I began to prepare for the long journey back by writing to Rebecca.

*Dearest Rebecca:*

*Unlike so many of the others who have died, I feel fortunate, but there was some damage to my left shoulder. The doctors do not say how much movement I will regain. I am sure God will continue to bless me. I am on my way home to you and will be there in about a week. I found out yesterday Jason Arde has deserted. He is reported to be in or around home. If you see him, turn him in to the authorities, for he is a coward. I thought him to be a friend. But I have it by several witnesses that he turned and ran even before the first shot was fired. I have been granted a six-month leave to heal and will be on my way to Galena by train at the first opportunity. I received the enclosed telegram.*

*Thomas*


*It has been some months since our last speaking, and I was telegraphed you were on the wounded list for Bull Run. I am sending this in the hope it will reach you, and the wound is not severe. The friendship we developed while we were at West Point brings back fond memories. I have written to Brigadier General McDowell about your situation and have asked that he consider any request from you for leave. If you so desire, I have also asked my wife Julia, to allow you to recover at the Grant home in Galena. I look forward to our meeting again soon. Please acknowledge.*

*U.S. Grant*
*Colonel, Seventh District Regiment, Illinois Volunteers.*


*While not wanting to offend him, I believe I won't pursue his offer. With you and your family present in Galena, it will more than satisfy my needs. I will try to pass the time by reopening my law practice. Please tell Julia Grant I am alive and will return to Galena. I will follow up here by informing Colonel Grant. You should know it is my intention to rejoin my brigade when I am able. I love you and can't wait to see you and your family.*

*Thomas*

The next morning, I got a surprise.

"Captain Hargrove, it is good to see you again, sir. What are you doing in Washington?"

"I have been reassigned to Douglas until the next field action. I wanted to see you before you left for home. I have your leave orders here. I wanted you to know I did the best job I possibly could on your shoulder. You must protect it from any injury for the next few weeks. It is my hope that you will regain full use of it in time. For now, keep it bandaged and continue to wear that sling. Have a doctor in Galena take a look at it when you arrive. It is still raw and subject to being reinjured. Take care Major."

Captain Hargrove left me to my own thoughts. It would be good to get home and rest. My hope is that the doctor is right and this injury won't be permanent. The next few weeks should tell the tale.

## 2

## A Little Dirt in the Eyes

The calendar had just turned to August. I switched trains in Indianapolis and saw a seat next to a lieutenant from a cavalry regiment. He was a man of about forty, stout in stature with a black mustache. He seemed to be gazing out the window without a care in the world.

"Excuse me, Lieutenant, is this seat taken?"

"No, Major. It's yours if you want it. I am Lieutenant Johnson, sir."

"Thank you, Lieutenant, I would like some good company on the way to Galena. It has been a long journey. I was wounded at Bull Run and am on my way home; how about you?"

"I am heading to Galena to join a cavalry regiment. My commission is with an Illinois regiment, and they are mustering in at Galena before leaving for Cairo."

The train lurched forward and began the slow, steady progression. The scenery soon began to blur as we left Indianapolis. My new friend and I settled in.

"I know what you mean about getting started; I bounced around myself a little at the beginning of the war. I am considering my options about staying in. If my shoulder wound doesn't heal, I may not have a choice."

"Major, I sense you have tasted battle. I . . . well, I have yet to experience it. What's it like?"

"Being in battle is the most frightening thing I have ever done. You can't disregard the death and carnage. I didn't think I would make it out alive. While I was in the hospital, I thought about my home and my girl

Rebecca. It scared the hell out of me to think I would never see her or anyone else again."

"Your girl must be pretty special. Do you expect to be married?"

"Maybe someday, do you have someone special?"

"Yes, I do. Lila. I got a letter from her today, wishing me Godspeed and wanting me home as soon as my enlistment is over. We plan to be married soon. Are you from Galena, Major?"

"No, originally from St. Petersburg, on the Mississippi River, but my girl and her father moved to Galena. Her father, Judge Thatcher, inherited a lead mining operation. He is thinking about running for Jo Daviess County Judge. The judge taught me law, helped me become a lawyer, and get into West Point. I am deeply indebted to him."

"Then I suppose you will go back to Galena when your enlistment is up?"

"Yes, I do expect to marry Rebecca if she will have me. But for now, we have a war to win, don't we?"

"Say, major, do you, by any chance, know General Grant?"

"Yes, as a matter of fact, I do. General Grant was in my graduating class at West Point."

"Here is my card. If you can arrange for me to meet him, I would be most grateful. I have a surprise for him. I know he lives in Galena, and I hope to serve in a regiment under his command."

We soon became witness to Galena's bustling streets with lots of wagons, people milling about, and smoke from the steamboat traffic choking the riverfront. A small port at the start of the war, it was now bustling with commerce and men in uniform heading south. I said good-bye to Lieutenant Johnson and got my baggage. I hired a wagon to take me to my first stop.

"Driver, if you could be so kind as to take me to the Widow Tompkins house on Branch Street. I have my personal belongings stored with her."

"Yes, sir, Major. I know where her house is. I delivered goods to her yesterday."

"Hopefully, my things have survived in better shape than I am?"

The driver helped me load my trunk and boxes onto the wagon. After dropping most of my things at the Widow Tompkins house he took me to the Desoto House Hotel. A long stay at the Desoto House was not possible as my military pay had not caught up. Fortunately, they gave me credit with the promise of payment. My second visit was to Rebecca. It wasn't long until I reached the Thatcher house. The anticipation of seeing her again made my heart race. I still remembered her perfume and felt a sense of stimulation. A knock at the door produced Judge Thatcher, and he greeted me warmly. When I entered the parlor, I was attacked from behind the window curtains. She rushed into my arms. It was an awkward hug with the sling in the way. I decided to take it off. Hugging Rebecca was more important now.

"Thomas, I have missed you so much. I don't know if I should kiss you or kick you. Why didn't you tell me you were going east? I cried so at the thought of losing you."

"I know. I know. I was stupid and selfish. Perhaps you can find it in your heart to forgive me. The one thing I did was keep you in my heart, even while I was lying wounded on the battlefield."

"I couldn't stay mad at you. I love you." She kissed me passionately, I blushed, and her father only smiled.

"I am staying at the Desoto House, temporarily. I want to begin looking for a place to live. Would you help me find something suitable?"

"Of course I will."

We spent the next few days together looking for a place where I could live, and possibly open a law practice. I was hoping for an all in one sort of home and office because I knew it may be temporary. I found an ad in the paper, and we went to take a look.

"What we have here is a fine little storefront on Water Street, which I am sure you will find accommodating. The leather goods shop has just closed, but the walls have been scrubbed and whitewashed. For the price you wish to pay, I believe this will be comfortable."

"Thank you, Mr. Blackwell, but I will reserve the decision until I see the inside."

"Certainly, Major. I am not trying to force the situation."

I began my inspection of the rooms. I liked the location, but there still needed to be some improvements before it would suit me. The whitewash reminded me of Aunt Polly's fence back in St. Petersburg.

"Well, Major Sawyer, what do you think? It is a real bargain for ten dollars a month."

"I think the office area is not much to speak of, a desk, a chair, and some shelves, but it might do. I have some law books to place, and the shelves behind the counter would be more than adequate. However, I still smell leather. Is there anything you can do to get rid of it?"

"I am afraid not, sir. We have scrubbed the place from top to bottom. If you sign the agreement now, I can give it to you for nine fifty a month."

I knew that look from Rebecca, and it was not a very good sign. She pulled me to the side to discuss the issue.

"Thomas, I like the location, but I am not sure about the building. Do you intend for it to serve your purpose as both a home and an office?"

"Yes, I think it will. It gives me plenty of room for storage and a small apartment in the back."

"All right then, I will trust your judgement, although it is sometimes faulty." She smiled.

I turned to Mr. Blackwell.

"If you paint the inside and provide three cord of wood for the stoves, you have a deal."

"Very good sir, if all goes well you can move your things in on Tuesday."

The most prized thing in my new office was the window. A whole dollar got "Thomas Sawyer—Attorney at Law" painted on with gilding and fancy letters. It was quite a job finding someone to do it. The fellow hired was from New Orleans and also painted riverboats for a living. There were three rooms off the office. It didn't say anything in the lease about living quarters, and the rooms were quite spacious. Two cast iron stoves would provide plenty of heat. As long as the lease didn't specify, I felt I could live at the location without a problem. I purchased a small cooking plate for one of the stoves, an old table, chair, and trundle bed and moved them into the smallest room. The judge, his wife Ida, and Rebecca came by to inspect the new place.

"Tom," the judge said. "The place seems to be a bit beneath you, son. I will look for a more suitable location for your office."

"Judge," I said. "With all due respect, sir, I don't think it matters what kind of fish you are seeking as long as you have the right bait." He laughed.

"Well, Tom, if you think this will work, the proof will be in what happens in the next few weeks. It is only a few blocks from the courthouse, and that would be convenient, I suppose. Have you given any thought to what you will do about the army once you are fully healed?"

Rebecca took a step in our direction with keen interest.

"Not yet, sir, I want to be sure I am in full fighting form before I consider my options."

"You might think about joining our mining company as a legal representative. You had quite a few dealings with companies back in St Petersburg and handled them well. I can pay you a handsome salary and move you into the mining office. The mine has some legal issues I think you could handle."

"Thank you, judge, but my first decision must be whether to return to war if my shoulder permits. I don't want to join the mining company only to be called away for service. It is better for me to remain independent."

A week went by with a noticeable dearth of clientele, and I began to think the judge was correct. When she came through the door, she looked like a farmer's wife with a white bonnet and a drab blue dress. Her petticoat was dirty from walking some distance in the dusty street. Her face was young, with just a few lines around the eyes, and her black hair was long and wavy. Her shoes were well-worn, and as I glanced back to her face, the expression changed to one of sincerity. My eyes became fixed on the necklace she wore, six small diamonds with an emerald in the middle. It didn't seem to go with the rest of her clothing. She glanced nervously around the room and appeared to be deciding if she should stay or go.

"What's that smell?" she asked.

"Oh, this place used to be a leather goods store, sorry but the smell is still noticeable."

She came closer to my desk and paused.

"Are you Mister Sawyer?"

"Yes ma'am, what can I do for you?"

"My name is Alice . . . Alice Reynolds. Before I say any more, how much do you charge?"

"My customary retainer is five dollars and expenses."

"That is a lot of money for me, but let me tell you my story. I am the sister of Jim McCready. He runs a livery stable here in Galena. My husband is Rob Reynolds. He is foreman of a mine about a mile from the north end of town. Mind you, I don't want to get into trouble, but I think he . . . well, he may be into some mischief."

"What do you mean mischief?" I asked.

"You see, he has been going out lately without telling me where. When he comes back, it's always the same answer, he's "checkin' on the mine". We live about a mile upriver north from Galena on the outskirts of town. It's a rented place, not much room for me and the kids, but we get along. I have been down to that mine, and it don't need to be checked on near that often. If what he says is true, he probably should have married the mine instead of me. I just have my suspicions, and I ain't sure what to think. I want to hire you to look into the matter. If need be, I want you to file divorce papers."

Now it was my turn to pause. This was only the fifth person to walk through my door, so I didn't want to dismiss her out of hand. But I was not taking hardship cases either, so I asked her straight up;

"I am not a detective, Mrs. Reynolds, but I have the means to look into the matter. My price is three dollars a day for investigation plus my retainer."

She reached around her neck and slowly took off the necklace.

"This here is all I got, Mr. Sawyer. You take it over to the bank and see how much it's worth. That will tell you how long you have to find out what's goin' on."

Something in the back of my mind told me I would regret this, but I consented to the arrangement. I wouldn't ask her to sign a retainer just yet. It seemed funny that this woman would be in possession of such a necklace. I needed to know more, and her giving me the bauble was no legal commitment. She turned to leave and then paused at the door.

"By the way, I found this note my husband had in his pocket. He came home drunk one night, and I found it when I picked up his clothes next morning. I thought it was strange and couldn't make anything out of it. It may be nothing, but you can have it." She handed me a scrap of paper, turned to leave, and stopped again. "You can't say anything about this to anyone Mr. Sawyer. If Rob finds—" Her face contorted in anguish.

She continued out of the office and went hurriedly up the street. If this turned out to be infidelity, I vowed to myself not to charge her for my time and give her back the necklace. I dismissed the note for now and headed to the bank to find out what the necklace was worth.

"Yes, Major Sawyer, can we help you?"

"I would like to know if you can tell me about this necklace?"

"I will have my assistant look it over. I will take about 15 minutes."

"I can wait." After around half an hour past I began to get nervous. Then the bank official returned.

"I must tell you it is part of a collection of jewelry that was stolen from the Desoto House two weeks ago. How did you come by it?"

"It was given to me by a potential client. I assume you will give it to the sheriff so it can be returned to its rightful owner."

"Yes sir, we will see to it. I will tell the sheriff, and you should expect to hear from him regarding the issue."

Evening was closing in when I grabbed my fishing pole and headed toward the river. There was something really beautiful about the river on a warm summer night. The stars were beginning to peak out of the dusk, and you could forget all about your troubles with a line in the water. The smell of the water and the sound of the gentle lapping against the bank made me relax. It didn't take long till I brought in my first catch. He fought me a bit, but I was able to pull him in. The fish was just about the size of my little finger but had some fight. I tossed him back in so he could grow up. I stopped long enough to light my lantern as the outline of the far shore began to fade. The river was beautiful enough during the day, but at night, it took on special meaning. The darkness was broken by glimpses of moonlight that glistened with silver ripples on the water. The lantern lights from a paddle wheel steamer pierced the blackness as it moved slowly by. The vessel was close enough to hear the leadsman call out the depth to the captain. He sounded, "Quarter Twain, Half Twain, and Mark Twain." The sound of the flowing water lulled me into a trance. One by one, lanterns peeked out of the dark across the bank. I closed my eyes.

> *I could hear the cries of the wounded soldiers; saw the exploding cannon, the volleys of shot, and the thick gray smoke of battle. I found myself in that ravine with the smoke shrouded rebels coming at me. That young Rebel in my sights, and the pistol fired. His eyes, those big blue eyes staring back at me. I was hit by the minié ball, spinning around and landing face down in the mud. The pain came back to my shoulder, and I felt myself drifting into the blackness of death . . .*

I came around with a start. Most of my pole was submerged in the water. It took me a few moments to regain my nature. I was still trying to forget the penetrating eyes of that young Confederate and remove him from my mind. He kept haunting me. I pulled my pole out, rebated my hook, and gave my line a toss. This time I brought in a three-pounder, dressed it out, wrapped it in newspaper, and placed it in my basket. This would make good eating with a few biscuits. I gave thanks to God for my catch and went back to the office. It was not long till I had that fish filleted, floured, in the pan, and dinner finished.

I suddenly remembered the note from Mrs. Reynolds. I took it from my pocket and looked it over. There were just a few words and some numbers. I could just make out 1+4=5 visible by imprint at the top. The rest of the numbers were, 36,40,34,34 space 15, 19 space 46, 48, 54 and 18 then a second line with 52, 27, 34 space 29 space 21, 21. The paper was torn on the edge like it was ripped from a larger piece. I spent enough time in the army to recognize a cipher when I saw one. I would sort it out but not right now. I was tired, and there was cleaning up to do.

The sun came up, and the heat started to build. By 10:00 it was nearly 90 degrees. Galena had an abundance of young people who could find trouble the same way I did as a child. I thought one way to help prevent this was to provide them with a bit of pocket change. I put the word out that I needed some temporary help. I signed up several lads to be my eyes and ears in Galena. For a remittance, they would let me know of any dealings in town that might interest me. I set the rules for payment and developed a sign to signify when I was in need.

The first order was to let Mrs. Reynolds know I would take her case. Overlooking the fact that the necklace was stolen, I was curious to know more about her family. It appeared Rob Reynolds or his wife may be mixed up in some illegal activity given she was wearing a stolen necklace. I took a red bandana out of my desk drawer and tied it to the hitching rail. Soon enough, the door swung open, and Jimmy Miller walked in. Jimmy handed me the bandana, saluted, stood at attention, and waited.

"Jimmy, I need you to go out to the Reynold's place about a mile upriver to the north of town. You are to wait till you can talk to Mrs. Reynolds alone if possible, and then tell her I accept her terms."

I paid him his due, and, as he started to leave, I said, "One more thing, let her know the terms are good for ten days. Then come back here and see me."

I didn't want to tip my hand about the stolen necklace just yet. I figured I was dealing with a criminal element and didn't want to draw suspicion toward myself or the delivery service.

"Yes sir, Major," he replied.

He gave me some semblance of a salute and headed out the door. Judge Thatcher told me the sheriff had gone to Springfield on political business and would not be back for about a week. His deputy would not do much, if anything, until his return. This meant he would likely not get word about the necklace until his return. It would give me a few days to figure out what was going on.

I needed to get more information on Mr. Reynolds, and a likely place might be Jessie Grant's leather goods store. Jessie told me most everyone in town passed by his store at one time or another. When his son Hiram left for the war, he hired Sam Skrogin as a clerk. Sam was a big man in town, not in status mind you but in size. He was nearly six foot five inches and weighed around 280 pounds. Sam was all muscle and could fling saddles and goods on and off the supply wagons with ease. The army rejected him because he sometimes had seizures that would render him helpless. When in the right state, Sam was a kindly sort and a reliable source for information.

"Good day, Major," he bellowed.

"Good day, Sam. This is such a hot day. Why don't you and I set here in the shade and play a game of checkers, if you have the time, of course."

"Okay, Major, if you still remember how to play."

We placed some chairs outside on the boardwalk and set up the board on an old flour barrel. We made small talk, and when I won, I said, "Say, Sam, have you seen Rob Reynolds lately? I had some business I wanted to discuss with him."

"Yes, sir, Major, as a matter of fact, I have. He came by here about an hour ago to pick up some new harnesses and leaders for his team. He said he was going over to the Desoto House to meet some friends."

"Thanks, Sam, for letting me win."

"You won't be so lucky next time."

On the way to the hotel, I ran into Jimmy, who was returning to my office. I trusted Jimmy as he was older than the rest and done work for me before. He helped me work on the judge's house when I first arrived in Galena. He was smart, a hard worker and a fair carpenter. I could see the war snatching him up at any moment. He had become a good friend, so I confided in him about the necklace.

"I suppose this means that Mr. Reynolds is up to no good. I did deliver your message to Mrs. Reynolds."

"Did you see Mr. Reynolds on your route?"

"Yep, I saw him all right. He left shortly after I arrived, and that's how I got the chance to talk to her."

"Could you identify him for me?"

"For two bits," he said, smiling. I handed him the money, and we walked to the back of the hotel.

"Go around to the front of the hotel and let me know if Mr. Reynolds is in there. Also, what he is wearing."

"I could have told you what he was wearing when I got back from the house."

"Just go on and look, will you?"

A few moments passed, and he returned.

"He's in there all right. He's still wearin' a brown hat, with a red shirt and brown trousers."

Jimmy walked off, flipping the coin as he went. He was a bright and clever kid. I waited, and in the heat of the day, it wasn't a pleasant wait. I began to feel the sweat trickle down the middle of my back, and my clothes began to stick to my skin. Soon I saw Mr. Reynolds emerge from the hotel with two other men. They moved to the side of the hotel on the long boardwalk and sat down at a table. I crept closer but couldn't get close enough to hear what they were saying. It was then that I noticed a broken piece of latticework covering the underside of the boardwalk. With Jimmy gone, I couldn't pass up an opportunity to find out more. I slid under the boardwalk and crawled on my back through the dust. The latticework let in just enough light to see, and I could make out images. After crawling about twenty feet, I could hear them clearly. A wider space in the boardwalk slats made my vision of the three fairly good.

The two men with Reynolds were rough-looking characters: the sort that would give you a good hand to hand fight on the battlefield. One was a short man with rounded shoulders and a large scar on his left hand. His complexion was ruddy, and he had dark ruffled hair. He was carrying a pistol and a large Bowie knife in his belt. He did have one other characterization I recognized. He had a gray slouch hat like I had seen on some of the Rebel soldiers at Bull Run. His cold dark eyes could look right through you. The other was a tall, lanky blond headed man. He was standing behind the short one with this whipped dog expression on his narrow face.

"Reynolds," the short man said. "Don't you back out on us. We will pay you fair, once the job is done."

"Okay, Nate, I won't," Reynolds said. "You know how important this is to me. You got to trust me."

"Trust," Nate exclaimed, "I'd more trust a rattlesnake than you. We remember what happened in Charleston. You turned tail and ran just when we needed you."

"I didn't!" Reynolds said angrily, "I was just going back for the rest of the money."

"If you did, you would have come back for us, you coward. If it weren't for your knowing the layout, we wouldn't even be talking."

Quick as lightning Reynolds threw a punch at Nate. They knocked over a chair and began rolling around on the boardwalk with fists flying. When they did, the dust began to pour through the cracks in the boardwalk. My eyes were hurting from the dust, and it was all I could do to keep from sneezing. The tall man broke up the fight, and they all seemed to regain their senses.

"Enough of this, you gonna do it, Reynolds?"

"Yea, I'll do it," Reynolds said, "just as long as you have my share. But I ain't a coward like you said and by the way, where's the money coming from?"

Nate responded roughly, "I got my sources, Rob. There are plenty of Copperheads, if you know where to look."

The three of them walked off together. I crawled out from under the boardwalk, and fortunately, there was a rain barrel close by. I washed the dust off my face. On the way back to the office, I ran into Jimmy. He started laughing the moment he saw me.

"What happened to you?"

"I was just taking a dust bath, it keeps the fleas off."

"You look like you crawled out of a sack of flour. Anything I can do to help?"

"You can stop laughing and keep this little incident to yourself."

"Will do, Major, just let me know if you need help brushing the dust off."

I readied a bath and took a look at myself in the mirror. My shoulder wound had started to seep. It was a lesson that I was not yet fully healed, and I needed to watch the physical activity. The warm water felt relaxing, and I cleaned myself off as best I could. My left arm would still not reach totally above my head, but the movement did improve a little each day. I could wash my hair now without much difficulty.

The next morning, I got a bite to eat and thought about going out to the Reynolds place. I waited an hour and got restless. I put the bandana out and soon Mort Rogers walked in. Mort was a little heavy set and he didn't move very fast. He liked assignments where he sat around a lot. It allowed him to make money with less effort.

"Hay Mort, I would like you to go to the Reynolds place about a mile north of town. Hang around there and let me know if there is any activity. At about dusk, you can give it up. But, if something significant happens, get back here and let me know straight away. Mind you, take care not to be seen."

"If this be one of your long-term things Major, it'll cost you a dollar."

"A dollar?" I said. "No chance, Mort, I'll give you two bits if you give me two hours work."

"No, Major, I really need the dollar you see my sister, uh . . . she is sick and all, and well, I need to get her some medicine."

"Okay, two bits now and the rest when you return. You can get the particulars on exactly where the Reynolds place is from Jimmy."

Mort left with the two bits in hand and the promise of the rest when he reported back. He returned in less than an hour.

"There weren't nothin' going on at the Reynolds place. In fact, they was nobody at home. The house was completely empty, people, furniture, kids and all. The front door was standing wide open."

"Thank you, Mort. I suppose you still want the rest of your money for such short work?"

"Naw, Major, you can keep the money. My sister made a miraculous recovery."

"Get out of here, you larcenist," I said teasingly.

This seemed odd that the whole family would up and disappear. My investment in the case was minimal, but there were questions in my mind. When Mort was gone, I turned my attention to the message Ms. Reynolds gave me. While I was no expert, I liked the challenge. The key had to be 1+4=5: it was the only formula mixed in with a bunch of numbers. But how do you make that into a message? I figured it might have something to do with the alphabet, so I laid out the string of letters a to z, and put 1+4=5 next to the letter "a" and put 1+5=6 at the next. I kept the number one in its place and continued all the way down the page giving each letter a formula. Then I took the value of each answer and tried it against the numbers that made up the note. So, if "a" equaled 5, then there were no letter a's on the paper. I assumed this was a dead end as surely the letter "a" was somewhere in the message. I took 1+4=5 and put it at the letter "z" position because if something doesn't work right side up, try it upside down. Using this system, the letter "a" would be 31. This looked more promising, but still, there were no letter a's. There was still something missing.

It was getting on toward noon, so I headed for the hotel. They served a good lunch, and I might be able to nose around and find out something more about Rob Reynolds or where the family had gone. When I entered the dining room, I glanced across the room, and the Thatcher's were just sitting down.

"Well, Tom, come and join us!" the judge exclaimed, "How is the practice going?"

"Great," I said with a smile. Not wanting to hear the lecture from the judge that would follow if I told the truth.

"Say, Judge, I wanted to ask if I could call on Miss Rebecca this evening."

"Certainly, Tom." the judge replied.

"Thank you, sir. I will call at seven tonight. There is a band playing here this evening, and I expect it will be a good social event."

I walked back to the office with a smile on my face. At seven, I made my call.

"You look beautiful, Rebecca. That pale blue dress and white shawl both suit you."

"Thank you, Major Sawyer," she said. "You are looking handsome, as well."

We strolled toward the Desoto Hotel, where melodious tunes were beginning to flow down the street. As we walked arm in arm, I got an idea.

"Rebecca, I have trusted you since we were children. I have a story to relate, and you must promise me you won't think me pretentious."

"Of course not, Thomas."

"I had this strange occurrence of a woman entering my office and offering to pay me with what turned out to be stolen merchandise. She wanted me to investigate her husband for possible infidelity. It turns out her husband is mixed up in what I believe to be some sort of secret activity. It is the Reynolds family. Perhaps you have heard of them? Anyway, their whole family has up and disappeared. The only clue I have is this cipher she left me. I have been working on it to no avail. It does make me wonder what is going on."

"Thomas, do you have the cipher with you?"

"Yes, I stuck it here in the pocket of my uniform jacket."

"Let me have a try, please?"

We slowed our walk and finally sat down on a storefront bench. Rebecca read through the formula, coded numbers and my work. She looked at it intently for some time. I didn't want to disturb her concentration, so I let the idea of the band rest.

"Thomas, hand me your pencil, will you?"

After a few minutes, she exclaimed, "Thomas, I think I have it! The trick is to take 1+4=5 as you did but add one to the first number going backward up the alphabet. That makes the numbers in the note make sense."

I huddled close to her, not particularly caring about the note at this moment but just wanting to be close to her. She applied her formula to each of the letter designations: *"Kill US Feb 18 Col N RR."* It was clearly a southern sympathizer message of some kind.

"Rebecca! This means that Rob Reynolds and his two cohorts are most likely Confederate sympathizers. I don't know what to think now. The note was written by someone who clearly has it in for the Union. Whatever was to happen would possibly happen on February 18th? Who was this mysterious Colonel N? Did RR stand for Rob Reynolds or possibly a reference to the railroad? It all had some significance, but what?"

Just then, Jimmy came running up to me.

"Major! Major," he said breathlessly, "you ain't goin' to believe this."

"What is it, Jimmy?" I asked.

"Just come on with me!" he said, grabbing my hand and pulling me along with Rebecca rushing to keep up.

We walked quickly back along the street to a crowd gathered around the sheriff's office. Sheriff Minor was standing on a wagon and began speaking to a crowd of citizens and reporters.

"This evening, it was discovered by a neighbor that several murders have taken place."

A muffled outcry shot through the crowd.

"The shallow graves of a woman and two small children were found in the backyard of a house a mile north of Galena. It was the wife and children of Rob Reynolds."

Gasps were heard and one lady in the crowd grew faint and fell to the street. She was helped to a nearby bench.

"When the bodies were uncovered, we found they were all shot at close range."

Additional cries welled up from the crowd.

"If anyone knows the whereabouts of Rob Reynolds, they are to report it to me or my deputies immediately."

I took a quick glance at Rebecca.

"I need to think this through," I said.

The thought flashed into my head: killing many men on the battlefield is justified, but when innocents are killed, we immediately try to track down their killer. We walked slowly away from the crowd. The news spread much faster than our pace. I knew it would be only a matter of time until my activities would be discovered, and I felt the best course of action was to let it be known. We doubled back and found the sheriff still outside the jail.

"Sir, I have some information that may be of interest," I said.

I related the story about Mrs. Reynolds coming to me, the necklace, the information my boys had supplied, the altercation I witnessed, and the man named Nate.

"Major Sawyer, I am asking that you come with me. I need to question you further in this matter."

I was taken by the arm and the two of us went into the sheriff's office. Rebecca went to get her father, and fortunately, she didn't have far to go. Word reached him of the murders and he was already halfway to the jail. Rebecca told him about the particulars as they walked.

"Sheriff Minor"

"Yes, Judge Thatcher"

"I wish to point out that Major Sawyer had no motive to kill Mrs. Reynolds or her children. He merely accepted a contract that was without merit and informed you of all his knowledge pertaining to the case. He contracted with the client of his own volition, knowing he wouldn't be compensated. Now, unless you intend to arrest Major Sawyer for the murders, I suggest that you release him."

"Judge, I merely wanted to question him regarding the murders." Looking at me he said, "Major Sawyer, don't leave Galena until this case is solved."

What I didn't mention to the sheriff was the coded message Mrs. Reynolds gave me. Rebecca and I were the only ones who knew about the note, and I wanted to keep it in confidence for the time being. I felt this was far bigger than three murders, tragic as they were; I needed to find out more.

# 3

## Sawyer To the Rescue . . . Sort Of

Rob Reynolds became a feared name in Galena. Everyone assumed he committed the ghastly deed and word spread quickly about his disappearance. Every time a crime was committed in Galena his name was mentioned. Wanted posters went out with a five hundred dollar reward for information leading to his arrest. The sheriff launched an investigation, but information was hard to come by. He managed to arrest the tall blond fellow I identified as one of the conspirators. Judge Thatcher told me he was not cooperating with questioning. I called together my network of boys and told them to keep their ears open for anything suspicious. A full dollar would pay for any bit of information on Rob Reynolds. Weeks began to pass, and the sheriff released the tall blond man as he could not connect him to the murders.

"I sent a telegram to General Halleck in Washington weeks ago about the message Rebecca decoded. I know the War Department has a lot to do, but a possible confederate plot should be important. Wouldn't you agree, Judge?"

"Yes, Tom, I would. You might try sending another just to stress the point."

"I will do so in the morning."

"What about this Reynolds fellow, have you heard anything about him?"

"Nothing at all; it has been a month since the murders, and no one reported seeing him. I do have my suspicions. In a chilling way, it seems that my involvement in the Reynolds case is giving my business a boost. Some curious sorts walk by the office and gawk at me because the sheriff may decide I'm a murderous rogue and arrest me. Some do come in for legal work. I guess they think my skills were worthy of their business. Regardless, Judge, I hate the fact the family was murdered. I gave the money for their proper burial."

"I am sure the family is grateful, Tom."

The calendar turned to Christmas Eve, and Galena was coated in a Christmas glow. I had dismissed not receiving a telegram reply from the War Department. Apparently they are preoccupied with running the war and are satisfied there is no immediate threat. Christmas was dampened by the death and destruction of the war. Snow blanketed the town. As I walked from the office to visit a client, a few lanterns shining through windows made cathedral-like shadows on the streets. Snowflakes danced in the wind and swirled around each corner. Except for the occasional whinny from a horse, it was peaceful. As I passed by First Presbyterian Church, I heard the choir rehearsing. It brought to mind that some in the church prayed for peace and compromise. Others prayed for an end to slavery and restoration of the Union. Seems it is for God to decide. I ran into Judge Thatcher.

"Tom, good to see you, Rebecca tells me she extended our invitation to enjoy Christmas Eve dinner with us tonight. We look forward to having you. Are you all right, Tom? You seem a little distant lately."

"No, Judge, I don't think I am. I seem to have periods where I lose touch with myself. I keep reliving that incident at Bull Run, and it haunts me. I don't know what to do about it. Perhaps I should ask the doctor on my next visit. I was on my way to visit a potential client, but it can wait till next week. It is, after all, Christmas Eve."

"It is a beautiful snow this evening Tom, it's so peaceful and calm. Let's head over to the house. I am sure Rebecca and Ida will want to see you. We don't want to miss the vesper service at church."

Over the next four weeks, I welcomed in the New Year by settling cases: one involving the arrest of an innocent fellow and the theft of dry goods, two assault charges and two property disputes. I wrote several wills and dealt with a number of mundane legal filings. One day, a familiar face came into my office with a problem.

"Sam Adams, how are you?"

"Not too good, Major, I have a problem I was hoping you could help with."

"What's wrong?"

"I have property in town that is rightfully mine. A man named Fisher is saying I have no claim. A month ago, I was in an altercation with Mr. Fisher over some money he owes me. I fought with the man and got the better of him. He swore he would get even. He has now claimed I owe back taxes on my property and has asked the sheriff to auction it off in two days. The county's records of my tax payments were lost in a fire, and he knew this."

"Let me ask you a very important question, Sam. Do you have any document that would indicate you own the property?"

"I have here the will from my father leaving the land to me. It has the appearance of a tea-stained rag, but I assure you it is real. I also have a document saying I filed for ownership at the courthouse, but I never received title. I could really use your help."

"I believe I can help you, Sam. Let's go down to the courthouse and have a talk with the probate judge."

We left my office and proceeded to the Jo Daviess County courthouse. Sam's fears began to escalate as we walked, but I assured him we would find a solution. Upon our arrival, I knocked on the judge's door.

"Come in, gentlemen. What can I do for you?"

Sam started to speak, but I grabbed his arm.

"Your honor, it is good to see you again. This is my client, Sam Adams. We are here to present to you some evidence regarding a property that is to be auctioned."

"Major Sawyer, I will entertain your evidence."

"Thank you, Judge. Your honor, I ask that you review these documents as evidence my client is the rightful owner of this property and that it shouldn't be auctioned. My client has tried in good faith to resolve this matter and shouldn't be punished as events that transpired that were out of his control. For instance, it is not his fault that Jo Daviess County didn't fulfill its obligation regarding the issuance of proper documentation certifying his ownership. In addition, my client is being harassed by a scoundrel who wants to discredit him and is using this auction to do so."

The judge leaned over the document and studied it for several minutes before he spoke.

"I will accept this will and application as proof of ownership. As a legal claim has now been established, that leaves the matter of unpaid taxes; therefore the property is still remanded for auction. Does your client have any proof of tax payment for the property?"

"No, your Honor. The county's own records were destroyed in a fire. My client did faithfully pay the taxes despite not receiving the deed."

"Well then, I believe that as rightful owner, Mr. Adams must have a record of payment. I am ordering him to pay one hundred dollars in taxes, and he can keep his property. I will order the county clerk to issue the deed to Mr. Adams as soon as payment is made."

"Your Honor, my client can pay, but I believe he has been grossly wronged in this action. The loss of records was not of his doing, and the county bears some culpability in this issue. I am asking you to reduce the amount to fifty dollars. My client has been under much stress regarding this issue and only seeks to put things right, according to the law."

"Very well then, fifty dollars and costs."

We proceeded to the clerk's office and took care of all the necessary paperwork, paid the fees assessed by the judge, and received the long-awaited deed.

I really liked Sam and didn't want to add to his indignation by charging him a large fee, so I asked for twenty dollars. He surprised me as we left the courthouse.

"You know, Major, I expected to have to pay those taxes again. So, I want to give you the same fifty dollar amount that you saved me as payment for your services."

"Why, thank you, Sam. Anytime I can be of service, just call on me."

Sam handed me the money, and I made my way back to the office.

The January snow certainly put a damper on traveling Galena's streets. Yesterday's mud holes were frozen over, and wagons slowly jostled and bounced along, breaking the ice in an awkward fashion. I was considering proposing marriage to Rebecca as I stoked the fire in my office stove. Most of the army was in winter quarters and there was no word of major engagements. With the war sure to heat up again in the spring, it seemed a foolish thought. The last thing I wanted to do was to marry her and then leave her a widow almost immediately. Sitting at my desk, I began going through the mail when I came across a letter from the War Department. I opened it with a mixture of dread and excitement. I was promoted to Lieutenant Colonel. With my acceptance, I was to report for duty immediately. I called on Judge Thatcher to show him the letter.

"Tom, it seems as though your decision has been made for you. I assume you will accept. But I think Rebecca may have other ideas. I will go and fetch her."

The judge strode off to gather his daughter while I paced the floor, trying to collect my thoughts. Rebecca practically flew into the room, and my arms, "Oh Thomas, what are you going to do? If you go, you will have to give up your law practice again, and worst of all, I will miss you terribly."

"I understand, dearest. I will miss you too. I have worked hard to rebuild my reputation as a lawyer here, but it is also important for me to fulfill my obligation to the army. I suggest we ask God for help."

With the Thatcher's standing with me, we all held hands and lifted the decision up to God. I went back to the office with a somewhat lighter feeling.

The next morning, I sat at my desk reviewing the commission letter. After I finished, I looked up and stared out the window at the falling snow. The large, fluffy flakes fell with hypnotic beauty. It was so relaxing I slipped into a trance.

*The guns fired a volley, and the cannons roared. The flashes from the muskets, the death that surrounded me, and that horrible yell as the Rebel line advanced. The young Rebel soldier appeared through the smoke. His eyes fixed on me and mine on him. The shots. I hit the ground once again, feeling the terrible pain in my shoulder.*

The trance was interrupted by a loud knocking at the door. It was Rebecca. She entered stamping the snow from her boots. I stood to greet her.

"Thomas, are you all right? For a moment there, I thought you were a statue. I knocked several times and you just sat there."

I tried to regain my composure.

"Yes, I believe so. I still am haunted by the ghost of Bull Run. I do so wish it would leave me alone."

"Thomas Sawyer! I know you better than most in Galena. I believe in your heart you want to return to the army, am I right?"

"I love you," I exclaimed.

"And I love you too, Thomas."

We embraced and held each other tightly for a long time.

She finally spoke. "I know your sense of adventure, and I know you won't pass up this opportunity. I also know I will miss you terribly. You will come back to me . . . Thomas? You will come back to me, won't you?"

She pulled away, and a tear began streaming down one cheek. I brushed it away with my finger.

"Rebecca, God willing, I will return to you."

I consoled her as best I could. After a few moments, we began the task of boxing up the law books. Hard work helped ease the pain in my heart. Most of the moving crates were still in the back room. I took a break from the work to scrawl my name across the signature line of the letter. We worked the rest of the day until darkness fell, and we were both very hungry. Walking Rebecca back to her house, we passed the post office. I mailed the letter to Washington and retired to the Thatcher's house for some late dinner.

"You are a fine commander Tom and congratulations on your promotion."

"Thank you, Judge," I said. "I do have some loose ends to tie up before I can leave. Could you see if Sheriff Minor is willing to rescind his order for me not to leave town? Even though the case of the murders has not been solved, I believe I have proven myself to be above suspicion. I also need someone to inform my clients that I am being recalled to service."

"Certainly, Tom, I can take care of these. Hanna, how soon until we dine?"

Hanna came to the Thatcher's about three years ago and was a freed slave. The Judge paid her a fair wage for her services. He also gave her room and board as she had no family in Galena. She was an excellent cook. Hanna called us to the table for a fine recipe of beef stew and biscuits.

After the meal, the judge took out a bottle of wine he was saving and proposed a toast.

"Here is to Tom. May he serve the army with all his abilities, be a strong leader, and, most of all, be in God's grace always."

A hearty "Here, Here," was said by all.

We retreated to the parlor and sat watching the fire. The judge had paintings on the walls reflecting a time before the war. One was a peaceful valley scene and another of an apple orchard in springtime. They reminded me there was still a chance to restore this nation and bring peace once again. Hanna entered the room and offered to make tea, but there were no takers. An occasional horse and buggy passed by outside. The crackling of the fire was the only other noise, and the room grew quiet. Rebecca broke the silence.

"Thomas, you will write to me as you have in the past?"

"Yes, I promise I will. I will miss Galena and my law practice, but there is the higher purpose of preserving the Union and ending slavery. Rebecca . . . would you walk with me back to my office. I want to continue packing for the trip even though I have no idea where I will be assigned or when."

Within a few hours, we had most of my things ready for storage. A few odds and ends remained that could be easily stored. In the morning, I would make arrangements for the furniture and books to be taken back to the Widow Tompkins' house.

A week passed since I sent the acceptance letter. This morning was a glorious one, the sun was out, and the temperature had warmed to melt some of the snow. I was staying with the Thatcher's now as my office was cleaned out. I got dressed, and after consuming biscuits, bacon, and coffee, I headed to the post office. I expected to hear from the War Department any day now about my re-assignment. What I received was a short letter from a friend.

*To Major Thomas Sawyer*
*US Army*

*I do not have much time as we are preparing for some actions in the field. My father informs me you have returned to your law practice while you healed. That is all well and good. I have been in touch with Washington, and they told me of your acceptance letter. I could use a good soldier to join my staff and help me in this fight. I have checked with the War Department, and they have approved your transfer. Please contact Colonel Oglesby at Fort Defiance, and I can explain more after you arrive.*

*US Grant*
*Brigadier General US Army*

I reread the letter, read the signature at the bottom, and an epiphany occurred. Of course, I thought, how could I have been so stupid? The code Rebecca deciphered was not referring to the United States, but possibly to General Grant himself. It may be an assassination attempt, and it was to occur on February 18th. I never heard anything from the War Department, and they had the same information. To make sure, I immediately went to the telegraph office and sent a telegram to that effect to General Grant and included my desire to join him. I ran to the Thatcher house and showed them the letter.

"It fits you well, Thomas, as you and General Grant are good friends," Rebecca said. "I suppose you will want to leave as soon as possible?"

"Yes, Judge, will you and Ida take care of the rest of my things?"

"Of course, we will, Tom."

"I need to go to the livery stable and collect my horse and saddle. Then I plan to secure passage on the next riverboat going south. I checked the schedules and it will be the first transportation taking me directly to Cairo."

Rebecca and I hurried to the docks.

"Yes sir, Major Sawyer, you are booked on the Fanny Harris heading south to Cairo. You will need to have all your things aboard by 10:00 PM. Passage for the horse, saddle and trunk is two dollars."

We left immediately for the livery stable to get my horse. I purchased him in Galena from a man who sold the finest horses. I paid twenty-five dollars for him, but he was worth every penny. He is an exceptional breed and built for speed. He is coal black, sixteen hands high, with a white diamond on his forehead and white markings just above his hoofs. He is indeed a splendid animal, and I named him Ares after the Greek god of war. I picked up my things and made my way toward the landing. Rebecca returned home to get her parents.

At fifteen minutes to departure, I was joined by the Thatcher family and about sixty new recruits from all around Northern Illinois. Rebecca handed me a telegram from the War Department. It was an acknowledgement of my commission and approval of my joining General Grant.

Without releasing the telegram, I looked at her with watering, but steady eyes and said, "My dearest, I will do everything in my power to come back to you. I promise to you that whatever happens to me, you will always be in my heart, in my thoughts, and in my prayers. Try not to worry if you do not hear from me right away, as I am sure I will be very busy."

She gripped my hands together and responded, "Thomas, I love you and want you to return to me. My heart will ache while you are away, and I will always worry about you."

It was dark and peaceful as the boat headed away from Galena. The water made a loud splashing noise on the paddle wheel as the steamer turned in a gentle arc and began to move swiftly downriver. I stood on the deck with a cold wind in my face and began to think about my new role. I imagined becoming a regimental commander or part of the general's inner circle of officers. That old excitement was coming back, and I was eager for a new command. Officers received a small room on board where I could get some rest. It took five days to reach Cairo, the only stops being for fuel and to change pilots.

The port of Cairo was bustling with soldiers, citizens, traveling gamblers, hucksters, and the like. Upon disembarking, I arranged for my gear to be delivered to the fort, and I took off on Ares. The timing of my arrival at Fort Defiance early in the morning was fortuitous as Colonel Oglesby was just leaving to join General Grant. He informed me there was an attack planned and the details would be sorted out when we got to the St. Charles Hotel where the general was taking breakfast. A Captain Rawlins met us at the hotel, and we were spirited into a back room to meet with the general.

"Colonel Oglesby, Lieutenant Colonel Sawyer," the general said. "I welcome you, gentlemen. We will be moving up the Ohio to the Tennessee River tomorrow with forces from Flag Officer Foote of the Navy. I will give an additional briefing as plans unfold. Colonel Oglesby, you will assemble with your regiment here in Cairo. Colonel Sawyer will join my staff as a courier. Yes, Tom, I did say Colonel . . . I have already made arrangements for your promotion to Colonel. Before you leave, gentlemen, get yourself some breakfast. We must be ready to move tomorrow morning."

"If I could have a word general," I said. "I am sure you are aware of my communication with General Halleck regarding a possible attempt on your life. I believe I can be of assistance in that regard."

"Colonel, I am aware . . . I also know that the entirety of the Confederate army we are about to face wants to kill me as well. While I do not ask you to decrease your vigilance, the priority here must be the battle to come. I feel I am well protected by the guard that has been posted and my staff. If you have any more details, please tell Captain Rawlins. I will inform the captain to make accommodations for you."

"Yes, sir."

Colonel Oglesby and I found a table in the dining room to get a bite to eat.

"Well, Colonel Sawyer, congratulations on your promotion."

"Thank you, sir, I will accept the promotion and am grateful to General Grant for making that happen. My concern continues to be for General Grant's safety and it dominates my feelings."

We were seated and soon served a sumptuous breakfast. There were fried potatoes, eggs, bacon, fresh biscuits, apple butter, fruit, and fresh coffee. I thought of how delectable this looked compared to the rations in the field. After settling in, Colonel Oglesby spoke.

"I understand about the General. He is my friend also. I would hate to see anything happen to him. Pass me the butter, will you?"

"My mind is a whirlwind; the upcoming battle, my new assignment as a courier on General Grant's staff, and telling my girl Rebecca that I arrived safely. I was disappointed I wouldn't be getting a command of my own. But I also know how fluid the situations are on the battlefield and how abruptly the need could arise for a field commander. On the other hand, the general or someone on his staff may have been aware that my horse Ares is a good specimen, and I am a fair horseman. This might have been the reason for my assignment as a courier."

"You will make a fine courier, Colonel. Your time for command will come soon enough." He took a long slow sip of coffee. "But remember, your job comes with the full authority of General Grant, and that means a lot. Don't be discouraged. Whatever part we play in the war we will both have the honor to serve. Let's toast to your new assignment."

Our glasses clinked together, and we both smiled. I felt better about where I was now as we finished our meal.

We left the hotel, and I joined Captain Rawlins for the ride to headquarters.

"You will find a tent has already been set up for you, Colonel. I have arranged for your provisions. If you need anything else, I am at your service."

"I understand, Captain."

"As General Grant's aid, I am responsible for his personal requests and much more . . . if you get my meaning."

"Yes, I believe I do. Everyone is aware the general takes to drink on occasion. I am sure it's an added pressure on your duties."

"Thank you for your understanding, Colonel."

"I am looking forward to a good rest when we get to headquarters. I am weary from traveling."

"I am afraid a short nap will be all that is possible, Colonel. As you know, we are preparing to move out."

There was a flurry of activity as the camp was disassembled. General Grant's party picked me up in passing, and in an hour, the entire army was on its way up the Ohio toward the Tennessee River. The General and his staff were gathered on the deck of the steamer "New Uncle Sam". The General revealed to us that we were going to attack Fort Henry. I glanced at a calendar in the officer's quarters, and it had February 6 circled in red. As we approached Fort Henry, the lead navy ships came under fire. We could hear Flag Officer Foote's forces returning fire. I stayed aboard the New Uncle Sam as preparations for the land engagement were made. Before General Grant could get the troops into position, the fort's commander surrendered. There was jubilation on the steamer, but the general didn't look happy.

"Rawlins!"

"Yes, General."

"Send this message to Major General Halleck. Ask if we can continue on and take Fort Donelson. It is just twelve miles away, and we have enough men, ammunition, and supplies to do so."

"Yes, sir, right away, sir."

When Rawlins returned, there was excitement in his face. He handed the General his orders.

"Major General Halleck says you can continue with all haste."

"Write up these orders, and I will sign them. General Wallace is to bring his regiment up to fill in the middle of the field. Flag Officer Foote is to continue with supporting fire when he reaches Donelson. I will issue others in time."

"Yes, sir."

"Colonel Sawyer, you will serve General Wallace and carry dispatches to me. Tom . . . I trust you as a friend and know you won't fail. Here is a map of the field. Take these orders to General Wallace. I want to have Donelson surrounded as quickly as possible."

"Yes, sir, right away, sir," I said with a sharp salute.

I road straight to General Wallace and presented him with the orders. Fighting was going on along the front, and I longed to join the battle, but the general had other ideas.

"Colonel, I have field notes and copies of the orders I have made. These need to reach General Grant right away. Please take them and hurry. The general has moved his headquarters to the cabin of a Mrs. Crisp. It is here on your map. Now go."

I arrived to find General Grant very busy issuing orders and preparing to leave for an inspection of gunboats damaged during the navy attack. In a matter of moments, he reviewed what I handed him, gave me new orders for General Wallace, and I was on my way back. The air was cold, the kind of day where sound carries a long distance. There were places on the road where water had frozen over. I noticed on my previous trip there was a short cut through a wooded area. It was nothing more than a pathway, but it was passable and brought relief from the cold wind. As Ares was making his way, I heard the noise of horses and equipment being moved. I glanced to my left, and through the trees, I saw a Confederate cavalry column moving down a small access road from Fort Donelson. They must have slipped away during the fighting. I needed to report this action to someone, but how? Should I ride back to General Grant's headquarters or proceed to the front and General Wallace? I didn't know if I was seen by anyone in the column. At that moment, some Confederates rode by very close to my position, so I stopped, and had Ares stand perfectly still. After they passed, we turned and quietly made our way down the path toward headquarters. Once the risk of being spotted abated, I began to ride hard. Suddenly, Ares stumbled on the ice, and it was just enough to throw me off the saddle. I landed with a splat in a mix of mud and ice water. Ares stood there with his breath and mine both billowing white in the air. He looked at me as if to say, "Hey, Colonel, what are you doing playing in the mud?" The only thing that appeared to be injured was my pride as a horseman. I grabbed the reins and tried to remount, but the mud hole was so deep I almost lost my boot. I led him off the road and into the woods where there was firm ground. I heard horses back on the path.

A voice said, "Well . . . where the hell did that Yankee go? I can't see nothin' in these here woods. We best get on back to the column."

I waited a full minute, which seemed like an eternity in the cold, and mounted my horse. Just then, from behind me, I heard the unmistakable cock of a musket.

"Hold it right there, Yank." was the command.

I twisted around on the saddle to look behind me, and there, in a Confederate gray uniform, was Rob Reynolds.

"Reynolds," I said. "You have taken me by surprise, and I surrender to you. I know you didn't kill your wife and children."

I think this comment took him by surprise. There was a pause and a quiver in his voice when he responded to me.

"And . . . and just how do you know that?"

"Simple. Your family members meant enough to you to settle in Galena and try to make a living. I don't believe you would murder your own for the sake of a cause."

"Well, I didn't kill them. It was Nate Wilson that did. We was going to make this robbery of an army payroll train, and he wanted to be sure I would go along. He thought if I didn't have no wife and kids, I would be more willin' to cooperate. Well, he was wrong. Now just get down off that horse, real slow like."

I could see the musket beginning to waver as he spoke. Clearly, the conversation was affecting him. My winter cloak covered my pistol, and as I began the dismount, I dove to the ground, pulled my pistol and fired as Reynolds fired his musket. Reynolds folded over and hit the ground. I quickly went up, felt for a pulse, and found none. I knew the shots would alert the Confederates, so I leaped onto my horse and rode as hard as I could back to headquarters. General Grant was away, so I reported to General Smith.

"Colonel Sawyer, what happened to you?"

"General Smith, sir, I have run on to a Confederate cavalry force, not half a mile from here. They are moving south, and I believe it could be General Forrest's men. I will submit a written report to tell you the rest."

"Thank you, Colonel, this is indeed important news. Major Tomlin, send another courier to deliver Colonel Sawyer's dispatches to General Wallace and send out a scouting party to determine the location, size, and strength of the enemy cavalry. Report back to me within the hour."

I was grateful for the break as it allowed me some time to wash up and get into a clean uniform. As I changed, I noticed a hole in my cloak from a minié ball. It seems Mr. Reynolds was a better shot than I knew. When I emerged from the tent, there was great confusion at headquarters. The Rebel army was making gains on the Union lines and attempting a breakout. This would open up an escape route to Nashville for the

Confederates in the fort. Without General Grant on the scene, the command was confused, and the situation dire.

"Colonel Sawyer, take these dispatches to General Grant and tell him he must return to headquarters at once. He has gone to assess the damage to Flag Officer Foot's ships."

"Yes, General Smith"

I rode to the river and then found the flag officer's command ship, the USS Saint Louis.

"Permission to come aboard, captain?"

"Yes, Colonel"

"Colonel Sawyer, what brings you here?" General Grant said.

"Sir, here are dispatches from General Smith. The situation is dire, and he is asking that you return to headquarters at once."

The general, his escorts, and I rode with rapidity back to headquarters. Under his guidance, the Confederates were pushed back to their original lines. They were once again bottled up in Fort Donelson, or at least what was left of them. I unsaddled Ares and turned him over to a sergeant for some well-deserved rest. The battle took the form of negotiations for surrender. I took the opportunity to write a letter to Rebecca, letting her know of the death of Rob Reynolds, his serving in the Confederate Army, and that this fellow named Nate Wilson was responsible for the killing of Mrs. Reynolds and the children. I didn't have long to write as General Grant came calling.

"Colonel Sawyer, I want you to take a regiment of soldiers for prisoner detail. Please see General Wallace and give him these orders. He will assign the regiment from his corps."

I was elated General Grant gave me a command, even if it was temporary.

"Yes, General, I will take charge of this right away. And thank you, sir." I hurried to General Wallace.

"General Wallace, sir, I have orders here from General Grant."

"Thank you, Colonel." He read the orders quickly. "I will assign you a regiment within the hour. The information you provided was invaluable as we now know General Forrest and his cavalry are no longer in Donelson. If we had only closed the gaps sooner, we might have captured them."

"Thank you, General."

"Oh, and Colonel, you can expect some of the men to be, shall we say less than battle ready. You will receive 100 reasonably fit men for the task. You are to march the prisoners out in two columns for transport to the steamers after feeding is accomplished. Once they are all aboard, your regiment will rejoin the corps. Wounded Confederates will be treated at the hospital, and all able-bodied will be transported."

"Yes, sir, thank you, sir."

My regiment formed ranks and spread out at five paces surrounding the group of prisoners. We didn't have far to go to the river, and I expected no trouble. We moved nicely and had just reached an area that ran along the edge of a wood when shots rang out.

"Sir, there are six prisoners that have attempted escape into the woods. Guards have hit two, and they are dead. The other four are still on the loose."

"Captain, take a detail into the woods and search. Have Sergeant Miller take another detail, go to the river's edge and work their way back to the woods. Report back to me with any updates on the situation."

"Yes, sir, right away, sir."

After a few minutes, the captain was back. "Sir, two of the Rebels were pulled from the river. We are still looking for the other two."

"Continue on, Sergeant. I will take the lead in the search for the last two."

"Yes, sir."

One of my men gave a visual signal, sighting one Rebel. Two shots were fired, and the Rebel surrendered. We cleared the woods without seeing the last one. One of my men found tracks, and we followed them as far as the river. When all the remaining prisoners were on board transports, I went back to headquarters to report on the missing prisoner.

"Sir," Captain Miller said. "The missing prisoner was found dead. He drowned in the river."

"Thank you, Captain. I didn't want to report that we lost prisoners on this mission. You may return to duty and reform the regiment."

I didn't know what was to happen next, but the last few days gave me my second taste of command. The army remained stationary while being resupplied, and there was some degree of normalcy attached to that activity. The conversation between Colonel Oglesby and myself kept coming back to me, and I tried very hard to convince myself being a courier was a good thing. General Grant sent Lt. Colonel Rollins to me with a set of orders.

*Colonel Thomas Sawyer has been temporarily assigned to Briga-dier General Charles Smith's Second Division, Third Brigade Commander, until relieved. He is to replace Colonel Cook, who is being transferred to brigade command in Washington.*

My heart leapt for joy. At last, I had an opportunity to command a brigade even if it was only temporary. This is what all my training, experience, and education prepared me for . . . or had it?

# 4

## Life on the Line

There was no pretense in thinking life in army camps was anything even remotely serene. In fact, a more common attribute would be misery with brief respites of relief. There were no standards for those who chose to cheat the government. Shipments of meat arrived rancid. Hardtack biscuits had mealworms. Vegetables, when we got them, were often in poor condition. After a battle, there were occasional shortages of ammunition and percussion caps. My responsibility was keeping the brigade ready for action.

"Colonel Sawyer, sir, there were two men missing from the 12th Iowa regiment this morning. I'll send out a patrol to get them back. If they are found, shall I hold them in confinement and report back to you as usual?"

"Yes, Captain."

It was gut-wrenching when dealing with deserters. Good men who couldn't take killing or the thought of being killed. They knew the punishment. It didn't matter the reason. They would be lined up before a firing squad of their own peers and executed. We have too much death on the battlefield to be killing our own. I would let them go except for the orders.

"Captain, we have some new recruits coming in today. Some will need to be supplied with muskets and ammunition. I have orders here for supplying the officers and men requesting uniforms. See that the quartermaster brings our needs up to date."

"Yes, Colonel. Here is my report on supplies. As you know, the battery has one 12 pounder with a broken wheel and axle. I am finding it difficult to find another wheel and axle. I have provided a list here of the other needs for the battery, and it is my hope the Colonel will provide some relief."

"I will see what I can do, Captain. In the meantime, tell Sargent Wheeler to pull another 12 pounder from reserves and reassign the crew. Don't waste time looking for replacement parts. That will be all for now."

So far as command was concerned, I was being bogged down with paperwork, not the kind of action I was looking toward. Our daily drilling was the only thing that got me away from my desk. With the victory at Fort Donelson, the men were all too eager to celebrate. Some of the men took to drink right away and were not fit for duty. The next morning, I was confronted by a private who was clearly full of drink. He didn't salute me but went into a wild speech.

"Say, Colonel, I reckon we showed them Rebels. We got the best of them and really gave them hell. Do you agree?" He produced a large knife and began waving it in circles. "Come on you rabbles, come and get me. I can whip all of you single-handed."

He waved his knife once more, stumbled forward, and fell to the ground in a daze. His uniform was of the 1st Missouri, and the kepi he wore bore the symbol of artillery. By this time, the confrontation attracted a small group of men who were laughing and cheering him on. I viewed this as a test of how I could handle the situation. I stepped up on a nearby limber box and began to speak.

"Most of you abide by the regulations regarding liquor. I expect this regiment to be the best in this army. You have displayed courage in the face of adversity, and I expect us to be tried even more in the weeks to come. The glory of God surrounds us, and as the prophet, Isaiah states: 'But they that wait upon the Lord shall renew their strength; they shall mount up with wings as eagles; they shall run, and not be weary; and they shall walk, and not faint.' I know you have lost loved ones, friends, and newly-minted comrades in this fight, and I grieve with you. I know the life of a soldier is hard, but we will persevere. We will be drilling tomorrow at sunrise. Anyone who does not report for duty, with the exception of those ill or wounded, will be disciplined."

Those gathered began to trickle back to their shelters and tents. All accept the private that began this impromptu meeting. He arose and looked at me with a sense of anticipation in his eyes.

"Nice speech, Colonel, but you didn't answer my question."

"Yes," I replied softly, "We did give them hell. Captain, take this man to our holding area. You will arrange to have him sit on a barrel in his underwear until sunset with a sign encouraging temperance around his neck. Hopefully, this will be humiliation enough to keep him sober and deter others from drink."

With no orders to move out, everyone began searching for better accommodations. As the camp offered little in the way of permanent shelter, the men built their own. Much to the aggravation of nearby landowners, men gathered limbs and sometimes whole trees from adjacent woods and constructed rudimentary shelters. Ideas for this type of housing were as different and imaginary as there were men. Some made tents covered with bound straw and crude wooden chimneys on one end. Others constructed more substantial structures out of entire trees, but this type of shelter took more time and resources. In any case, whole streets sprang up, including services for meeting basic needs. I spent each morning prior to drill walking along the line of tents and shanties of our brigade. One afternoon I received a letter from Rebecca.

*Dearest Thomas:*

*I hope this letter finds you in good spirits. I love you, and I pray for your return to me soon. I had a long talk with Reverend Clark today about my spiritual health. It seems he is worried about my not attending church lately. I am fearful something will happen to you, and it affects my wellbeing and probably my health. But do not be concerned, my love, as I will persevere. I love you very much and miss you. Mother and Father send their love also.*

*I wanted to thank you for the letter regarding Rob Reynolds. That poor family has been taken from us now, and we shall probably never know the whole of the story. I have conveyed the information to the Sherriff about this scoundrel Nate Wilson. I do so hope they catch that fellow and bring him to justice. It will do me, and much of Galena, good to see that happen. I suspect he has fled the area as there has been no report of anyone in Galena seeing him. Father and Mother are well, and Father has more work now than ever before. I think of you often and the last meal we shared together before you left.*

*There is a rumor from some that President Lincoln may come to Galena. I do not see much truth in it as I am sure the President has much to do in Washington. Father says he will have his full support should he need it in the future. He has made some past contributions to his campaign and hopes to someday meet him personally. I want to see him succeed because I know if he does, you will be supported in your cause as well. I will close for now but will be writing again shortly.*

*Rebecca*

"Sir, did you say in the dark?" was the response from Captain Davis during our officer's meeting.

"Yes," I said. "In the dark. We need to be ready to form ranks and attack regardless of the time and place."

"With all due respect, sir, we never fight at night."

"Captain, we will do this, and I will take full responsibility, dismissed."

With the early morning came the grumbling of men as assembly sounded at two a.m. Fog from the river crept into camp overnight. Moonlight filtered through the fog and projected everything in eerie black shadows.

"Captain, here are my orders. Have the men form marching ranks, then break into battle formation, place cannon on the ridge, ammunition wagons behind, and then the reserve corps in the woods. I have copies here for each officer. We will begin promptly at two fifteen."

Falling, bumping, howling, and cursing penetrated the fog and darkness until torches were lit.

"Colonel, with all due respect, sir, this is impossible. We are forming ranks by feel and can't find the proper places for our regiments in line of battle. The cannons can't stay on the road. It is a disaster."

"Captain, tell the officers to use the maps provided and verbal direction. We will continue to try this till we succeed. Place the four ordnance pieces on the rise to the south of the line with ammunition supply wagons to the rear."

"Form ranks!"

"Colonel, some of the men are refusing to obey orders."

"Captain Davis, we will discipline any able-bodied soldier who refuses this exercise. I will not tolerate insubordination. Inform the regimental officers I deem ten minutes to be an acceptable time. Anything longer, and we will repeat the drill from its starting position."

"Yes, Colonel, right away."

With all back at the start, we tried again. On the third try, we reached the ten-minute mark. It was nearing daylight, so I issued the order to dismiss for breakfast. Some fresh potatoes had arrived in four supply wagons, enough for a few bushels for each regiment. I hoped this treat would ease their pain.

"Colonel, General Smith has requested you come to headquarters."

"Thank you, Captain."

I went to see General Smith, and with every step, I got a gut-level feeling of trouble.

"Colonel Sawyer, take a seat. I hear you were performing night drills with your brigade. Did you receive orders from me to conduct such a drill?"

"No, General."

"I remind you that you are only temporarily in command of the third brigade. If you wish to continue in this command, you will check with headquarters before conducting any night drills. Were it not for the fact that you are a West Pointer and a friend of General Grants, I would have you relieved. Do you understand, Colonel?"

"Yes, sir. Begging the Generals pardon, sir, I was trying to give the men preparation for what I feel would eventually be a reality. Our brigade just accomplished a night maneuver in ten minutes. I believe it quite an accomplishment."

"I understand Colonel, but you must check with headquarters and let me determine the usefulness of such maneuvers. However, I do admire your forward thinking, dismissed."

I would not make the same mistake again. I needed to think of a way to get back in General Smith's good graces. The next day consisted of marching drills accompanied by boredom and the next more of the same. We didn't extend any invitations to civilians who sold goods to the army or "sutlers" as we called them. Some were tradesmen selling war souvenirs of Confederate medals, pieces of uniforms, kepis, or weapons. Permission was granted to some who provided vital information, but despite the posted guards, others would slip through and mingle among the troops. My concern was always Confederate spies. Toward evening, one sutler was caught without a pass. After an angry altercation, he was shot and killed by pickets from my brigade. There was a loud protest from followers outside the camp. It had the potential to become serious. I sent a note on the situation to General Smith, looked over evidence presented to me, and proceeded to the scene. A hush fell over the crowd as I knelt beside the body and prayed aloud.

"God, I ask your blessings on this poor unfortunate soul. This man didn't deserve to die. This poor man was merely trying to get along in life. Lord, I want you to accept this man's spirit into your care and open the gates of heaven to him this day."

I stood up and spoke to the crowd.

"I know most of you are kind at heart. You must also know I desire this army to be the best it can possibly be. Captain Davis informs me this man had papers on him linking him to the Confederate army. Our job is to protect your homes, your livelihood, and, most of all, these United States from the Rebels. I implore you to turn in any information you might have on Rebel activities. The more we are distracted by this kind of incident, the less protection we can offer you. I bid you go now in peace, and if there are no claimants, we will bury this man." I paused and waited for someone to speak up, but there was only silence. I turned on my heel toward the captain. "Captain Davis! Take charge of this body and see to it a burial detail is formed. See if there is anyone who can identify this man."

"Yes, Colonel."

After a long pause, sutlers began to trickle away from the scene.

It was early the next morning when Captain Davis came to me. It was an unusual visit as I was still in my bed.

"Yes, what is it, Captain?" I said wearily.

"Colonel, I think you should know a person came to claim the sutler's body. She said the man's name was Wilson, Craig Wilson. She said his brother Nate would be none-to-pleased to hear he was dead. She took the body away in a wagon, so I dismissed the detail."

That name shot through me like a bolt of lightning. I saw no family resemblance when I viewed the body, but if it was the same Nate Wilson that committed the murders in Galena; this would serve to fuel his anger toward the north.

"Submit your report on the matter." He paused with a look of anguish on his face.

"Is there anything else, Captain?"

"Sir, there are three privates who didn't report for picket duty this morning."

"See that they are replaced on the picket line and dispatch a detail to search the camp."

"I have already done so."

I got out of bed, dressed, and put on as presentable a face as I could muster at four in the morning. I found the men already detained in the holding area and standing at attention.

"Men, might I remind you that you men are soldiers first and foremost, and such actions will not be tolerated? Do you have an explanation?"

"Private Williams, sir, and this here is Private Jackson, and that's Private Starnes. Well, sir . . . you see, sir . . . we was just . . . well, sir . . . lonely, don't you see, and it was Jackson's idea to visit them ladies."

Private Jackson made a lunge, and the two went rolling on the ground. They tumbled about for a bit, and then Jackson pulled a small knife from his boot. One of the guards used the butt of his musket. This blow cut his arm and drew blood. Jackson fell to the ground. When he stood up again, blood was beginning to run down his arm to the hand that once held his knife.

"Take him to the doctor," I said. "Once he is seen to, take him to holding. Now, Private Williams, you were saying?"

"We was wrong, sir, and we powerful regret it now, especially since we missed duty call and all. We ain't got no excuse, sir."

"I understand you have basic desires Private but not at the expense of your duties to protect this regiment. I won't tolerate such actions. The three of you will be kept under guard until a decision is rendered by General Smith concerning your dereliction of duty."

In the morning, I saw the three secured by their wrists to a tree branch with their feet just touching the ground. Private Jackson was gagged using a bayonet wrapped in cloth. I assumed this was for stating his opinion to General Smith during the interrogation. He had a bandage on the wounded arm. Other soldiers taunted them. Letters scrawled on a piece of wood next to them, indicating the same punishment for others if they failed to do their duty. They could have been executed so they were lucky the general was in a conciliatory mood. This type of discipline spawned some hatred for General Smith and the rest of the command, but it served to keep order.

The next few days were spent working on logistics and keeping the regiment in the best shape possible. On occasion, I visited the sick call to see men lined up to visit the regimental medical staff. The reasons for my visits were twofold. One was to visit with the men who were truly ailing and the other to flush out the malingerers like quail from the brush. One sergeant standing in line seemed to be in much distress.

"What is your name, sergeant, and, where are you from?" I asked.

"James, sir, James Lancaster, from Cairo, Illinois, I head a cannon crew. I got hit at Donelson . . . it weren't much then, sir, but it's got a grip on me now."

"Captain Davis, get this man to see a doctor right away. Tell them to give him special attention and report his condition to me. Men who are able to head a cannon crew are in short supply."

I continued my visit by entering the hospital tent.

"Hello there, soldier," I said. The patient's dark blue eyes slowly opened.

"Hello, Colonel," he said, "You here to meet with the dying?"

"No. I am here to wish you well and to pray for your healing." He raised his head slightly.

"Won't do much good now, Colonel, I already lost my leg, and I can't be of any use to you . . . or to anyone for that matter. I have a farm near Milwaukee and plan to get back there as soon as I can. I have a wife and two small children that need tending too. Listen, Colonel, could you get this to my wife?" He handed me a letter addressed to a Mrs. Goodlet in Milwaukee.

"Yes, I will be sure this gets to her."

"Thank you, sir," He lay back in his bed and closed his eyes.

It was Sunday, and a chaplain came into the tent to conduct services. He brought with him another soldier with a guitar. At the singing of the first hymn, the mood in the tent seemed to improve. They sang "Rock of Ages." It sounded good to hear a chorus of voices praising God, even if some were barely capable. One soldier who was shot through the jaw couldn't sing but waved his hands in the air. Others got slowly out of bed and stood to sing. With the singing of "My Faith Looks Up to Thee," most were putting forth an effort to participate.

It didn't matter where we were from or what condition we were in. We were all just a congregation at worship. My thoughts went to Rebecca and gazing out the window of the Thatcher's home so long ago. It seemed so odd that in this hospital tent, my thoughts were of serenity. I wished that kind of picture could be shared with all of those soldiers. Then the chaplain attempted a few words of encouragement.

"Men, it matters not what we do here on earth, but what God has in store for us. If you have been faithful here on earth, you will be blessed and received into heaven."

He went on to deliver a short sermon on morality. Unfortunately, it did little to cheer the men. The brief respite of serenity yielded to pain and suffering. I talked with a few more men and left. There was little else I could do except pray. On the way back to my tent, I paid the three-cent postage and posted Private Goodlet's letter.

I didn't have long to relax in my tent. I was summoned to the edge of camp to settle a dispute. Captain Davis reported to me that pickets from my regiment found a hog wandering in the woods close to camp. The men did not often get fresh meat, and the temptation proved too great. They shot the animal and had it immediately cut, cleaned, skewered, and placed over a large fire. When I arrived at the edge of camp, a farmer asserting to be the rightful owner of the hog came looking for the animal. He was about 50 years old, his face wrinkled from the sun, clothes, and boots muddy from the fields. He was riding on an old draft horse. As I expected, he was not in a jovial mood.

"Colonel," he exclaimed, "My name is Shiras Combs. I have just come from a three-mile ride to find my animal. This sergeant here tells me that your men have shot and killed my hog. What do you intend to do about it!"

"Mr. Combs, my sergeant tells me that pickets found the hog wandering in the woods." "It ain't so," he said. "Some of your men took my hog from the pen, loaded it on a wagon, and run off down the road. I have a family to feed, and the meat from that animal was to last us until spring. What am I supposed to do?"

"Calm down, Mr. Combs. Just give me a few minutes to get to the bottom of this."

At that moment, a wagon approached, kicking up dirt as it came. It was driven by a tall thin man with a balding head. He wore thin horn-rimmed glasses and a rumpled shirt. He reminded me of a disheveled accountant. He was a comical sight as he drove right into the middle of the group, stopped, and climbed atop the wagon seat.

"I have driven some four miles to rescue a hog that was taken from my farm. You need to return that animal to me as it is my rightful property."

Mr. Combs spoke up,

"This man is Clinton Walters. He lives about a half mile down the road from me. He must have seen your men leave the house with that hog. Clint, the nerve you have, comin' down here to claim it is your hog. I ought to whip you right now. I'll tell you, Colonel, this man is a liar, a cheat, and you can't believe nothin' he tells you."

At that moment, Mr. Walters jumped down from the wagon and grabbed Mr. Combs from his horse. The two men began exchanging punches. Mr. Combs got in a good right hand that bloodied Mr. Walters' nose. My pickets separated them and held them at some distance from each other.

"All right, enough!" I said. "Captain Davis, assemble the men on picket duty this morning."

After the pickets were assembled, I reviewed the line. As I walked along, there were three men who stood out to me. I dismissed the others, took the three aside, and began the questioning.

"You men want to tell me what happened here?"

One saluted and began to speak, "Private Macklin, sir, we were on picket duty in our usual places and we heard this noise in the wood and went to investigate. When we saw this hog, we shot it and brought it into camp. That was it."

"You are lying private, now tell me the truth."

They all stood silent, and minutes passed. Finally, one of the other two spoke.

"I told him this wouldn't work. You idiot, you got us in big trouble here. It was Mack's idea, sir. We passed this farm yesterday and saw the hog in the pen. Mack said we ought to get it when we were on duty today. That's when we took the animal and shot it."

"I can't have thieves on picket duty protecting my men," I said. "Captain Davis; take these men to our prisoner holding area. I will let the general decide their fate. Have Mr. Walters escorted out of camp. Perhaps having his nose bloodied will convince him to leave Mr. Combs alone."

"Now, Mr. Combs, we were discussing proper reparation for your animal. I do not wish to burden you or your family. I can't return your animal, but I will make reparations. I will pay you a fair price for your hog. I am prepared to give you a voucher for five dollars."

At that statement, the farmer's face began to turn a bright scarlet red.

"Damn man, that's not a fair price, its robbery. A friend told me your government vouchers take forever to receive payment. I can't replace the hog nor buy sufficient food with such a paltry sum."

"As my men are already in the midst of roasting your hog, I can't return him to you. My final offer will be to pay you a voucher of ten dollars, provide a barrel of flour, and a barrel of salted beef."

"I suppose I will have to accept your offer though I think the hog worth more."

"Captain Davis, take care of this, will you?"

"Yes, Colonel. Say, Colonel, how did you know those men took the hog?"

"The mud, Captain, Mr. Combs had mud on his boots from the farm, and that same color mud was on the shoes and pant legs of those three. If they took the animal, then it must have come from Mr. Combs' farm and not from the woods as they claimed."

As I watched the procession leave, I thought of all the innocent people in this country swept up by the effort to feed armies on both sides. Young or old, rich or poor, this war touches everyone. As I proceeded back to my quarters, I was stopped by Captain Davis.

"Sir, I bring you a message from the medical staff."

> Colonel Sawyer—Sergeant James Lancaster is expected to return
> to duty in four weeks. Dr. Raymond.

The message gladdened my heart.

It was dusk when I made it back to my tent. The sun's bright red glow moved under the clouds, and the sky was filled with an orange hue. The bottoms of the clouds were painted orange with bits of blue sky intertwined. It seemed everyone in the regiment stopped for a few moments to take in the sight. It was breathtaking. For a moment, the sunset was bigger than the Union army, bigger than the Confederates, bigger than this country of ours. It was somehow reassuring that God put an end to the day in this way. Amongst all the misery and death, there was a sign that at least some beauty was present. The regimental band was playing in the background as I settled down in my tent. After taking a small meal of hard tack, and a bit of pork from a certain roast hog, I was content. I heard distant conversations amongst the men about what might be next for the army.

Toward the end of March, the improving temperature brought improved mood in the troops. When I awoke this day from a sound sleep, it was just before dawn. Unfortunately, recent rains made the ground like mush, and it meant the men would be drilling in the mud. This would make for some grumbling in the camp as cannons, limber, and wagons, almost anything that was supposed to be mobile wasn't.

"Sir, this message is from General Smith."

"Thank you, Captain, well it seems as if our general has sanctioned a horse race for the division. A course will be marked off at half a mile and a return to the start-finish line. Each regiment will select one man and horse to participate. Captain, I suppose we need to put this to a vote. At assembly tomorrow, you can hand out slips for the men to write down their choice, collect, and tabulate them and bring the results to me."

"Yes sir, but then you have the best horse in the brigade. What if the men elect you to ride for us?"

"We will cross that bridge when we come to it."

When the vote was in, I was chosen to represent our brigade in the contest. I respectfully declined, citing the prowess of Ares as among the fastest horses in the Union army. The regiment then turned to Captain Henry Davidson of the 52nd Illinois. His horse could give Ares a good contest.

"Sir, General Smith requests that you report to him at second division headquarters. He said it was urgent."

Captain Davis seemed quite nervous. I was used to having things happen quickly in battle, but this message seemed a bit unusual. I was feeling troubled as I arrived at headquarters.

"Have a seat, Colonel Sawyer. I received word from General Grant that you are to enter the horse race tomorrow. General Grant had a long correspondence with a Judge Thatcher regarding your character and past experience. He feels that you would be well suited for a special mission we have in mind."

"But what will I tell the men, sir? I have already declined participation in the race."

"I will take care of this. You must lag back in the pack at the start of the race. The rider representing the 1st Brigade will crowd you and will strike you from the right, so be prepared for the blow. You will exclaim that you are injured, remount, and ride directly to the medical tent. My staff will be there and have been directed as to what to do. That is all for now."

"Yes, sir."

I was hoping that whatever the assignment, it would help with General Smith's opinion of me. After breakfast, an aid brought my horse to the tent saddled and ready to ride. It was a beautiful day. There was a clear blue sky, and a delicate crispness was in the air. Among the soldiers, there was a good deal of excitement for the race. It had definitely increased morale. Some brigades held elimination races to determine their champions. Regimental flags lined the route the horses were to run. Men lined the course and were cheering each champion as they made their way to the start. Of course, there were wagers made. This gave things a sense of urgency among the men. When I approached the start line, there was a howl of protest. At that moment, General Smith appeared and made an announcement that I would be riding for the general and his staff. Before there was a chance for the protest to grow, a corporal from the signal corps at the far end of the course waved the start flag.

I made sure that Ares lagged back in the pack. We reached the turn, and the horses slowed. I was bumped as planned, only the bump was harder than I expected. It turned my horse, and I was spirited to the ground. I was immediately picked up off the ground by two members of the general's staff and carried to the hospital tent. I kept asking if Ares was all right, and I was assured he was. I finished brushing off any effects as General Smith entered the tent.

"Colonel Sawyer, you have an opportunity to serve your country that will require your utmost skill and cunning. For the moment, you will be isolated here in the medical tent. I will tell the men in your regiment that you have been severely injured and may not return to duty for some time. I will have your things gathered and sent to Galena, including your horse. Here are your orders from General Grant."

As I took the orders, I felt a great surge of anticipation. I had no idea what to expect, but whatever it was, I prayed to God I would be up to the task. I knew that, if General Grant was involved, I would do my best to meet the demands.

# 5

## Desire to be Undercover Tom

*Colonel Sawyer:*

*You will be provided with documentation saying you are a merchant from Philadelphia, Pennsylvania, in the dry goods business. You must assume this civilian role until you reach your destination. We cannot risk the Confederate armies knowing your location. It is imperative you tell no one where you are going.*

*You are to proceed to Mound City, Illinois, via the USS Louisville. You will be accompanied by a military protection detail dressed as civilians. At the docks, you will report to the Mound City ironclad. Once on board the ship, you will report to General Frèmont and Major EJ Allen to receive further orders. I can't tell you how valuable your service has been and will continue to be. Please destroy this message.*

*US Grant*
*Commanding—Army of the Tennessee*

I felt a churning of exhilaration in my body. I had not felt this excited in a long time. I met Major Allen once before and knew of his direct connection to President Lincoln. His real name was Allen Pinkerton, but he went by Major Allen while in the military. It made me heartsick to be ordered not to tell Rebecca anything. There was no one I trusted more than her. But I didn't want her to worry. I was worried enough for both of us. The papers for my new identity fit neatly into the jacket pocket of my new clothes. I met Jacob and Jim, the two men assigned to protect me.

We traveled rapidly by horseback to the USS Louisville. We boarded the waiting steamer. As things slowed down I took the opportunity for casual conversation.

"Well, Jacob, nice weather we are having, don't you think?"

"Pleasant enough, sir."

"You have any place you like to eat around here?"

"No, sir."

All the while, Jacob was continually looking up and down the deck. His concentration was clearly on the surroundings and not on my questions. It was also clear I wouldn't be getting information from him. His associate, Jim, had the same attitude. They were unlike anyone I ever met in the service. Both were tall, strong, young, men, and I believe they were specially selected for this type of work. They were trained to be ever vigilant and well-disciplined, something that did not reflect current military training. Then Jacob approached me and said, "Sir, I suggest you turn in below deck and get some rest. I have orders to keep you below deck for security reasons. Good night sir."

The journey took several days and I was asked to stay below deck as much as possible. I passed the time by praying, playing solitaire and carving a small doll. Chance sometimes forced me to talk with others passengers and I was quick to assume my new identity. Jim would intervene in some conversations and come up with an excuse for me to return to my quarters. Jim and Jacob were continually watching out for anything suspicious from the other passengers. On the fifth day Jacob awakened me at three fifteen in the morning. After a small breakfast of potatoes, eggs, bacon, and coffee, we left the ship in a small skiff.

"Sir," Jacob said. "Once we dock we are under orders to see you safely to the Mound City. General Frèmont and Major Allen are waiting for us."

We walked at a brisk pace with Jacob leading the way and Jim trailing. The Mound City ironclad blended into the morning darkness. She was painted black and her outline barely recognizable. The crew was in dark blue uniforms and moved about the darkened ship with ease. Jacob, Jim, and I approached the commanding officer.

"Permission to come aboard," Jacob said.

We all went below. Three men sat around a table veiled in cigar smoke. I recognized Major Allen right away. Another, General Frèmont, fought in the Mexican War. Our paths had never before crossed.

"Colonel Sawyer, I am Major General John Frèmont." He shook my hand vigorously. "I think you know Major Allen."

"Colonel Sawyer, good to see you again," Major Allen said, "This gentleman is Albert Richardson. You probably have read some of his work in the New York Tribune. He has been of invaluable service to the military, in an undercover capacity."

We all sat down. Jacob and Jim were standing and ever vigilant in the back of the room.

"Colonel," General Frèmont continued, "It will become obvious to you in a few moments why you were chosen for this mission. I must ask you all to remain silent while our visitor is with us."

He made a motion with his hand, and Jacob and Jim left the room. When they returned, they had with them a Confederate army officer. They positioned him in the lantern light. He raised his head, and I was stunned. This didn't seem possible, and I thought this must be a dream. I felt as though I was seeing myself in a mirror. He was the same height and build as I was, except his hair was longer. There was a pause as everyone assembled took in the sight of the two of us in the same room.

General Frèmont finely spoke, "Colonel, the Confederate major standing before you is James Blake. Major Blake, do you have anything to say?"

"I am Major James Blake, Confederate Army of the Potomac."

He stared at me with a pained expression, and I am sure I returned it with something similar. We could not stop staring at each other. It was almost as if the rest of the people in the room disappeared. General Frèmont made the same motion with his hand, and Major Blake was removed. There was a long period of silence, and I assumed it was to let Jacob and Jim escort Major Blake away from the ship.

General Frèmont began, "Colonel Sawyer, as you are probably aware, the Union and Confederate armies have been conducting prisoner exchanges. There will be a prisoner exchange with the Rebels on June 13th at Aiken's Landing, Virginia. Major Blake is on the list of those to be exchanged. Colonel, you not only look alike, but your voices sound similar. You can see why we have taken safeguards to get you here. We would never have discovered this amazing coincidence were it not for General Grant. He noticed the similarity when Major Blake was on a prisoner transport that passed his way. Prior to his capture, Major Blake served on the staff of Confederate General Robert E. Lee as an orderly and courier. I am sure by now, you can see what we have in mind. We are in the process of organizing a select group of men we are calling the Jessie Scouts. This select group will conduct clandestine activities behind the Rebel lines."

There was a knock on the door, and Jacob and Jim returned with a second man.

"Colonel Sawyer, this is Daniel Blake," Major Allen said. "He is James Blake's younger stepbrother. Daniel is a northern sympathizer who has proved his worth by providing us with a good deal of intelligence on the Confederacy. Daniel now lives in Philadelphia but spent his younger years on the Blake Plantation. He left home at seventeen after an argument with his father. Daniel is willing to teach you everything he knows about James and his family. The potential benefit of having a Union man in General Lee's inner circle goes without saying. Mr. Richardson is accomplished at this kind of work. He is here to help you regarding your undercover work. Do you have any questions?"

"Major Allen, I have a million questions. My first question is—do you actually think this would work? Even if I managed to get into Lee's camp, I don't know how long I could play this role. You have gone to a lot of trouble to get me here and protect my identity. I don't think this mission has a chance in hell of succeeding."

"Colonel," General Frèmont said. "You are being ordered to seize a rare opportunity to serve your country. Your mission is to find out and relay as much information as you can to our Union Forces. You will relay that information through our scout network. You can accept this mission or resign your commission. The choice is yours. Remember, the prisoner exchange date is set for June 13th. Until you make a decision, you can remain under our protection, but you must not leave the city or be seen by anyone."

Jacob, Jim, and I left the ironclad and headed to a nearby residence. The house was three stories, well-appointed, and had, what appeared to be, the latest in furniture. At least the army wanted me to be comfortable while I thought this over. You could hear the anxiety in Jim's voice as he bid me goodnight. I had come there with nothing in the way of personal items. The army supplied me with a nightshirt. I sat in the overstuffed bedroom chair and was consumed by my thoughts. What about the war? Fighting against Union troops without missing a beat? Could I get that close to General Lee and keep up the masquerade? These were big issues. But then Major Blake was serving as an aid to Lee, and there may not be a need to fight against my own troops. It could be the opportunity of a lifetime or the chance to die a martyr's death. I feared the latter. I had no idea how this was going to work. Would the information Daniel Blake provide be accurate? Could he be trusted? Was there an escape route? All this kept me wide awake. I needed to learn more about this optimistic plan. I prayed hard.

> *"God, help me in this fateful decision. Alleviate my fears no matter what I decided to do and to help me. Our Father, who art in heaven . . ."*

I finally drifted off to sleep in the chair. I awoke late in the morning. The sunshine was filtering through the bedroom windows. It shown through the crystals from a lamp on the nightstand, and there were tiny rainbows all around the walls. It may have been just the way it always was when the sun came through those windows, but to me, it was a sign. I thought about Rebecca's words when she helped me pack, and they echoed through my head,

> *"I know you will do the right thing."*

I dressed and went downstairs to the dining room, where Jacob and Jim were eating breakfast.

"Good morning, Colonel," Jacob said. "Have you come to some decision?"

"Yes," I responded, "I have. You can inform General Frèmont and Major Allen I will do it."

"Very good sir, I will do so right away" he immediately left the table.

I didn't tell them half the reason I said yes was a morbid curiosity to see what they were planning. I sat down to a breakfast that was wonderful in every respect. There were biscuits, bacon, corn cakes, apples, fried potatoes, ham, and honey. It was a feast compared to the food in the camps. When Jacob returned, he had Albert Richardson with him. We retired to the parlor where Mr. Richardson began my training,

"First off, we need to get you educated in the spy business," he said. "You will refer to me as *scarlet* in all communications. That is my code name. Your code name will be *fox.*"

"If you don't mind, I would like to choose my own."

"And what might that be?"

"Huck," I said.

"Very well then, Huck it is. You will refer to yourself in all messages as Huck. I will provide you with a list of scouts and their code names. Any one of them may be your contact while you are with the enemy. You must memorize both their real and code names. Only use their code names in correspondence. I don't need to remind you that your safety and the safety of those in the network depend on secrecy. I have here some daguerreotypes of the individuals, and we will study them over the next few days. This will allow you to know the contacts by sight. I will brief you on each of their characters."

He produced a large feed sack from the parlor closet. Reaching in, he took out a canteen.

"This canteen appears to be normal with a flat spiral design on both sides. However, if you press on the center of this spiral, take a knife and carefully pry on the exposed notch, it loosens the spiral plate and exposes an inner chamber for placing notes or a map. It is specially made, so there is no difference from a regular canteen in the amount of water it holds, and the cover is made with a close enough fit that water and dirt won't penetrate. I suggest you leave it in your tent, so it won't draw suspicion."

Next, he produced a Confederate sword from the sack.

"This is a remarkably fashioned Confederate officer's sword. What makes this sword unique is that the hilt is detachable. By pressing a small lock button at the innermost point of the guard and applying a left-hand twist, it pops off like this. Once the hilt is detached, you will notice it is hollow on the inside for notes or maps. Put the hilt back into place on the blade by pressing down and giving a right-hand twist, like so. Once locked into position, it has the strength of a normal sword. Only by a very close examination could one detect the button. It is recessed to avoid accidental activation. These three cigars are laced with opium. Smoking one for a few minutes will bring on unconsciousness, but we are not sure how long it will last. This is a bottle of disappearing ink for notes and a cipher wheel for encoding messages. It is hoped the canteen and sword can be exchanged without notice. They will be the primary means of communication. Duplicates of these items have been produced so they can be exchanged. You will have scouts around you from time to time, so hopefully, that will be of some comfort."

For the next few hours, I made clumsy attempts to correctly operate both the sword and canteen. With Mr. Richardson's help I began to get fairly proficient.

"Colonel, I need to leave now, but I wish you the best of luck. I will be sure your identity and code name are shared with the scout network. We will be in contact."

It was well after lunchtime when Jim brought in some water, boiled potatoes, crackers, and apples. After lunch, I was alone with my thoughts for a few moments. It was a lovely spring day, and I wanted very much to go outside and take a walk. That thought was interrupted by a visit from Daniel Blake. I noticed he was sweating a great deal, and it seemed too much for the weather we were experiencing. His clothes were a bit rumpled, and he was rather pale in complexion.

"Colonel," he spoke in a raspy voice, "This is by far the most difficult thing I have done for the cause. I still love my stepbrother, although I do not condone his actions with the Rebels. I believe in the Union cause, and I can understand if you have some reluctance to trust me. I will do everything I can for you. When this war is over, I pray we will once again be a country. I know you will do the right thing."

I thoughtfully looked over this Virginian. He ended his statement with the very same phrase Rebecca used. This was somehow reassuring to me, and any doubts vanished.

"Well," Mr. Blake, "I believe you are ready to school me on your stepbrother, so, shall we begin?"

"My father Jesse and mother Martha own a tobacco and cotton plantation just south of Clarksville, Virginia. Father was married once to a woman named Millie Toliver, but she died. After her passing, my father moved to Clarksville. James was a child of that first marriage and came with him. He met my mother and married her within a year of his arrival. My two sisters and I were born in Clarksville. Laura is the youngest at eighteen and married to Roger Clark from Roanoke, Virginia. They live in Roanoke and have two children. Mary is twenty and has not been married. She lives with our parents on the plantation. It would be best if you didn't contact them while you are behind enemy lines. Any messages to them must come from me. Once I receive word that you are with General Lee, I will write to my parents and tell them James has returned to the war. James was never one to write letters, so they won't think it strange to hear this from me."

Daniel went on to tell me about family life on the plantation and what he could remember of their childhood. He told me the family had about twenty slaves that worked the plantation. I repeated back the details several times until he felt I grasped them. Then we went on to James' personality.

"James," Daniel began, "has a gift for keeping track of things. He worked every day on the family's finances and kept track of selling our tobacco and cotton. He courted a girl named Sally Turner and was almost married, but Miss Turner rejected him. James took this very hard. He still talks about Sally as the love of his life. James does have a temper, but it is rare that he shows it. He was cheated once by a tobacco merchant and became enraged. There was a fight that ensued, and he beat him to near an inch of his life. He was acquitted of charges because there was testimony from witnesses saying the merchant provoked the fight. Most generally, James is quiet, does his job, and stays out of trouble. He has a nervous habit of rolling the material of his clothes between his first and second fingers of his hands. He doesn't smile much and keeps himself neat with a short beard. He will keep his hair medium length."

"Is there anything unusual about his walk or anything?" I asked.

"No," "Other than the thing with his fingers and his love for the Confederacy, he is pretty much normal. You must try hard to learn the way James spoke certain words. Words like "tobacca" not "tobacco" and "confedrat" not "confederate." I will teach you all I can."

I was confined to the house in Mound City for several more days working with Daniel on my articulation of words. Jacob and Jim continued to be ever vigilant and most curt with their conversation. Jacob did tell me Major Allen left and would return with additional orders. I was now able to look at the daguerreotypes and identify all the scouts. Proficiency with the tools was better. The tiny button and release of the hilt on the sword was the most difficult. There were times when I wanted to throw the sword out the window of the house, but I restrained myself. After Daniel left I made a list of words and worked hard on the pronunciations. The hardest part of this isolation was not being able to send letters home.

The schooling was not done. One morning Major Allen came to see me with a young woman.

"Colonel," he began. But I cut him short.

"Miss Van Lew," I said, recognizing her from her daguerreotype.

"Colonel Sawyer," she said. "I must confess I didn't expect to meet you personally. My station is in jeopardy of being exposed while I am here. Therefore, I shall be as brief as possible so I can return to Richmond. President Davis is more confident than ever the South will be victorious. He continues to deliver this message to the troops and to his military leadership. While I have other business that has brought me here, General Grant asked me to warn you Lee's army at some point may push north. I do not know when this will happen, but you must not miss this opportunity. I am sure you will be taken to his headquarters once exchanged. I wanted to meet face to face with such a courageous man and wish him good luck. I look forward to working with you."

She pulled a cloak over her head and hurriedly left the room accompanied by an escort. After two more days, Major Allen returned. Jacob and Jim escorted me back to the ironclad that evening.

"Colonel Sawyer, I have a special note for you, but before we get to it, I think you must know something important. In these past few days, we have suffered a major loss of troops and equipment near a place called Pittsburg Landing. General Grant has managed to stave off a major attack by Confederate troops but at a heavy cost."

Gloom settled over the room for a few moments, and we both sat without speaking. Then Major Allen handed me the note.

*Colonel Sawyer:*

> *It is with my sincerest gratitude that I write this note. I understand that you have the distinct opportunity to provide your services on a special mission. I would be personally grateful, the country would be forever in your debt, and our cause would be made better for your acceptance. Although we have never met, others speak to me of your bravery and tell me your character is above reproach. Your service in Mexico, at Bull Run and under General Grant, has readied you for this mission. The least slip on your part will result in a threat to not only your life but to those who support you. It may mean you will sacrifice yourself for the secrecy of the mission and the good of our county. I pray God will be with you.*

*A Lincoln*

A note from the president himself was indeed an honor. I read the message again and was awestruck the president would even take the time. Major Allen then spoke,

"Colonel, I have here some items that will be a necessity. Part of the reason for Miss Van Lew's visit was to bring this map of the Confederate troop positions. She risked much to deliver it through enemy lines. Here are General Lees' headquarters and the names of the regiments in his command. In questioning, it was discovered Major Blake also performed courier duties for General Lee. As an aide to the general, he was also in charge of provisions for General Lee's staff officers. At the time of his capture, he had this notebook. It contains likes and dislikes for officers and mention of his duties. Be wary of any questions concerning the notebook as the enemy may know it has been in our hands. I would advise you to pretend you were beaten while in captivity and your memory a bit faulty. That would explain your inability to recall the intimate details of your duties. Hopefully, they won't see through the ruse. The Mound City will be leaving tomorrow for Cincinnati. Once in Cincinnati, you will travel by train to Washington. You will travel in civilian clothing, with Jacob and Jim seeing to your safekeeping. We will supply you with Major Blake's Confederate uniform. When the time comes, you will board the steamer New York with other Confederate prisoners. You will be taken to the landing to be exchanged. Good luck, Major Blake."

There was constant traffic along the river. Supplies, men, and materials were being moved by almost any conveyance that would float. This made the waterway very congested. Our captain was kept busy, avoiding the abundance of wrecks dotting the river. Some were evident as part of the vessel was exposed in the water while others were not. We put ashore several times during the journey, slowing our progress. I spent my time going over the documents I was given and hoping my brain could hold most of the information. Major Blake's notebook was my main interest. Name abbreviations like CM, WT, CV, TT, AL, and RC, followed by listings of personal likes and dislikes. I studied these carefully but was not positive who these individuals were. I asked Jacob if he could find out some full names to go with the initials. We reached Cincinnati without incident, and Jacob and Jim made sure we got to the train station without incident.

By now, the month of May was almost over. Our train traveled on a circuitous route and was delayed several times as the Confederate cavalry had torn up the tracks. I used this time to full advantage by studying the notebook. Upon arrival in Washington, we didn't leave the car until a carriage was summoned. The carriage was the covered, black lacquered kind with dark side curtains. As we traveled, smells of sewage filled the air. I couldn't resist the temptation to peek through the curtains as the swaying carriage yielded brief glimpses of the outside world. I was greeted by a stunning sight. The unfinished capitol dome served as a backdrop for a chaotic scene. Citizens and soldiers alike filled the streets. We passed by several hospitals. Soldiers without arms and legs, their wounds still bearing bandages, moved slowly up and down the streets. After some minutes, we arrived at a back entrance to the Willard Hotel. My room was on the top floor. Jim stood guard at the door while Jacob accompanied me in.

"Well, Colonel, how are the accommodations?"

"Fine, fine, it will probably be a long time before I am in a hotel room as grand as this."

"If you don't need anything else, sir, I will leave you and check on your departure time. Colonel, you will need to keep this door locked at all times. Jim will be leaving with me, and we do not want to draw suspicion regarding this room. However, we will be keeping a watch on the hallway on a regular basis."

Jacob left the room, and the weight of my decision began to consume me. The night was now descending. I knelt beside the bed and began to pray for guidance from God.

> *"God, you have been my protector from the time I was born. Please watch over me in what some may say is a fool's journey. I ask you to spare me any trials to come, but if there are any, I ask for the courage to endure them. Please be with Rebecca and comfort her and her family while I am away. I ask that my role may be to shorten this conflict."*

The next morning Jacob announced his presence with a special knock and a verbal command. I opened the door carefully, making sure no one else was in the hallway.

"Colonel, I have some news about your request. Our scout network has put what we think are some names to the initials in Major Blake's notebook. We believe CM stands for Charles Marshall, the WT is for Walter Taylor, and the CV is for Charles Venable. Hopefully, you will be able to pick up the rest in conversation. I have some procedures regarding your integration into the Confederate ranks. On Tuesday of this week, you will change into Major Blake's uniform and be taken to the steamer New York. At this time, you will be integrated with a group of Confederate officers from Alton prison. After this, you will be regarded as one of the prisoners. Do not expect any special treatment. For purposes of the mission, you will be Major James Blake."

In some respects, I felt like a condemned man at the gallows. I still had an opportunity to back out of this whole affair and resign my commission, but something wouldn't let me. It was the thought of how many lives I could save. I envisioned myself as a hero and tried to bolster my resolve.

# 6

## Into the Lion's Den

I didn't sleep much the next three nights. The first night I lay awake in the darkness. What kept coming to mind was the night in the cemetery when Huck and I saw death up close. We saw Injun Joe stabbing Dr. Robinson to death with Muff Potter's knife. The same vision was repeated the next night. But on the third night, I saw myself testifying against Injun Joe. I had summoned the courage as a youth to mark a man for murder. This is the Tom Sawyer I know is deep inside me. It is the man I have come to be, and I drew on this strength. I can and will overcome any trial set before me. Time passed agonizingly slowly, and the rations they placed me on seem cruel even by military standards. I was told it was necessary to adapt me to Confederate rations. I read the scriptures every day and prayed for guidance and protection from all evils. Jacob gave me information that the US Navy had taken the port of New Orleans last month. I sat down to write a last letter to Rebecca, not knowing if it would ever be mailed.

*June 12, 1862*
*Dearest Rebecca:*

*I have been sworn to secrecy regarding the mission I am about to undertake. I can't lie to you; it will be a dangerous one. I do love you and wish I could hold you close, especially at this difficult time. I am unsure of what lies ahead, but I will do everything in my power to return to you. I enter into this mission with every confidence I will succeed. I pray God will be with me in every step I take. I ask that you and your family pray for me in earnest. Please ask those in the church to do the same. I will admit I am frightened, but some of the fear helps me be more alert. I am sure this makes no sense to you now, and it sounds like I am babbling, but if given the chance, I will explain it all.*

*I remember our childhood together, the adventures we had, and what I now recognize as joy when we were together. Such memories will help to sustain me when I get into difficult circumstances. Be assured I love you; I will always care for you and want the best for you. Please tell your father I appreciate all he has done for me. Getting the appointment to West Point and my military training has prepared me well for what lies ahead. I have looked death in the face many times, and I am not afraid to die. Daniel walked into the lion's den, and so I go to face my biggest challenge yet. He made it through, and I believe I can also.*

*I love you very much and am sorrowful at not being with you. I must compose myself and fold this gift to you with all my heart. You won't get letters from me nor I from you until the end of this journey.*

*Thomas*

I was awakened the next morning by Jacob, I handed him the letter.

"Colonel Sawyer, the situation on the battlefield in Virginia has changed. We have word General Lee is now in command of the Army of Northern Virginia. General Johnston has been severely wounded at the Battle of Seven Pines. Major Blake is now in prison in Washington under heavy guard. Sir, you need to prepare yourself."

The Confederate uniform fit, but the smell was, in a word, obnoxious. I considered it one of many trials to come. After a breakfast of two pieces of bacon, coffee, and some hardtack biscuits soaked in bacon fat, we left for the steamer. I was transported in the same black carriage that brought me to the hotel. As we approached the New York, I got my first glimpse of the other prisoners under guard at the docks. As I got out of the carriage, I was immediately seized by two guards and shoved into line with the others. We were all escorted onto the steamer and taken to a large room below deck. There we were told to sit quietly until the steamer got underway. I was thankful no one was allowed to talk. I tried to put my best face on and tried to belay any nervousness. Some of the men decided they would break into the song Dixie, but that was quickly quashed by the guards.

Late in the day, we reached Akin Landing, and the New York belched and chugged into the dock of the plantation. We were escorted off the steamer and told to sit on the grass by the dock. In a few moments, a group of Union officers and enlisted men were escorted past our position and onto the steamer. I sat with my legs crossed and head down, so none of the Union soldiers saw my face. Thankfully, they passed by without incident. We stood up, and the Union guard returned to the steamer. I turned to see it depart, and the thought occurred to me that it might be the last time I see any friendly faces. Turning back, I came face to face with a Confederate colonel I didn't recognize. He approached me, and I saluted. He returned the salute, and he reached out to shake my hand.

"Major Blake, it is really good to see you again. General Lee is expecting you at his headquarters this evening."

"Thank you, sir, it is good to see you again, and I look forward to getting back to duty. However, I must tell you I have some memory problems. I took a blow to the head at the time of my capture and may need some assistance."

He looked at me reproachfully.

"Half a Major won't do, sir. You will be dismissed from duty at the slightest mistake. You must be in top fighting form for General Lee."

We were approached by a sergeant with two additional horses that were saddled and ready to ride. The sergeant said;

"Colonel Taylor, we are ready, sir."

This told me I was in the presence of Colonel Walter Taylor, adjutant to General Lee.

"How are things in Norfolk these days?" I asked.

"Fine, Major, I expect to hear from Elizabeth when we return to headquarters. Major, you have some duties to attend to when we reach headquarters. I have here some notes from General Lee regarding your additional responsibilities."

"Thank you, Colonel."

He handed me a thick pouch, and I tucked it away in my jacket pocket. It was clear there was no suspicion as to my true identity. I began to get some confidence this grand scheme may work.

"Tell me about your experience in enemy hands, Major."

I hadn't anticipated this question.

"Horrible sir, just horrible, after I was captured, I was taken to Alton prison in Illinois. There I was mistreated shamefully. They gave me little to eat or drink, the cells were cold; we slept on the hard, stone floor with only a blanket for cover. I am moving slower now as a result. The prisoner exchange came just in time to rescue me from the smallpox as it was breaking out again."

This seemed to satisfy the Colonel's need for information, and we rode along silently for some miles. I did have one thing to cheer me up. The weather was good, and the ride was not difficult. We came across a picket line and were halted briefly for inspection.

"Rain barrel," Colonel Taylor shouted.

"Very good, sir, come ahead."

"Colonel Taylor and Major Blake for General Lee," he said.

As we approached General Lee's headquarters, I could feel my heart rate climbing, and my head began to pound. The camp seemed to be in a great state of excitement. I was sure it was because of the change in command. Colonel Taylor dismounted and went in while a sergeant and I waited outside. He returned in a few minutes.

"Major, the General can't see you now, he is in a meeting. Your orders are in the pouch. Sergeant Craton has seen to your belongings. He will show you to your tent."

My tent was located some thirty yards from headquarters, so it was a bit of a walk. My heart returned to my chest where it belonged, knowing I had a momentary reprieve from meeting the Confederate commander. I read the orders carefully.

*Major Blake:*

*I wish to welcome you back into service with the Army of Northern Virginia. Due to my recent appointment to command this army, I am asking you to accept a role to which you are somewhat unaccustomed. For the moment, I need you as a courier. Having lost three of my most valuable men in this role, I hope you will accept this important mission. You will report to Colonel Taylor tomorrow and meet with the other members of the staff. I hope your imprisonment has not affected your abilities as a leader in this army. I need every officer to be fit for command and ready to serve. You will be relied upon as an integral part of this army.*

*Army of Northern Virginia*
*R. E. Lee, Commanding*

I pondered the meaning of the orders. Had he heard about my prison treatment excuse? Stupid, I thought, as the orders were written long before my arrival. Being a courier meant that in times of action,

I wouldn't be stationary, and it might be difficult to communicate with the scout network. I discovered many of Major Blake's things were kept for his return. A small trunk was in the tent, and I began to explore. A daguerreotype of what I assumed was Jesse and Martha standing in front of their plantation house. A worn Bible with an inscription inside the front cover, *"To my dear son James, May God bless you and protect you with love, Mother July 1860."* His frockcoat with the infantry major's gold stars emblazoned on the deep-blue collar. Infantry was not something his stepbrother mentioned, but then I failed to ask. Any moment I could be placed in command of Confederate soldiers in battle. This really frightened me. I would probably look for an opportunity to end this charade and make my way back across the lines. I was in need of rest, but the necessities prevailed, so into the woods I went.

When I returned to my tent, a canteen was hanging on my tent post, and a sword was tossed into the tent. I opened the compartment on the side of the canteen and withdrew a small piece of paper. The note read, *"Pick up tomorrow, 1:00 AM, destroy."* I checked the sword, and there was nothing in the hilt. It was nearly 11:00 pm now, so I felt the urgency to get some kind of information to send back in the next two hours. I went out into the darkness. There were pickets standing watch around the General's headquarters tent, and some of his staff still there making arrangements for tomorrow. A group of officers were sitting around a fire, so I slowly made my way up.

"Major." One of them called from the other side of the flickering flames.

"Yes, sir, couldn't sleep," I responded.

We were approached by a captain.

"Colonel Talcott, sir," the orderly snapped, "General Lee requests your presence at once." He arose to leave and came around the fire, so I saw his face clearly in the firelight.

"Good to see you again, Major."

"Same to you, Colonel, I replied."

"Major, I hear you are going to be a courier. General Lee is reorganizing the army, and we will be moving out in the morning. You might want to get your gear together."

"Yes, sir, I will, sir."

I returned to my tent and scribbled a note about the reorganization of the army and moving out, signed it "Huck," and placed it in the canteen. I knew it wasn't much of a report, but at least it was something.

The past few hours told me two things, how the system was going to work for passing information, and another scout had close access to the Army of Northern Virginia. I hung the canteen where it was discovered and lay down to sleep. The night proved to be a lot shorter than expected.

"Major . . . Major, wake up, it is near dawn. The troops will be awakened soon, and we will be moving out. You need to get some breakfast."

"Yes, sir, Colonel Taylor."

They were announced to General Lee by Colonel Taylor, each one of them as they came; Longstreet, Magruder, Smith, Stuart, Ewell, and Hill. I stood close by and tried to commit their faces to memory. After an hour meeting with the general, they departed. A few minutes later, General Lee immerged from the tent. His looks and conduct befitted his reputation. His uniform was spotless; his beard closely trimmed, but in his face were the lines of weariness. He mounted his horse. The tent was immediately taken down, and gear packed away.

"Major Blake," he said.

"Yes, sir," I replied.

"Good to have you back, mount up, and fall in. Colonel Tayler, take the lead."

I learned the new Confederate general was not going to let any grass grow under his feet.

"Your mount, sir," said Sergeant Craton.

"Thank you, Sergeant. Remind me to put a good word for you with the General. This is a fine-looking animal you have brought me."

"Begging your pardon, sir, this is your horse. We kept him for you while you were away."

"Sorry Sergeant, I guess I didn't recognize her in the morning light."

"That's okay, sir. Just take care she don't get shot out from under you."

My first slip and I was praying Sergeant Craton wouldn't mention my not recognizing my own horse. We were followed closely by supply wagons and reserve troops. As we got closer to the Chickahominy River, you could hear minor skirmishing. We reestablished a headquarters at a farmhouse owned by a man named Hogan.

"Couriers stand by for orders!" Colonel Taylor shouted.

The sound of cannons signaled a major battle was underway. We all mounted our horses to await dispatches.

"Major Blake, take these to General Longstreet and await a reply. Here is a map of the field and where General Longstreet is located. Do not lose this map."

"Yes, sir."

I rode in the rear of Confederate troops moving northeast toward the Chickahominy River. The path I was on began to change, and I found an opportunity to pull up in trees lining the road. I pulled the dispatch from my pouch and opened it. It was instructions for General Longstreet to conduct a diversionary attack and hold the line until General Jackson could arrive. I could not delay without suspicion, so I delivered the message to General Longstreet and was given a reply. I mounted my horse and suddenly was frozen in place.

> I heard the cries of the wounded soldiers; saw the exploding cannon, the volleys of musket fire, and the smoke-shrouded gray line coming toward me. I saw that Rebel in my sights and the pistol fire. I felt myself being hit by the minié ball and spinning around. The pain came back to my shoulder, and I felt myself falling. The smell of the earth, the look of Private Lars Winston, the blackness, it all came back to me.

It was then that I heard the voice, "Major! . . . Major! You need to get your ass out of here!"

It was one of Longstreet's staff screaming at me above the gunfire to get going. I regained my senses, apologized with a loud, "Yes, sir, sorry," and galloped off toward headquarters.

Things were happening fast, and I wasn't sure of my direction in relation to the field of battle. I moved through a grove of large pines, and the path narrowed. I came across an unexpected sight. Through the trees, I could make out a form coming toward me. It was clearly a man walking and leading a small mule. The mule carried two baskets of goods and rolls of goods strung across its back. A small flag of the Confederacy flew on the side of its harness. It was being led by a scruffy looking character with ragged brown clothes and a dusty Confederate slouch hat. He had a gray speckled beard, and his hair twirled down nearly below his beard. This was not one of the scout's pictures I memorized.

"Howdy Major. My name is George . . . George Washington. I'm lookin' for a way around all this fuss over yonder. Can you tell me what direction is best? I'd like to find General Lee's headquarters."

"Well, sir, I can tell you the direction you are headed is right back into the fighting. You best take this trail back south. Are you a sutler?"

"Yep, sort of makin' my own way, if you know what I mean."

"Can I offer you a cigar for the journey?"

"No, thanks, too much chance of being drugged, you know." He paused briefly and looked me in the eyes. At that moment I saw a man much younger than he first appeared.

"We must pretend you are interested in my wares," he said.

I took out some notepaper and scrawled a message about the orders just received by General Longstreet. I opened the hilt of my sword and placed the note in the compartment. Closing it all up, I handed it to him.

"George . . . you will see this gets into the proper hands?"

"Yes, sir, I surely will. Oh, and, Major, you might need this sword as it has similar handiwork."

As we parted, I looked back to see him cutting across a field toward the Union lines. This time he was mounted on the mule and traveling much faster. He also changed the flag on the mule to one of the US. I continued my journey back to headquarters. As I rode, the firing increased. I spurred my horse onward and rode hard to make up for lost time.

"Colonel Taylor, Major Blake reporting with a message for General Lee."

"Very good, Major, wait here while I inform the General."

"General Lee, sir, Major Blake has arrived with a message from General Longstreet."

"Very good, Colonel, send him in."

The General was seated at a small table. He was looking over maps and occasionally writing on neatly stacked paper. His spyglass lay across one of the chairs along with several courier pouches. I glanced at the maps, and they appeared to be battle plans. I had little time to prepare myself for meeting General Lee, and this was a real test of my ability.

"General," I said. "I have brought this message from General Longstreet, sir."

He looked up at me with an air of calmness, took the message from my hand, and opened the pouch. He read the note intently, smiled, and said, "Well, it looks as though old Pete will be carrying the day." He only glanced again in my direction. "That will be all, Major."

I saluted, turned abruptly, and left the tent. My heart was pounding in my throat, and I took some deep breaths to calm myself. Despite our being on opposite sides, there was an aura of greatness in this commander.

His demeanor was calm and his movements deliberate. With the battle raging, I was sent out several times with other communications. Each time I learned a little more about the battle around the Chickahominy River and the Confederates were holding their own against superior numbers. There was no evidence of my friend on the mule after that single encounter. Darkness put an end to the fighting as I approached headquarters. I was bone-tired and ached to get off my horse. I passed my last pouch to Colonel Taylor, and he said I was dismissed. At least I had proven that, so far, my cover was solid.

"Major Blake." The voice came from behind me.

"General Long, how good to see you again," I said.

"You also, Major. I assume you are excited about your new role. We will miss your personal attention to our affairs, but we are all making sacrifices."

"I understand, sir. Sacrifices for the cause."

"Major, it is important we have good communication with all concerned. I hope you will apply your thoughtful considerations to the courier position. A report came back from General Longstreet's command you may have had a brief lack of attention to your duties, is that the case?"

"Well, sir, there was an issue this morning where I did have a small mental lapse, but it won't happen again."

"Very good, Major, see that it does not."

I drew a small bit of rations and returned to my tent. Except for an apple, I had not eaten all day. The hardtack and bacon tasted a little better with a cup of coffee. I needed to get into the headquarters tent, if possible. There was a treasure trove of information my troops could use. Tomorrow would bring another day of aiding the enemy, and I was struggling to keep up the role. I hoped a bit of sleep would help, so I blew out the lantern and lay down gingerly. A short time later, General Long approached my tent and called me out. The expression on his face was one of deep concern.

"Major, I have been informed that your time in captivity may have taken a toll on your abilities. I have orders here requiring you to take some leave to go home and rest. You will be leaving tomorrow for your home in Clarksville. I have assigned a horse and saddle for you and will give you orders for a safe passage. I believe this is the best course of action given the circumstances."

"I do appreciate that, sir, but I won't let this affect my actions in the future."

"Major, if it was up to me, it would be fine, but the orders come directly from General Lee. If all goes well, you can return to his command in three months' time."

"Sir, would you please see if the General would reconsider?"

"I will do what I can, Major, but for now, you will be leaving us in the morning."

That damn Confederate nightmare put my mission in peril. I could attempt to escape and cross back to the Union lines. I could go south with the hope of gathering information on troop movements behind enemy lines and then escape. The last thing I wanted to do was to go to Major Blake's home. Daniel warned me not to go there. I kept asking myself where I could do the most good. That is when I noticed the canteen on my tent had been moved ever so slightly. It must be a message. I hurried into the tent and opened the canteen side to reveal a note. The message was in a cipher, and needed decoding. It read, *"Blake escaped, doing everything possible, be on your guard. Scarlet"* I put the canteen back together and tried to quell my emotions. I wanted to strike out at someone or something, but there was no escape. I was in a Confederate prison without walls. Tears of frustration etched my face as I tried to sleep.

I arose the next morning at the bugler's call, dressed, and went out to breakfast. Thankfully there was no sign of the real Major Blake. Someone on the General's staff procured some eggs. I gathered around the campfire and was soon served one fried egg, hardtack, bacon, and coffee. As I sat down to eat, Colonel Taylor approached me.

"Major, now that you are going to Clarksville, General Lee has some assignments for you. There are important dispatches here that must be delivered. One is for General Hill and the second from General Early to his family. A courier will meet you in Lawrenceville to take General Early's correspondence on to his farm in Franklin County. This is an important family matter, and he does not want it delayed by the postal service. The courier who will meet you in two days' time is Lieutenant Chase. I will again have your things packed away for when you return. Do not delay as these must be delivered to General Hill in Petersburg today and to Lieutenant Chase by tomorrow."

He didn't need to tell me not to delay. If the real James Blake came into camp, I would at least be some distance away. I needed to get a message to the scouts that I would be moving south and why. I placed it inside the cover of the canteen and left it in the tent. This would be the best

I could do under the circumstances. Colonel Taylor came out and wished me well.

"Get some rest, Major, and get yourself in shape to return. We need every man at his best. Give my regards to your family."

"Yes, sir, I will."

The thought crossed my mind I would make a break for the Union lines as soon as I could, messages or not. As I rode away, I tried not to panic and go tearing out of camp. I was now on another journey. This ride was unexpected and potentially much more dangerous.

# 7

## Tom On the Run

T he sun was high in the sky, and the air was searing. My leaving was delayed and it was now the Fourth of July 1862, our nation's birthday, but there was no celebration. Word in camp is that Confederate troops were just attempting to break McClellan's line near the James River. Wounded soldiers came flowing back through the camp. Riding a few hundred yards, I stopped within sight of the headquarters and lingered for a few moments. I dismounted and pretended to check the saddle and bridle adjustments glancing back every now and then. It was then that I saw George and his mule with a Confederate flag waving from his harness. He was making his way through camp selling his wares. There was a chance my message would get through.

The road south was heavily patrolled. General Lee kept his supply lines well-guarded, and this would make escape more perilous. I steeled my resolve not to let this misdirection dissuade me from my mission. There still may be a way to get to the Union lines with information in hand. I rode two miles before I discovered a small grove of trees. A check in all directions satisfied me there was no one in sight. Settling back against a large pine tree, I opened the correspondence for General Hill. It was a directive from Lee outlining the expansion of the fortifications at Petersburg to the south and included a map of what was to be done by engineers. I made a copy of the map and directions and inserted them into the pommel of the sword. The other document was a deed for some property near the Early plantation in Franklin County. I could see why the General was in earnest to get this information back to his family.

Ownership of land would be of critical importance as the war progressed. I tucked the documents away and got ready to ride.

The next stop on the way to Petersburg was the Half-way House, so named because it is halfway between Richmond and Petersburg. It was good timing on the ride because my canteens were empty.

"Major, where you headed?"

"South to my family. Barkeep, would you fill my canteens?"

"Certainly, there is a fee of two bits for each canteen."

"What?" I said. "That is an outrage. You charge for water?"

"Times are tough, Major. With the war and the blockade, we need to make money somewhere." He pulled out a pistol and pointed it in my direction.

"Just a moment, I want no trouble. I have just come from General Lee's headquarters and am on my way south. All you need do is fill my canteens, and I will be on my way."

"Major, it don't matter to me where you come from. This land has changed hands three times in the last three months, and I don't much care whose side you're on. That will be four bits, or you won't need water anymore."

"I have no quarrel with you. Like I said, I want no trouble."

"You best be careful, Major. It's a hot day out there, and it can disturb a man's brain."

I paid the money and left. As I approached the lines outside Petersburg, sentries hailed me. I recited the password and showed them the correspondence for Major General Hill. An aide to General Hill greeted me and took the parcel.

"You're welcome to rest your horse, Major," the aide said.

"No, sir," I said. "I am indeed anxious to continue south, but I appreciate your generosity."

"Very well then, you can draw three days rations from our mess sergeant over there."

After about an hour's additional ride south, I crossed a small stream, and my horse decided it was time to take a break. He headed for a cool drink. I dismounted and found some shade. The trees were old and gnarled with roots jutting up and down the bank to find the liquid gold. Unsaddling my horse, I let him graze nearby.

The sun's reflection made the tops of the water glisten as it flowed. My thoughts turned to Galena and the river back home. How I ached to see Rebecca. I dozed off for a few minutes, and when I awoke, my horse was gone. I began to search frantically. I found tracks leading along the creek and back north. I walked just a hundred yards when I saw him munching on some tall grass. The last thing I needed was to lose my horse. Stupid, not securing him, I said to myself.

The Virginia countryside began to open up with many large plantations. Slaves worked the fields. It pained me to see them toiling under the threat of the lash. The road forked, with one going south and the other to the northwest. The road northwest could possibly take me to Union troops. Union cavalry units were menacing the roads south of Petersburg, and I might run into a patrol. My thoughts turned to what I would say to any Confederate troops. I was attempting to return to my command, and the plans for meeting Lieutenant Chase had changed. I rode for several hours and found no soldiers, Confederate or Union.

As I topped a small hill, I saw four riders coming in my direction. They bore no colors for identification and didn't seem to be in military dress. They were traveling fast, but I felt they hadn't seen me. I pulled my horse into the best cover available, which was an outcropping of rocks about twenty yards to the west. I secured my horse and hunched down behind the boulders to await their crossing. Minutes passed, and I began to think the worst. I was right. I heard the cocking of several weapons from behind me, and a gruff voice called, "Well, well, looks like we have got us a Rebel major. What you think of that, boys? You raise up right slow now, Major, and we won't shoot you—yet."

I stood up and slowly turned to look at my attackers. There were only three now, and they were covered in dust. They looked and acted like highwaymen out for whatever they could get.

"What do you want?" I asked.

"We want all your goods and your horse. We got one horse that's wore out, and we are in a powerful hurry. You just keep your hands in the air where we can see them. Caleb, bring that lame horse up here and get him unsaddled."

"You boys ought to know that I am a scout for Major General Hill," I said. "There are cavalry troops not too far behind me. If you don't get out of here, you will most likely be shot or hung."

"Well . . . we happen to know from the newspapers General Hill is snug as a bug in a Petersburg rug. Besides, it's money we're after. You need to shut your trap and empty your pockets."

"Max, just shut up, he don't need to know nothin' about us."

Caleb took my money, papers, sword, pistol, and the deed. They backed away slowly and were in the process of gathering in my horse when one of them pulled its halter too hard. The horse reared and knocked him backward in my direction. I grabbed him and held him in front of me just as another attempted to shoot. As he fired, I dove behind a nearby outcropping of boulders. The round passed through his friend and splintered against the rocks.

I managed to squeeze between two large rocks and into what I soon realized was a dead end. At least there was only one opening for them to come through without heavy climbing. I wedged myself up as high as I could on one of the rock faces close to the entrance. I still had a small dagger hidden in my boot. As one entered the opening in the rocks, I jumped him from behind and slashed his throat. As I turned away, I was hit by a hard, right fist to the face. I fell backward to the ground, and my knife went flying. This man was on me in a flash, and I took several hard blows to the ribs. I was having trouble breathing and felt I was on the verge of unconsciousness. I managed to kick him away, but then he pulled out his large Bowie knife and came at me full force.

"Now we are going to finish this, Major," he said.

He came forward and struck down with the knife. I grabbed his wrist with both hands and held on with all the strength I could muster.

"This is how it will feel to be a dead man, Major. Your time is up."

Just then, I felt him being lifted off me as if shot backward by some mysterious force. I saw him fly airborne before smashing against a rock headfirst. I looked into the glare of the sun and saw the outline of this enormous figure of a man.

Then I heard a familiar voice, "Well, Major Tom, you almost got yourself killed again, didn't you?"

"Silas, how in the world did you get here?" He paused for a moment.

"Well, Major, you see, we got overrun by them rebs an' they caught me. They says they is goin' to turn me in to my old master right straight as there is a reward of one hundred dollars for me. They put me to goin' south under guard, but I escaped them an' run off. Then I spent five nights on the run. I got caught up by them fellows that come after you. They had the same idea of getting the reward money, so they tied me up on the saddle. When they sees you, I guess they figured to get you, too. When they went to jump you I worked loose, watched for my chance an' pult him off you. I didn't know it was you in that Confedrut uniform till I saw you fightin'. Is you okay, Major?"

I stood up slowly and caught my breath.

"Yes, I think so."

I leaned back against one of the rocks to actually take stock. I thought my ribs might be bruised, and a small cut on my left arm was trickling blood. I didn't bother to tell Silas I was now a colonel. It didn't seem to make much difference. At any rate, we were now a burial party for two men and guard for another. We tied the survivor to a nearby tree. I retrieved my things from the body of the one they called Caleb. There were four horses . . . three worth riding . . . with saddles, some additional weapons, and a small food supply.

Silas and I went through the pockets of the dead men. Caleb's last name was Donner. We found several personal letters on him. One was from a First Lieutenant John Mosby, indicating they were to meet on August 15th for the purpose of enlisting in the Confederate cavalry. Two others were from different women, each expressing their love for him. The second man, Max Hardy, had some Confederate dollars, a gold watch inscribed to him by a girl named Lela, and a daguerreotype of a woman. We assumed this to be Lela and left it in his pocket so he could take her to the grave.

Silas and I spent the next four hours digging shallow graves for the two less fortunate and an additional hole to bury the gear we couldn't take. The soil was rocky and made digging tough. We did have the aid of a small shovel and a pick that was strapped onto Caleb's saddlebags. We laid out each body, stood at the graveside, asked God to bless the departed souls, and began to cover the graves. We managed as best we could and piled on rocks to finish the job. We lay in the shade to rest.

"Say, Major, you mind if I keep that watch?"

"You can have the watch. Mind you, if you are caught with it, it might go worse for you."

"Can't get much worse than it already is, they is goin' to hang me sure if I gets caught."

"Silas, I think I will keep this Bowie knife. It might come in handy on this trip. We best get moving."

By this time, it was late afternoon, and we took a bite to eat. Our prisoner was coming around, and we gave him a few sips of water.

"Say there," I said. "You clearly don't discriminate when it comes to choosing your victims. Black or white, Union or Confederate seems not to matter. What is your name?"

"Frank," he responded.

"Well, Frank, why were you in such a hurry?"

"We were goen' . . . to enlist."

"Riding hard so you can enlist doesn't make sense. Why don't you tell me the truth?"

This question was met with silence.

"This could go well for you as I might consider letting you go for the truth." Frank made no comment.

"You just think about it for a while."

Having Frank tied to a tree for a few more hours might change his disposition. In the meantime, I would try to see where I stood with Silas.

"Silas . . . what do you want to do now?" I asked.

"Major Tom, seems we is both in a fix. I got a wife an' children at a plantation an' I mean to get 'em back. Since I is so far south now, an' so close to 'em, I figure I could steal 'em an go north. I met this abductor named Tubman, an' she promised me she can get us to freedom. She is goin' to help us if I can get my family to Danville in the next few days. I met this abolitionist from Danville while I was on the run. He showed me where he lives, an' he know the way north."

"Where are they, your family, I mean?"

"Clarksville," he replied. The name shot through me like a bolt of lightning.

"Clarksville, Virginia?" I exclaimed, just to be sure I heard him right.

"Yes, that's the place. Major . . . I know you is beholden to the army an' all an' if you don't want to help me . . . well, I understand. Beside, God don't choose one side or the other, just cleans up the mess that's all."

Silas helped me get Frank onto one of the horses. We tied his hands securely and placed a rope on the halter with a leader to prevent Frank from riding off. We had already stripped the lame horse and turned him loose. The sunset was offering up a golden hue as we began to move. We spotted a grove of trees in the distance.

About thirty yards into the woods, we came to a clearing with a half-finished cabin. Three of the four walls were standing, so it offered some protection. We dismounted and set up camp for the night. I thought the walls would offer enough cover for us to have a small fire. I retied Frank so he would be sitting down for the night against a suitable size tree some ten yards from camp. I thought that maybe spending a night tied to a tree would give him more incentive to talk. When I returned to camp, a cool breeze kicked up, and the air began to smell moist. We were in for some rain. I made sure my ammunition was well protected. Silas and I bedded down for the night. Unfortunately for Frank, at the base of the tree there was a nest of red ants. He began to yip and yap something dreadful, and we got up to investigate.

"Well, Frank," I said. "Do you feel like telling me what you and your gang were up too?"

"I ain't tellin' you nothin'. You killed my friends, and you will likely kill me too."

"Evidently not," I said, as I started to walk away.

"Wait. Wait." came the cry, "All right, just get me the hell off this anthill."

"What do you have to tell us?"

"Well, we was going to drop this here runaway back to his master, collect the reward, and then join up with the army. We were headed toward Clarksville when we got wind of a payroll shipment. It's comin' down to Petersburg through Richmond by way of the Wilmington Railroad. There was a plan to meet up with six others at Bellfield in three days, intercept the train and relieve it of the money. There is supposed to be nearly 100,000 dollars in Confederate cash on the train. Guess it don't matter none to Caleb and Max . . ."

His words spilled out quickly, so I waited for him to take a breath and finish.

"Being as you're a Confederate major and all, I guess you're going to shoot me now that you know the truth. I ain't done much in my life, so I figure a fitting end will be to get struck down by a Confederate ball."

I loosed him from the tree. He stood with his eyes closed, waiting for me to draw my pistol and shoot him. Instead, I led him to a different tree and tied him again. He was well out of sight of our camp now. Back at camp, I whispered to Silas, "What say we turn our friend Frank here loose. Any disruption he can cause the Confederates will help our cause. I will pretend to go to sleep. You wait about half an hour and quietly sneak over to Frank with his horse. Tell him you will offer to cut him loose if he will forget about the reward on you and make straight for Bellfield. You got that?"

"Yes, Major, I got it."

I knew there would be some risk, but I was also hoping his greed would send him north. I went to my bedroll and lay down, keeping my head cocked to listen. After what seemed like an hour, I heard a stirring of the horses and then heard hoofbeats. Our prisoner rode to freedom. He would most likely be riding wet as a misting rain began to fall. There was enough tree cover to protect us, and the breeze cleaned the hot air and washed it away. I rolled over to see Silas coming into camp with a big grin on his face.

"Well, Major, we just let the mean ol' dog out after them chickens."

"We surely did, Silas, we surely did." I turned over and went to sleep.

By morning, the rain passed, and the sky was beginning to brighten. The dampness was just enough to prevent a fire. Silas and I got a breakfast of hardtack and honey from Caleb Donner's saddlebag. I knew that the heat of the day and the moisture on the ground from the previous night's rain would make things hot and sticky.

"Silas, how do you plan to get your family away from the plantation?"

"Well, Major, I figure I would sneak them out in the early mornin' dark. That-a-way we could have a small head start. There is a rail fence I can shinny cross an' get up close to the cabin. Then, if they don't make no noise, I can sneak 'em out with enough time to get away. There is four-o us an' there is this old plow horse my young-ins can ride. Kind of worked out how we got this extra horse now if you'll let me use her, I will be grateful."

"Well, you seem to have things in order, but you realize traveling at night will be slow and dangerous. Even with a head start, you may be tracked down."

"Yes sir, I do . . . but that is the only way I know to gets them out. I plan on takn' them in a direction so we will be hard to track. Major, can you help me? I sure would be beholden to you."

"Yes, Silas, but you know that if you and your family are caught, there is little I can do to prevent a hanging."

"Yes, sir, I knows it. But the life they have now don't 'mount to much, and I figure God will protect us."

He turned to me with a grateful expression on his face, wiped his eyes, and said, "Major, isn't anyone any better than you are."

We paused and looked into each other's eyes. I was determined to help him in any way I could.

"We best get moving then," I said.

We started to break camp and tried to remove any signs of our presence in the woods. We were on a mission together, and I was determined to make at least the beginning of this rescue happen.

"Silas, we still have some distance to reach Clarksville from here. By now, the Confederate army may be looking for me, and you have a price on your head. That will attract lots of attention. You can't mention to anyone about being with me while we are in or around Clarksville. I will do the same for you. We need to be extra vigilant. Do you understand?"

"Yes, Major, I does, so you can count on me."

It was comforting not to be traveling alone. We began to run low on food. As I predicted, the temperature and humidity made traveling hot and sticky. We made slow progress toward a road turning south to get to Clarksville. We saw a farmhouse in the distance where a woman was standing on the front porch. She scurried inside and closed the door. I took a rope and quickly faked some loops around Silas to give the appearance he was tied to his horse. We rode on and approached the house.

"What y'all want?" she shouted from an open window.

"Begging your pardon ma'am," I said delicately, "I am Major Blake of General Lee's staff. I suppose it looks a might funny an all me bein' out here with this runaway. I'm under orders to deliver him back to his master and collect the reward. I'm powerful hungry and would appreciate anything you might have."

There was a long pause, and the door slowly opened. I don't know if it was the mention of General Lee or returning a slave, but she seemed to have warmed to me.

"We ain't got much, Major, but I can spare a little for you. That runaway o'yours needs to stay outside. I got some berries here and a few apples. You like some buttermilk an a few biscuits?"

While she was scurrying about the kitchen, I put two apples and some biscuits in my jacket for Silas. I finished as quickly as I could.

"Well, ma'am, I want to thank you for your kindness."

I stood to leave and noticed a newspaper on the entryway table. I picked it up and looked at her quizzically.

"Thank you for filling the canteens. Do you mind if I take this?"

"No, you can take it; mind you, it is a week old. It was tossed aside by a passing Confederate cavalryman. Major, I got my husband and two of my boys in the fight. I got myself and my youngest son and daughter to run this farm. I ain't lost any men yet that I know of, but I don't know how much longer I can keep this farm a-goin'. You tell General Lee he needs to make this war short as he can. If it lasts till harvest, I may have to give it all up."

"Yes, ma'am, I will do my best to shorten the war as much as possible."

My heart went out to this lady. I said a small prayer that her trials be brief and her men return home. I gave Silas the food, and he ate it as we rode. We moved cautiously up the road toward Lawrenceville, keeping a watchful eye for troops. According to the map from Colonel Taylor, there were two stage line roads running into Lawrenceville. If I was going to help Silas and myself, I had to deliver General Early's deed. I was hoping this would give us more time without drawing suspicion from the Confederate army. All this time I was wondering about the real Major Blake and if my cover was compromised. We crossed over the Meherrin River and came up on Lawrenceville from the south. We found a small patch of woods off the road, and it appeared to be a perfect campsite. There was a briar patch to the north and west of the woods, limiting access.

"Silas, why don't you wait here and make camp. I will ride into Lawrenceville and deliver this package to a Lieutenant Chase. I should be back by nightfall."

As I entered Lawrenceville on this late afternoon, I found the streets mostly deserted. I found one gentleman sitting in a chair on the porch of the blacksmith's shop. Judging from the scuffed-in grooves on the boards, it was a well-used location.

"Sir," I asked, "could you tell me if a Lieutenant Chase has been here?"

"No, sir, but you might try over at the hotel stage stop. They most generally see everyone that passes through here."

I soon arrived at the hotel. "My name is Major Blake. Can you tell me if a Lieutenant Chase came by here and left a message for me?"

"Yes, sir, Lieutenant Chase came by here yesterday. He said if you came by, you was to meet him at the Brunswick Mineral Springs. It's a big place just up the road a piece to the east."

I rode out to the springs. As I approached the long drive to the main house, I heard a good deal of commotion. A fire in the slave quarters was beginning to grow larger by the minute. Lieutenant Chase was attempting to organize a bucket brigade.

"Form a line, form a line," he shouted.

"You there, get your people over to the spring and start handing buckets," I said.

"Form another line to get the empties back, be quick about it," he said.

"Keep that water coming, we are almost there."

After an hour of hard work, the fire was out. The slave quarters were heavily damaged but appeared repairable. Lieutenant Chase and I sat on the porch of the main house. A woman appeared on the front porch with servants. They brought with them wash water and two glasses of lemonade.

"Thank, thank you for your work," Lieutenant Chase stammered, "you must be Major Blake."

"You are welcome, Lieutenant. I regret I did not arrive sooner. Perhaps, more might have been saved."

I gave the Lieutenant the pouch for General Early's family. Just then, a buggy pulled up to the house, and a gentleman introduced himself.

"I am John Ravenscroft Jones: it appears I am indebted to you both for your efforts to save my property. I intend to reward you by providing you a good dinner and accommodations this evening."

"Sir, I am Major Blake. I thank you for your generosity, but I must decline. I desire to be on my way to my family in Clarksville. I will leave it to Lieutenant Chase to determine his length of stay based upon his orders. Perhaps you know my father, Jesse Blake?"

"Yes, I have heard of Mr. Blake but not made his acquaintance. I understand your need to see your family. I will, of course, give you something for your travels but you must at least spend the night. I will have my best accommodations for you both."

I looked at Lieutenant Chase, and he nodded his affirmation.

"I must apologize for my leaving, but my desire to reach Clarksville calls me to put in a few more miles before dark. Again, I thank you for your hospitality, but I must be on my way."

Mr. Jones directed his servants to bring out some ham, biscuits, and a jar of peaches. He filled my canteens with mineral water from the spring. I mounted, spun my horse around, and rode off in the direction of Clarksville. As soon as the mineral spring was out of sight, I doubled back to find Silas. I approached our camp in the wood with caution. When I reached the campsite, all the horses and equipment were still there, but not Silas. With a price on his head, I thought the worst. Suddenly, Silas appeared from the woods.

"Major, I is surely glad to see you. I wasn't sure who was coming, so I hid."

"We best break camp and get moving if we are going to rescue that family of yours." He grinned broadly.

"I sure does, thank you, Major; I told you in the field hospital you was going to live. God, he does provide."

We headed southwest sticking to back roads. Occasionally, we would ride past a farmer tending his fields. These were generally old men or women as the younger men were enlisted in the service. We kept on moving until nightfall and found another wooded area that seemed a good place to spend the night. I took the opportunity to share the food from Brunswick Mineral Springs with Silas. As night fell, the stars began to glisten in the sky, and the moon shone brightly. We built a campfire amongst the trees, unrolled our bedrolls, and lay down under a canopy of limbs mingled with the stars. I pulled the newspaper from my pocket and began to search the content. After a few minutes, I saw Silas get up and slowly pace back and forth.

"You best get some rest, Silas," I said. "You will need all your strength for tomorrow night."

"We is so close now," he said.

He lay down to sleep. I formulated an idea that might help, but it would keep till tomorrow.

# 8

## Rescue Times Two

We arose early, to start before the heat of the day. We rode most of this day without stopping and put in about twenty miles. The next day we did the same. At around noon we began getting close to Clarksville.

"Major, I has to get round to the north of town to rescue my family. The plantation is bout a mile north of the town. We need to have the dark afor we can get them out. I'm sure I can do this. I really want to do this."

"Okay, let's go north and see if we can find some cover. You have come this far. Are you sure you're up to this?"

He didn't answer.

We rode on with Silas in stone-faced silence. I knew he was working up the courage to place his whole family at risk. I was hoping his family would be ready to do the same. I would also be risking a lot as well if this plan of mine failed. Silas knew where he was going in this area. But I needed to see for myself if this was going to work. The ground he must cover with his family in just a few hours would be dangerous in itself but more so in the dark.

"Silas, according to the map, if we circle north, there is a road heading south running near the Roanoke River . . . I am formulating a plan, but don't have it entirely worked out."

"We has to come in from the north Major. It's the only way to get them out."

"Ok, we will ride up three miles north and look for shelter. We need to get some rest before we go out tonight."

The old barn sat back off the road some sixty yards. It was just large enough to hold the horses and us. The outside was weed-choked and in bad need of paint. Apparently, it was unused for some time. We approached the barn slowly. I saw no signs of others visiting the place recently. After forcing the door open, we found it deserted.

"Too risky for a fire," I said. "It would likely burn the place down. Why don't you get some water from the creek we passed? I will get some food ready."

We ate a dinner of ham, hardtack, and honey unrolled our bedrolls and soon were fast asleep. I awoke at twilight and prodded Silas. We were fortunate the moon was full and afforded us some light through the slats in the barn.

"Major, the plantation is two miles south of here along the river. Once my family is with me, I'll take 'em north along the river bout twenty miles to the safe house. From there, Miz Tubman say the people will smuggle us north. I has been plannin' this for some time. I know where the house is and how to get there."

"Silas, I want you to take what is left of the food. It will be something to feed your family on the way."

Saddling our horses was no small task in a dark barn. But with that accomplished, we moved out slowly. The moonlight cascading through the trees gave some light on the road. The two miles passed quickly, and we approached the area of the plantation. Unfortunately, Silas neglected to tell me the ground north of the plantation was full of briars. We dismounted and began to walk around the area, encouraging the horses as we went. It did not last long. I thought this might be the reason why Silas thought this a good escape route. No one would think of them escaping through this prickly area.

Finally, the silhouette of the plantation came into view. It was a large stone structure set on a hill. There were eight buildings on the property, the main house, two smokehouses, and most important to Silas, the slave quarters. The quarters set back from the main house about twenty yards. Silas also neglected to say anything about the guinea hens in the yard. They would be an early warning system for the folks in the main house. I turned to Silas.

"You are going to need as much of a head start as possible to get to the safe house by morning. I have come up with something that just might work."

After briefing Silas, I mounted my horse and skirted the property. It was nearly eleven o'clock as I rode quietly down the long entrance and approached the house. As expected, the hens began to raise a ruckus, and a dog began to bark. I soon saw a lantern light in the main house.

"Halt! Who are you, stranger?" a voice from the front porch declared. "I have you in my gun sight."

"Major James Blake here," I replied, "and I am asking for hospitality."

The man with the lantern came closer and shined the lantern light in my face.

"Goodness sake, you are a sight, James. What are you doing way up here? Did your family know you were coming? Your mother and father are so worried about you, boy. Get yourself down, come on in, and clean up a bit."

I dismounted, tied my horse very slowly, and took my time walking up the steps. Lanterns were lit, and the misses of the house came down after a few minutes.

"James, James, I do declare, you lost boy?"

"Well, no," I stammered, "I was just coming by this way, and it was getting late. I delivered a message for the Confederacy today and was bone-tired after riding from Lawrenceville."

"Well, as long as you're here, you might as well make yourself comfortable. Take off those clothes, and I will give them to Jane to be cleaned. I have an extra suit of Fulwar's you can wear, in the meantime. Have you had anything to eat?"

"No, not recently," I said.

"Jane," she said. "Get James some buttermilk and some of those muffins in the pantry."

"I certainly do appreciate your hospitality."

I changed into this man's suit and reappeared. When Jane entered the room, she made eye contact with me and managed a slight smile. Her movements were precise, as she served the family members first. When she got to me, she leaned close and poured the buttermilk in my glass. She handed me the buttermilk on a tray and whispered, "They is gone."

She stood up, turned to the lady of the house, and said, "Will that be all Mrs. Skipwith?"

"Yes, Jane, that will be all," she responded.

I sat down at the table and began to eat. A strange man and his wife were sitting across from me. Their pictures were on the wall with a large coat of arms in between, with labels indicated the names of Fulwar

Skipwith and Mary Skipwith. At least this was something to go on, but I needed to be very careful what I said.

"Well, how long has it been since you have seen my family?" I asked.

"It was about two weeks ago at a tobacco sale in town," Mrs. Skipwith said. "We sat and talked a while with Jessie and Martha. They miss you terribly, James, and want you to come back and help run the farm."

I suddenly remembered the war wound story.

"Well . . . I was hit in the head while I was in prison in the north. This has affected me, and I have trouble remembering things. The doctors told me it would improve with time."

Mary spoke up, "I suppose that is why you were so far north of your folk's home. You can spend the night if you wish and start for home tomorrow."

I awoke early. As I gazed out the bedroom window, the golden hues of daylight were just beginning to grace the morning sky. However, my appreciation was short-lived. The overseer reported to Mr. Skipwith that three of his slaves ran away. There was no sense of panic in the household, only anger at a loss of property. I came down the stairs in a borrowed nightshirt and found Mr. Skipwith fully dressed and walking out the door. He had a pistol tucked in his belt and a musket strapped to the saddle of his horse. There was a haversack with what I presumed was enough food for a few day's ride. Evidentially one of the slaves gave him the northerly escape direction.

Jane brought me my uniform. It was clean and looked in reasonably good shape. I went to a room and hurriedly changed. When I came back down the stairs, I was greeted by Mrs. Skipwith, who had this motherly look of concern on her face.

"James," she began, "I am sorry you have been through so much. Being in a Yankee prison must have been real traumatic." I nodded in affirmation.

Jane brought out a breakfast of bacon, eggs, and buttermilk. Mrs. Skipwith offered grace.

"Dear God, bless this meal of which we are about to partake. Bless this food to the nourishment of our bodies and bring us peace, Amen. You need to eat something, dear boy." I stood up from the table.

"You must excuse me, Mrs. Skipwith, but I need to be going. I only have a small amount of leave time, and as you have said, my parents are anxious to see me."

"Certainly, James, I understand. You told me of your memory problem last night, so I made you a map of how to get to your family's farm."

She left the room for a few minutes and came back with a crude drawing of roads leading south through Clarksville and position of the road leading to the farm. While she was gone I ate the food presented to me.

"You must come back and visit again, James. We would be glad to have you and your family."

"Yes ma'am, we will do that if the opportunity presents itself."

I gathered my things and went out to saddle my horse. While I was readying, Mrs. Skipwith came to the front porch.

"When Fulwar returns, I will give him your regards," she said. "You know, James, what you are doing is fighting for Virginia and plantations like this one. We support the cause, and Fulwar has given all he can for the Army of Northern Virginia. It is good to have you on our side. Here are some apples and water to get you home. Be safe and take care."

I could abide by the last phrase. I mounted my horse and rode down off the hill. I managed to give Silas and his family as much time as I could. Knowing it would be unwise to go into Clarksville, I headed south long enough to be sure I was out of sight of the plantation. I circled around to the north near where Silas and I started our approach. I needed to get back to the Union forces as soon as possible. I was doing no good for the cause here. The real James Blake could pop up at any moment. If he made his way back to General Lee, the whole masquerade would come tumbling apart. Hopefully, the Confederate army wouldn't come looking for me right away. My Confederate mission was fulfilled, and I was presumed to be at home convalescing.

I found a bridge and crossed the Roanoke River above Clarksville and kept heading north and east, being careful to avoid the major roads. I would soon need additional food and water if I was to continue north, so I set my sights on Boydton. I began the ride feeling fine, but within an hour, I began to feel sick. I took water from my canteen, but there was a pain in my stomach that wouldn't subside. I rode along a few minutes more, and the pain increased. I began to sweat hard and found it increasingly difficult to stay in the saddle. My breath became shallow and quick. I left the contents of my stomach along the trail. I sipped water, but the pains became more intense. I pulled my horse into a shaded area and slid off the saddle. It was all I could do to secure him to a tree and lay down. My vision began to blur, and I lay there in pain for several hours.

I was there on the battlefield, again facing that Confederate and firing. The Confederate bullet struck me in the shoulder, and the pain came. I passed out.

When I regained my senses, it was near dark. The pain in my stomach subsided some, but when I tried to mount my horse, I was too weak. I took an apple from the saddlebag and began to suck on the juice. I took a few swallows of water. After a short nap, I realized that my sweat had soaked my uniform. I lay back on the ground and closed my eyes.

I awoke in a bed with the sound of water tinkling into a bowl. I felt the coolness of a cloth being applied to my head. My vision was blurry, but I recognized the women's face.

"There, there, dear, just lie still. You've had a rough two days. Papa and I are here to take care of you. Papa! Come here quickly, James is awake."

That was all I heard. When I awoke the second time, I was still in a room with the moon shining brightly through the window. There were deep shadows of curtains at the window with a flower print barely visible. The bed I was in had a curved brass railing at the foot and a quilt matching the curtains. I rolled over and saw a nightstand with a daguerreotype of James' stepmother and father. I must be in his room, in his home, and this frightened me more than anything I faced on the battlefield.

> My thoughts were racing. Could I bring myself to portray my assumed role to his family? I had no choice now. How was I to conduct myself? This couldn't be happening. What if the real James showed up? Oh, God, what am I to do? Damn. Damn. Damn.

I struck the bed with my fists over and over again. This was really more than I could bear. I thought I was about to lose control of what sanity I had left.

A lantern light appeared outside the door to the room, and Martha Blake entered. She seemed taller than in the daguerreotype with gray-streaked hair and a lovely, smooth complexion. "James," she said softly, "Are you awake?"

"Yes."

"How are you feeling, son?"

"I am not myself. I have been in prison, beaten, shot, and can remember little of my life here. I am asking for your forgiveness. Do not think me bad as my sacrifice for the cause has been enormous. Please,

please, forgive me, mother. I should never have gone away to war." I was praying this would work.

She looked at me lovingly and bent over to kiss my forehead.

She said, "There, there, James, you have been sick with a fever for two days, and you need to rest."

She left the room, and I lay looking at the ceiling, wondering what happened in the intervening days. After a few minutes, Jessie came into the room.

"Well, son, you certainly gave us a fright. We thought we lost you to the fever. Colonel Taylor sent us a telegram you were coming days ago. We never thought you would arrive in this condition. It was a good thing Mr. Skipwith found you and brought you back to us. Otherwise, you would have died."

Martha came in and began to straighten up around the room. She said, "Mary has been asking to see you, but I told her to wait a day or two so you could gain some strength. You will need it for her. Molly will bring you a bite to eat when she has it prepared."

I awoke again late the next day as the sun was casting high shadows across the room. As I lay in bed, I began to put the pieces together. Mr. Skipwith must have gone after Silas and found me on his way back to the house. He probably delivered me here because he thought it was James' parents' responsibility to take care of me. There was a knock at the door, and a soft voice asked,

"Mr. Jim, is you awake?"

"Yes."

"It's Molly, and I bought you somthin' to eat."

She entered the room and set the tray down. Apparently, she was the Blake house servant. She was a light-skinned, negro woman and was dressed in a plain green dress with a light brown apron. She moved slowly but deliberately toward me.

"Thank you, Molly," I said. She sat down the tray and turned to me.

"Mr. Jim, I hope you is feelin' better now. You just rest an try an get your strength back."

"I will, Molly, I will."

She tucked my covers up on the bed and left the room. As I began to take little bites of the chicken stew, there was another knock at the door.

"James, can I come in?"

"Yes, certainly."

Another woman entered the room, and I knew from a daguerreotype this was Mary, James' stepsister.

"Mary," I said, "how wonderful to see you."

"Well, James, it seems you do have some memory problems. You have never addressed me like that before. James, I have come for you to hear me out. I know the real reason you left the farm, and you best get your mind back together and quick."

"Why, Mary, what is wrong?" She began pacing up and down the floor.

"Don't play games with me, James. You know very well what is wrong. Ever since you enlisted, Father has wanted to tell you, but our stupid brother keeps responding for you. Father sent letters to both you and Daniel. Did he ever let you see them? Did he tell you?"

"No, I just asked him to take care of the correspondence for me while I was in the field. When I was captured, there was no mail delivered to me in prison."

Her angry look softened slightly when I told her this, but she continued to pace.

"Mary, whatever it is, you can tell me. If I can help the situation, I will try."

"All right, Sally Turner is with child. She has been trying to get in touch with you to let you know. I am outraged that Daniel didn't tell you."

"Well . . . um . . . no, he didn't say anything to me. After I was captured, they moved me around from prison to prison. I didn't get any letters. How could I have known? Her family, what are they going to do?"

"They are planning to send her away, of course, to her aunts in Atlanta, so she can have the baby there. Her aunt is desirous of a child, and this won't raise much suspicion."

"How can you be sure the baby is mine?" She stopped pacing and looked heatedly at me.

"Oh . . . really, James, you are the one. She told me in a letter you visited her shortly before your capture. How could you do such a thing? You don't know how much you have embarrassed this family—and me?"

Mary began to turn red in the face and left the room, slamming the door as she went.

I knew I could do nothing about that situation, so my thoughts turned to my own. The choices were grim. I needed to try to leave the house without being shot, either for being promiscuous or for not being

James. I struggled out of bed, felt weak, and flopped back down. I was clearly in no condition to make an escape attempt.

I spent the next several weeks regaining my strength, seldom leaving the bedroom, and being waited on by Molly. There was no sign of the real James, and nothing indicated I was compromised with the family. Every day, I became more guarded, worried that I might make a slip, and have anyone in the house could recognize me as a fraud. Martha made regular appearances to tend to me. She would often sit and read the papers aloud about what was transpiring regarding the war. I suppose she thought this to be of some comfort. Of course, the articles were biased toward the south, and they painted a dismal picture of Union efforts. She read of a battle on August 28, where Generals Lee and Jackson whipped the Army of the Potomac under General Pope. The engagement sent Union forces scurrying back toward the Washington defenses. The paper said there were indications Lee was moving northward.

Whatever the disease, it sapped my strength. I had the notion this may be why I was so prone to falling off my horse. Molly kept encouraging me with each tray of food. I was being held prisoner in the house by my own body. Fitful nights of sleep formed dark circles under my eyes. I was beginning to look like a ghost. Fall was fast approaching, and I was worried the real James would show himself. One evening Mary entered my room, towing her anger with her like a heavy chain. I expected her to pull a pistol and shoot me every time we met.

"Well, James . . . what do you have to say for yourself today?"

"Mary, I still do not have the strength to do anything at this point. You need to try to calm yourself. Would it help any if I said I would do the right thing by Sally when I am well enough to travel?" She simply scowled at me.

"It is too late for that now, James. When the baby is born, it will be given to relatives, and Sally will come back to her folks. She will, of course, be completely disgraced if word of this ever reaches anyone in town. You must never see her again. Mother and Father will, of course, continue to dote over you. You have always been an angel in their eyes, but I am the one running this plantation now. You have not only disgraced her, but our family will also suffer as a result. This even tops Daniel defecting to the north. I don't know if I can ever forgive you, so, as soon as you can, you must leave this place."

With that, she whirled on her heels and left the room. Refreshingly, it felt as if an oppressive storm just lifted.

I saw less of hurricane Mary as she was busy with a late harvest. Since James wasn't around, it fell on Mary to be responsible for harvest, curing the tobacco, get it to market and record the sales. Her father offered to help, but she and the slaves would handle it all. She was right about one thing, Jesse and Martha did dote over me, and it appeared I could say or do little wrong. One evening I was in the parlor alone, and Jessie entered.

"James, at least you had the good sense to join the army and fight for the south. Our way of life depends on each state being able to govern itself. Up to now, Virginia has been good to us, and we like our life here. Of course, I don't need to tell you that, my boy. We are so very proud of you, son. That stepbrother of yours has no brains. Before he left home, we suffered a bad argument about the slaves. I have no feeling for him now. Last week we sent a telegram to General Lee letting him know you were ill. I am sure you want to get well so you can rejoin him."

"Yes, sir," I said with a slight smile. "It would be really good for me to get back in the field."

At this point in my recovery, I was able to walk down the stairs and sit in the parlor. I became accustomed to the furnishings and the pictures on the walls. One oil painting in the parlor intrigued me. It represented Jesse and Martha with five children stair-stepping down with James being older and taller than the rest. The artist must have been one of those traveling types and painted in a hurry. The images were not very clear. I guessed about Laura, Daniel, and Mary, but there was another child about the size of James in the background.

"Father, can I ask you something?"

"Sure son, what is it?"

"How did you feel about having this picture painted?"

"It was your stepmother's idea. She wanted something to pass down through the family. I went along with it, and that is the story. Except for the fact that your mother wasn't in it the picture, it is complete. She's passed away a few years before I moved to Virginia." Tears welled up in his eyes, and he looked at me.

"Your mother loved you deeply, and it is my fault she died. I should have gotten her to the doctor sooner. You don't know the half of it."

He turned and left the room. I felt I couldn't say anything more without raising suspicions about myself. I stood there, wondering what it was that caused him to hold such grief. Early the next morning, I was in the parlor chair when Molly came into the room.

"Good Mornin' Mr. Jim," she said. "I hope you is feeling chipper this mornin.'"

"Not too bad, Molly," I replied.

"Mr. Jim, Miss Mary just been like this powerful whirlwind ever since you left. That's why it's sure good to have you back, even if it's just for a little while. We is makin' sunshine today, Mr. Jim." She smiled and went back down the hallway.

"We is makin' sunshine today," was her favorite thing to say, and she said it often. She would say it to me on a regular basis as a term of joy and use it as sarcasm to fend off Mary. Her attitude never changed, and she would always be humming something sweet and melodious or singing a spiritual. Even though she had her chores to attend to, it didn't seem to change her. As the day began to heat up, I went out to the porch to set in the sunshine. There was a small white fence surrounding the house, and trees lined the road leading past the property. Because of the trees, you couldn't see travelers on the road until they passed by the access road to the house. I began to get drowsy when I noticed someone make the turn and come down the access road.

When the figures got close enough for me to recognize, I was astonished. It was a mule with a small Confederate flag on its halter and George leading him on. As he arrived at the fence, so did Jesse.

"You best be getting along peddler. We got no use for you or your goods here."

"Wait," I said. "I know this man and have had some dealings with him. He has been near General Lee. Well, George, it's good to see you again. Perhaps, you bring us some news of the war?"

"I do, sir," he said. "The war is going well for the south, and we anticipate many more victories." He turned to Jesse and said, "I met James near Manassas and sold him some buttons and thread. I wanted to let him know General Lee is expecting to see him any day now. He said I should deliver the message as no one else was coming this way."

"Thank you, George," I responded, "I believe I am fit enough to travel now and can make the trip back north." George looked at me with a glint in his eye and winked.

"You best be on your way, as there is more urgency than you know."

With that, George turned his mule to leave. He paused and said, "Major, if you need anything in the way of supplies for your journey," He tapped the mule's baskets. "I will be camped three miles east of here."

I went back into the house and dressed in my Confederate uniform.

"Mother, Father, I regret I must leave your kindness, but I must return to General Lee. Where is Mary? I want to say good-bye to her."

"I am afraid she won't come out to see you off, son," Jesse said. "She is still angry with you for your mistake with Sally. Her hatred burns deep son and I am afraid it will not end."

"We wish you well, son." Martha said. "Here are four days provisions for you. It should be enough to get you back to General Lee. Be safe and come back to us."

I rode away from the farm, thinking what a relief it was to be out of that emotional jail and I had survived. I rode the three miles north and then doubled back to the east. After I rode about two miles, I saw a thin stream of smoke rising from a wooded area and thought it might be George's camp. I approached the site carefully and found a smoldering fire, George's mule and gear, but no George.

With no one around, I grew suspicious. I took my horse deeper into the woods and secured him to a tree. I concealed myself behind some large bushes near the camp. George was a fellow scout, and I would help him if he was in trouble. An hour went by, and then I heard some movement in the woods. From the sounds being made, it was a small party of riders. I was close enough to hear them clearly, as they came into camp.

"Well, I told you so. You didn't believe me, so I had to prove it to you." It was George's voice but under a great deal of stress.

"You proved nothing." One of the others said. "We will wait here until Jake gets back from Clarksville with supplies. Then we will go to our sources and find out the truth."

They dismounted and gathered near the smoldering fire. Peeking out to get a better view, I saw three men. They were covered with dust from riding hard. I felt this tightening in my gut because one was Nate Wilson. I must have become too lax in my vigilance. The next thing I knew, there was a pistol pointed at my head and someone telling me to get up and move.

George and I were placed together, with my captor keeping watch. I assumed this was the missing Jake. We were told to stand some ten feet from the others gathered around the campfire. George began whistling a tune, and our guard told him to shut up. He kept on whistling, and as the others turned to look at us, I found out why. His mule began to bray loudly and kicked a large log into the air. It was enough of a distraction. We pounce on our guard. I grabbed his head, and George pulled out a knife concealed in his boot and dispatched him quickly. As he doubled over, I grabbed his pistol, and George grabbed a nearby musket. We both hit the ground and began firing. George only had one shot, so he made it count. I managed to hit one other with pistol shots, and they both went down. However, in the fray, Nate Wilson grabbed a horse and rode out of camp.

"My mule hates that tune. George said. And it's a good thing too!"

I filled George in on Nate's background and the family he killed back in Galena. He just shook his head, and we kept on digging. About twenty minutes and one grave later, I had to ask, "What was that all about?"

"Well," he began slowly, "It was about a plot to murder President Lincoln and who was going to carry it out. Our paths crossed while I was on my way back to camp from seeing you. I managed to wile them with stories of my connections to General Lee. It seems this Nate fellow was a recruiter for volunteers to do the job, and I told them I wanted to join. He became suspicious of me, and I had to lead him to a Confederate outpost to verify I was on his side. Initially, we headed in different directions. They doubled back and followed me a ways. I tried to lead them away as I knew you were coming, but they didn't fall for it. My guess is this Nate will be headed north as he used the name Antonia when talking with his conspirators. I believe he was referring to Antonia Ford, whom we suspect of being a Rebel agent."

We finished burying the dead, saying a blessing over the bodies, and cleaning up the camp, so there was little trace of our being there. There was some daylight left, so we packed up, took the horses supplied by the desperados, and left for the north. To travel light and fast, we needed to leave George's mule, his supplies, and the extra horses with a farmer outside Boydton. George knew him as a Union sympathizer and one of his sons was fighting with a Wisconsin regiment.

Nothing was working out as planned. I was nowhere near General Lee, but I was somewhat thankful for that. I was exposed to the Blake family and came out alive. I still did not know where James Blake was. George and I were now on a journey together, and we needed a plan. I suggested finding a Union line.

# 9

## The Journey Back

O ctober crept up on us, and the smell of fall was beginning to fill the air. After four days of hard riding, switching horses, and dodging Confederate troops, we made it to the outskirts of Charlottesville, Virginia.

"It's a good thing you are still in Major Blake's uniform." George said. "I have no way of contacting a scout until we get nearer to the border. What say we camp for the night?"

"Very well, you do look a little worn out. I will go on into Charlottesville and see if I can get any information on Confederate movements."

I didn't mention it to George, but we were running low on supplies. Even though I had little in the way of cash, I was looking for a store to buy food. Everything seemed to be closed for business, and the streets fairly deserted. I did run on to a man sitting on a rail fence.

"Good evening sir, I am a courier from General Lee's staff. I have been on leave and am working my way back. Can you tell me how close I am to the Confederate army lines?"

"No, sir, I can't," was the response. "You might check with Mr. Michie. His place is just north, around Earlysville. He might be able to help."

I rode out in that direction, and a small two-story building came into view. There was a sign saying Michie Tavern over the door. From the looks of the place, it had not been a tavern for some time. There was a lantern glow showing through the window, so I knocked at the door. I was greeted by a man in his thirties,

"I am sorry," he said. "But the tavern is no longer in service, and this is my family home. For now, all I can offer you is water."

His eyes glanced over my appearance, and he must have approved. He motioned me to enter. He went around the room and lit another lantern. The additional light revealed a dusty gathering place with several tables and chairs. I took a seat at a table near the door, just in case I needed to make a fast exit.

"I am Thomas Michie," he said. "What brings you here?"

"I am after news of Confederate forces in this area and was told, perhaps, you could help."

He seemed slightly annoyed at this statement.

"When the stages were running, perhaps, but now I don't see many travelers come this way. I haven't seen any soldiers in more than two weeks."

He went over to a counter and brought back a newspaper and laid it on the table.

"I am afraid this is the only news I can supply. Say, what is your name, Major?"

"Major Mason," I responded, "I am on leave and on my way to rejoin the Army."

"Just why didn't the Army tell you where they were?" he said.

He kept pressing the issue, so I tried to deflect the conversation.

"I am headed for Petersburg, but I will eventually be returning to General Lee's command, so I can't talk about my duties. I am under orders. I thought you might save me some time in the saddle."

This seemed to work as he sat down on a chair in the corner and placed his feet up on a table. Information about the war was plentiful, and articles covered much of the paper. There was much about the Confederate cause, the inflation of the Confederate dollar, and an article on a speech by President Davis. The article that caught my interest was news of Lee moving his forces north into Maryland. If Lee was moving north, it left Virginia with fewer Rebel troops. If George and I went due east from Charlottesville, we should run into either the Union lines or Confederate cavalry, it would be a perilous journey, but worth the risk.

"Thank you for the information, sir. I bid you a good evening."

We set out to the east and skirted around Charlottesville. Our plan was to go south of Petersburg to reach Union lines and then on to Fort Monroe. We felt sure we would be able to catch a ship to take us north.

"George, with me in a Confederate uniform and you in your ped-dler's garb, we could both be shot by Union pickets before we even reach the lines."

"Yes, that thought occurred to me too."

"If we have a choice, maybe you should make contact first. They would be less likely to shoot a peddler."

"Depends on if I am recognized by one of those boys I cheated."

"Thanks, George, that's not very reassuring."

While we were riding, George began to tell me about his past. He was such an accomplished scout, I was not sure if he was telling the truth, but the story was a good one.

"I learned early on from my daddy. He was a slick and crafty sales-man spending most of his time on the road. We lived in this small cabin in Pennsylvania, just a few miles south of Philadelphia, and it was a hard life. Momma did sewing to bring in money for the family. I left home at fourteen to see the world. I managed to sell enough subscriptions to a paper to get as far as Washington. There I found a job as a store clerk selling shoes. I would send money back home to mom from time to time when I could afford it. Life got pretty dull, and I became depressed. I began to drink a lot more than I should and soon found myself in debt and in jail. I got word to the family through a friendly jailer. My father arrived about a week later and paid my fines. Through his contacts, he got me a job working on the Philadelphia Wilmington & Baltimore Railroad as a security agent. I traveled up and down the railroad lines until that became boring."

"The railroad had a contract to build a rail bridge over the Susque-hanna River. I was selected to be the head of security for the project but never got to see a lick of the bridge being built. That was because I met Allen Pinkerton. He must have recognized something in me that I didn't see in myself. It was early on, just after the start of the war. Allen came to me and asked if I wanted to scout for the Union army. This scout stuff sounded like an adventure, so I said, "sign me up." My first assignment was to take a coded letter across the Union lines and into Confederate-held Virginia and contact one of his scouts, a fellow by the name of Dave Graham. He said I would recognize him because he had a stutter in his voice and gave me his general area of operation. I gussied myself up and was given a letter from Jefferson Davis himself to travel across the lines. It was fake, of course, but it was really well done and looked authentic. Mat-ter of fact I still have the letter with me. You never can be too careful when you travel around here. Anyway, the message I carried was ciphered, so I didn't know what it said. I passed into a Confederate camp near Manassas Junction early last July. I told them I was just passing through to get to Richmond and wanted to stay the night before continuing on. I found this Dave fellow trying to sell needles, thread, buttons, and such, and I pretended to be interested. Late that night, I told Dave I had a letter for him from his wife and slipped him the coded message. I left the next morning. After riding several miles toward Richmond, I doubled back to the Union lines. It wasn't long before I was getting deeper and deeper into the scout business. I developed this persona because of the way I saw Dave work. It wouldn't hurt things for this war to have two peddlers wandering the lines."

"Say, George, I have a question for you. Your name . . . is it really George Washington?"

Before he could answer, we topped a rise and saw riders in the far distance. It was a long column of Confederate cavalry and moving rapidly north across our path. I surmised from there urgency they must be screening General Lee's forces. Fortunately, we were not discovered yet, and we quickly pulled off into some tall grass, dismounted, and got our horses on the ground. There was no other cover, so we were hoping the three-foot-tall grass would be enough. We waited for some quarter of an hour. Guessing it would be enough time, we began our journey again. I also knew by now the Confederate army could be in search of me as Major Blake, the deserter.

An hour before dark, we paused outside the town of Farmville. We were both getting hungry as I failed in my attempt to get food in Charlottesville. I noticed a train heading east toward Farmville with several freight cars. This was most likely a shipment for Confederate troops. As we rode across country, I suggested we intercept the train. George looked at me like I was crazy but followed along. George and I raced across country at an angle to intercept the train. We were about two miles from the fort at High Bridge over the Appomattox River. We approached Confederate sentries at a rapid pace.

"George," I said. "let me do the talking." I began hollering at the sentries, "Don't shoot! Don't shoot! We are coming from Farmville with some urgent news."

As we pulled up, a sergeant looked at us suspiciously.

"Tell me what y'alls business is before I have you hung."

"George," I said. "Show the good sergeant here your letter from President Davis."

He showed him the letter of passage, and while he was reading it, I said to him with as much urgency as I could muster, "Sergeant, you must signal this train to stop as there is a conspirator on board who is desirous of assassinating President Davis. We have this on the highest authority from the Confederate government. I have a telegram here from Richmond if you'd care to read it, but we can both see that there isn't time."

Just then, the train appeared in the distance with the smokestack billowing black smoke. There was this look of panic on the sergeant's face, I recognized it as indecision.

"Look," I said, "what harm will it do to stop the train for a few minutes and find out the truth? If the saboteur is not on board, they can continue. If he is there, you have saved the life of our president."

There were a few moments of silence, and the sergeant returned the letter to George. "Signal the train to stop," he shouted.

George and I sat confidently on our horses as the train slowed to a stop. A Confederate Captain came forward from the first car.

"What the hell is going on, Sergeant? Why, on God's green earth would you signal this train to a stop short of the outpost? Explain yourself!"

"Well sir," he said sheepishly, "This major here said there was a saboteur aboard that was going to kill President Davis. I couldn't take the chance they were right, and they got this official letter from President Davis, giving them the right to travel. The major says also he has a telegram to back it up." The captain turned toward us.

"Sir," I spoke up confidently, "We are agents of the Confederacy on a special mission for President Davis. We have it on good authority from Richmond you have, in your company, a Corporal James that is involved in a plot to assassinate President Davis. Can you bring this man forward so he can answer to these charges?"

"I have no such man on this train. The only corporal I have is Corporal Denison, and he can't possibly be mixed up in such a plan. I can vouch for his character."

"Then send this corporal out so we can see him for ourselves," I demanded.

After about a minute, the corporal appeared in the failing light. I acted as if I had seen a ghost, and George played along to the hilt.

"But . . . but, Captain," I said. "You don't know this man the way our sources do. This sir is a saboteur using the name Denison to get passage to Richmond with the intent of killing President Davis. You, Captain, have been taken in by his calm demeanor. His real name is Allen James."

At this accusation, the captain turned to look at the corporal with some suspicion. A look of anger spread over the corporal's face.

"Look here, Randy, you've knowed me more than a year. You knowed I wouldn't do no such thing."

Just as the Captain turned back to us, a massive explosion and gunfire erupted from a hill on the opposite side of the train. Some powder onboard one of the boxcars ignited and sent boards, iron bolts, and chunks of exploded wooden boxes raining down on all of us. The remains of the boxcar began to burn, and the Confederates started working feverishly to unhook the car. The Captain began shouting orders to his men and more exited from the train. They moved in unison toward the hill and seemed to ignore us. George and I quickly dismounted and led the horses slowly away from the train toward a ravine on the same side of the tracks. The Confederates were now engaged in a fight to save the train. A token guard was left at the train, and this made for easy pickings. We had to act fast as the Rebels in the fort were sure to have heard the explosion. We subdued the guard on our side of the train, and George and I quietly crept up and opened one of the boxcars. We helped ourselves to all the rations we could fit into our shirts and promptly made for the horses. It was soon going to be completely dark, so we rode at a right angle away from the action keeping a low profile until we reached our original route.

George looked at me, quizzically.

"Say, Colonel, I am all for taking chances, but that was ridiculous. You could have gotten us either hung or shot. I was sure we were in for it till the firing started. Did you know the soldiers were there?"

"I was pretty sure, but I was playing a hunch. As we were approaching Farmville, I noticed the tracks from a large party of riders heading for the railroad. There were some two-wheeled limber tracks, so they were pulling cannons and wagon tracks from pulling artillery pieces. I saw some evidence of freshly-bent rails at one crossing. Destruction like that would only have been done by Union Cavalry. That hill was a perfect spot for an ambush. I merely sweetened the pot for them a little by stopping the train. It's too bad we couldn't get to the ambushers before any Confederate reinforcements arrived."

We looked at each other, turned our horses south, and began a methodical pace in the dark. We were soon weary of trying to pick our way in the dark, so we decided to make camp. It was hard to find a suitable place, but we managed to locate a small patch of trees about a quarter mile off the road. We unsaddled and secured our horses. Then we unrolled our bedrolls, ate a bite of food, and settled in for the night.

We awoke to light rain and a cold wind from the northwest. We got the horses saddled and began the journey south toward Blackstone. I pulled my rain cape out of my saddlebag, and it kept me somewhat dry. George was not so lucky. He snugged up his coat and tied a blanket around his shoulders. We made fairly good time reaching the outskirts of Blackstone just before dusk. By then, the rain stopped, and the sky lightened a bit. A traveler came down the road toward us in a horse-drawn wagon loaded with supplies. He stopped his rig, and George presented him with his fake traveling paper.

I spoke up and said, "We are traveling to Petersburg with some important papers for the government. Can you tell us about the military activity in the county?"

He looked quizzically at us.

"I am Major Blake of Clarksville, Virginia, a fine upstanding infantryman serving with General Lee. If you would give us a word, we would appreciate it."

"There are no troops in these parts that I know of. I have been but fifteen miles from here today. If you want more information, you can go just a few miles south of here to Colonel Guy's place. He might be able to tell you more. Just follow Jordan's road, and you can't miss it."

"Much obliged, sir."

About fifteen minutes later, we came within sight of a plantation. Even though we were soaked through and the wind was beginning to bite our skin, we decided to ride on. After a few miles, we heard riders coming up behind us. We veered off the road and into a wooded area to await their passing. We waited and waited, and they didn't pass. I knew instinctively something was wrong, and George looked at me with the same pained expression. I signaled to him we should make a break for it. I held up three fingers and began the countdown. Three, two, one, and we spurred our horses out of the woods.

Our escape came to an abrupt halt facing a line of Confederate soldiers with weapons drawn. They were a unit of the fifth Virginia cavalry.

"Well sir," the colonel in charge exclaimed, "We have been looking for you for some time Major Blake, if that's who you really are. We contacted your family, and they said you left Clarksville two weeks ago. It don't take much to figure out you been on the run. Take them." A sergeant quickly grabbed our weapons from behind. "Colonel, what do we do with this other fellow here?" the Sergeant said.

"Bring him along. We have our orders."

Deserters and spies were usually executed on the spot. There must be something else going on. Our hands were tied, and we proceeded out along the trail and north toward Petersburg. We stopped at dusk to make camp, and we were placed under guard at the far end of the camp. The rain began to fall again, and we all sat in the open. Our only consolation was the guards assigned to watch us suffered the same conditions. George and I looked at each other and fell to the ground as closely as we could for warmth. We simply opened our mouths to get what water we could. For the first time in my life, I felt as though my life was worthless. I began to pray for God to protect me, for Jesus to enfold me in his arms and comfort me. I began to recite the Lord's Prayer over and over again. I don't know if George was a religious man, but I was praying aloud. If I were to die in the morning, at least I would be with God, my heavenly Father. There was a changing of the guard in the dark, and their silhouettes stood out against the firelight. The replacements were not happy about having to guard us instead of finishing their meal. I tried to enter into a conversation with one of them.

"Hey soldier, you heard what they plan to do with us?" I exclaimed.

"Yea," he replied, "They plan to stretch both your necks with a rope at noon-time tomorrow. Sides, your Yank friend will look better with a longer neck."

Suddenly, George piped up.

"I got this secret you all might be interested in," he said with a loud voice.

"What's that?" one soldier replied.

"Come a little closer," George said. "I want to share it with you alone."

There were two others standing guard, so there seemed to be little danger in his drawing within about five feet of the two of us.

"You and your guards want to make a lot of money?" said George.

I thought he was crazy, but I knew by now he was the best at his craft. As the guard drew near, George kept a lower voice.

"I want to tell you I can get you five hundred dollars right now. You interested?"

"Maybe," said the soldier.

"I can give you five hundred dollars in your own script and another thousand in a hiding place where only you can find it. All you need do is look the other way and give us a five-minute head start."

"You got nuthin' on you, we searched you," he replied.

"Oh, but I beg to differ, my friend."

"Okay, came the reply, prove it, and I will keep what you got. Maybe, just maybe, I will make this deal. If'n you don't give me somethin' now, then you got nothing, and you ain't a-goin nowhere."

"Well, sir, you drive a hard bargain, but I guess I have no choice. You need to cut me loose for just a few seconds to prove it."

The guard drew and cocked his pistol, then released George's bonds.

"One quick move and you're a dead man."

George calmly reached into his coat and began picking at a thread near the top of the collar. Once he got it loose, he began pulling. As the seam unraveled, there appeared the edges of Confederate bills. When he got to the bottom of the jacket, a large number of bills appeared. He handed them over to the private without a word. The private smiled, tied George's hands, turned, and began to walk away.

"Thanks, Yank," he said. "Y'all are gonna die with a little less cash."

As he was walking away, George spoke up again.

"Aren't you interested in where the rest is?"

He paused and stood there for what seemed like an eternity. Then he approached us again looked around nervously.

"Okay, Yank, this is the way it is. Y'all have five minutes, and then I sound the alarm. I will tell my two friends about the deal, so they won't shoot. Now, tell me where it is."

"A mile back down the road, there is a turn off with three big rocks. At the edge of the largest rock, there is a small tree. Just behind the tree and under the rock is the rest of the money."

"Thanks," the private said. "Now you will hang, and I will profit even more."

He began to walk away, but one of the other guards came up to us. He cut our bonds.

"You go ahead, and I'll take care of snarled tooth here. A man's word is a man's word."

We didn't have to hear the invitation twice. We bolted for the edge of camp at a dead run. The guards were true to their word, and five minutes later, a ruckus of firing and shouting could be heard. We rolled under a fence rail and continued to run until we were out of breath. We stopped only momentarily to try and determine which way to go. We could hear the hoofbeats of horses all around us in the dark, but we chose a good spot to stop. It was the middle of a briar patch, and the horses didn't like being scratched up, so they balked at going into the area. We lay flat against the ground with a lot of foliage for cover and held our breath as the searchers went by within a few feet of us. After they passed a few hundred yards beyond our position, we sat up and took a deep breath.

"George, I whispered, are you all right?"

"Just a few scratches," he said. "I suggest we make haste as they would be returning soon." We stood up and began to run in different directions.

"Wait," I said. "What are you doing?"

"I am going back where they would least expect us to go—back to their camp."

"Are you crazy? Do you want us to be captured again?"

"No, but we need food and transportation. The closest place to get them is back at their camp, and I think, with some luck, we can borrow both while most of them are out looking for us."

We crept back to the edge of the camp, all the while assessing the guard's locations. They carelessly situated watch fires at each end of the camp and with a couple through the center, but none on the outskirts. We slipped under the back edge of the command tent. There we found food stores and two nicely maintained saddles. While we were there, I couldn't resist looking at the maps and plans on the table. We stashed the saddles and food at a nearby creek. Now we needed to commandeer some horses. The guards were standing by the fire, and their heads kept darting about. We moved slowly and cautiously toward the corral. One of the sentries wandered away from the fire and came our way. He was leisurely checking the herd and looking about as he came.

George whispered, "I can take him out without a sound, you wait here."

He lay down in the grass and slowly crept up behind the sentry. As the sentry walked by, he sprang up from the ground, grabbed the sentry around the neck, and took him down, twisting his head. We untied two of the mounts and slowly led them away from the camp. Fortunately, the horses didn't make a sound. When we were ready, we rode in a line directly away from the camp for a few hundred yards and then headed due east as the parties searching for us went south. Hard riding in the dark was the order for about half an hour. Exhausted from our ordeal, we needed to stop. We spotted an old farmhouse and several outbuildings just down the road. We rode in from behind the buildings and slipped into the small barn on the outskirts. As we slipped off the saddles, we noticed we possessed the very horses we were captured on.

"What are the chances of that happening?" I said.

We smiled, shook our heads, and lay down on the earthen floor to rest.

"Say, George," I asked, "What about the money hidden behind the tree and under the rock?"

"What money is that?" he responded with a chuckle.

Exhaustion took over, and we were soon asleep.

We were awakened at first light by the sounds of muskets firing, and this was serious firing, not some skirmish. It meant there was at least a corps or two engaged in battle. Two shells landed near the barn we were in, and a cannonball came through the wall with splinters of wood just missing us and slightly wounding one of the horses. We quickly saddled and mounted our horses, burst through the open door, and exited lying low in the saddle and riding hard down the road. Minié balls whizzed by us from two different directions, and we were running blind. Suddenly, we saw troops in battle formation just ahead. My eyes searched for a battle flag, recognition of a uniform, anything that would give a clue. I finally recognize in front of us was a Union cavalry unit, dismounted, and firing directly toward our position. Behind us was a Confederate cavalry force charging up the small rise we just traversed. George and I flew to the ground and hit it hard as shots rang out over us from both directions. We managed to get the horses down but were helplessly caught in the crossfire.

As the battle raged over our heads, we felt the Confederate line getting closer. Just as they were about to overtake our position, the Union cavalry got support from an infantry brigade. The counterattack drove the Confederates back to their original lines. Horses thundered all around us. The Confederate line began to collapse, and they fell back quickly. The Union horses bolted by us as they broke through the center, and the rout was on. Confederates scattered in all directions. Some Rebels were rounded up and held by guards while others were shot as they tried to escape. All this time, George and I lay motionless. There was a quiet that ensued as the Union bearers were making sure the fighting was well beyond their position before taking the field. We staggered to our feet, and that's when I noticed the blood, not on me, but on George. He was shot in the leg, and the wound looked serious.

"George!" I said with a start, "You've been hit."

"Yea," he said. "This might be my last assignment," and he collapsed to the ground. Union soldiers placed him on a blanket and carried him off the field.

"Soldier, I muttered, I know I am in a Confederate uniform, but I am Colonel Thomas Sawyer, US Army. Please take me to your commanding officer."

With that, I was first led to the hospital to be checked out by doctors. I was taken to an old farmhouse commandeered for use and ushered into the parlor. All the furnishings were removed, and there was only a table and three chairs in the room. The doctor examined me quickly and found only scratches from the briars. I was taken into another room in the house, and unceremoniously had my hands tied behind my back. I was then tied to a chair with several strands of rope. I was so taken aback I couldn't say anything for several minutes.

"What, what's going on?" I stammered.

A colonel came into the room and addressed me.

"Sir, I am Colonel Paxton with a detachment of Colonel Averell's brigade. I am placing you under arrest as you fit the description of a Major James Blake of the Confederate Army. Major Blake escaped from our prison with the help of some Confederate sympathizers. We have orders from General Burnside, that your capture and return to prison are a top priority. We will be taking you back to General Burnside's headquarters for further questioning. Sergeant, escort the prisoner to a holding room."

I decided the whole mess would be cleared up tomorrow. I was cut loose from the chair and taken to another room. There were several Confederate officers in the room with me, and they seemed indifferent about their capture. A guard brought us some coffee and hardtack, which we ate without a sound under the watchful eyes of our captors. My thoughts turned to George. I didn't know where he was or if he survived his wound. This was undoubtedly not the greeting I expected when I reached the Union lines. Somehow, someone must recognize the truth.

# 10

## The Real Colonel Sawyer

The next rays of morning found me wide awake, cold, and hungry. I was separated from the other Confederate officers and taken to a wagon. I was assigned two guards. I knew that was never done to a regular prisoner. I suspicioned it was because they weren't sure who I really was.

"Say, you fellas know I am no Rebel. My hometown is Galena, Illinois. You ever been to Galena?"

"No," came the reply. "And we don't know any such thing. Right now, you are a Rebel and will remain under our guard until we reach headquarters."

The wagon jostled down the road, occasionally hitting a rut and jarring my teeth. I took a long slow drink from a canteen trying to get the upset feeling in my stomach to dissipate. We pushed east toward the coast and picked up a company of cavalry. I thought about George again and what happened to him. The parade of wagons and cavalry turned south and, judging from our direction, we were heading toward the Virginia border. It was going to be a long journey back.

We went through Charlottesville and passed the same little tavern where I gathered information. As we traveled east, it became evident there was some urgency in our journey. Two rainstorms slowed our progress. Twice we were warned of enemy movements by negro sympathizers and changed our course. I overheard a conversation between soldiers about a battle that was about to take place near Fredericksburg. They also said that was our objective. We increased our pace, and my physical condition deteriorated.

*It would be hard to explain to the angel Gabriel that I died as a prisoner of the very army I was supposed to be fighting for. Worse yet, I died in the back of a wagon as a broken man. I hope Gabriel would say, "Okay, Tom, It could have been arranged for you to die at Bull Run. You have fulfilled your mission and done all you could. But you have died at the hands of the country you loved. The rest of your loved ones can enjoy the freedom you fought for. You can enter the kingdom of God, good and faithful servant."*

We reached Fredericksburg on December eighth by skirting the city and crossing the Rappahannock River at Barnett's ford. We linked up with the Union army's right flank at nightfall. Preparations were underway to build pontoon bridges across the Rappahannock and move the Army of the Potomac to strike at the Confederates. It was also apparent General Lee and his army would meet this challenge with one of his own. Confederate sharpshooters were already picking off workers trying to construct the bridges. I was taken to General Burnside's headquarters.

At last, I thought, I would be a free man and able to assist somehow in the upcoming battle. I was stopped outside the headquarters. I could see and hear what was going on through a window that was slightly open. General Burnside glanced about the room, his dark eyes flashing from officer to officer. He raised his voice in anger.

"Gentlemen, I must implore you to keep our engineers moving forward. Time is of the essence, and we must get those bridges finished. Dismissed."

The staff left the room, and I was brought forward.

Colonel Paxon spoke, "Sir, I am Colonel Paxton of Averell's brigade. We were under orders to bring a man fitting his description to your command if he was captured."

"Damn, man, I do not have time for this nonsense. If he is a Rebel, then take him to prison or parole him, but get him out of my headquarters."

"Sir, we are under orders to bring this prisoner to you. The order comes directly from Major General Halleck in Washington, sir."

"Aha, yes, I remember the directive now. It involved a Major Blake, an escapee from federal custody. As I recall, Washington was putting a great deal of importance on bringing this man in. Place him under guard, and we will deal with the issue as time permits. Right now, I have bridges to build and an army to move."

"I am not Confederate, I am a Union officer, Colonel Thomas Sawyer, someone, anyone, please tell General Grant I am here."

"We can't take the time to do that now. Colonel Paxton, you have my orders, you are dismissed and take the prisoner with you."

The next morning, I was taken to a prisoner holding area adjacent to the main camp. I was weak from lack of sleep and meager amounts of poor quality food. We were packed into wagons and taken to Fairfax, Virginia. Again, I pleaded my case dropping as many names as I could think of, and again, I was rebuffed by the guards. We were loaded onto railroad cars. As many as 75 to 100 per car, and we began a long cold journey north and east on the Orange Alexandria line to Washington. It was a long trip with few stops along the way. If we had to defecate, we used a corner of the boxcar. I was in and out of consciousness on the train ride and found it difficult to walk when we reached Washington. We disembarked, and all Confederate officers were taken directly to the Old Capitol Prison. I saw another chance at freedom as we came to the prison entrance. A young major was registering names of the prisoners, their rank, and where they were from. When I approached, he looked at me, and without asking a single question, he said, "James Blake, Major, CSA, Clarksville Virginia, Next."

"Wait, please wait, I am not James Blake, but Colonel Thomas Sawyer US Army."

"Don't mess with us, you were in here once before, and you escaped. We ain't about the let you do that again."

"Please, I am asking you to check with General Grant."

"Move along."

They led me to a floor with several other Confederate officers dressed in what was barely recognizable as uniforms. I passed the other prisoners and was placed in a solitary room no more than five feet by seven feet. Apparently, the real James Blake was no model prisoner.

Again, I went to the door and shouted, "I am Colonel Thomas Sawyer . . . check if you will."

There was no response except jeers from the other Confederates. I slouched back in my cell and began to weep. Was it possible I would spend the rest of the war in this prison cell? What would happen if the real James Blake was killed and his body buried? I was scared on the battlefield many times, but this overwhelming, silent fear was by far the worst. They brought in some food consisting of watered-down cornmeal and water to drink. I ate with solemnness and returned the pan and cup to the guard.

Someone from the sanitary commission came through and passed out pencils and paper for us to write letters. This was an opportunity for me to get word home that I was still alive. It would take some doing to get the letter passed the censors. I decided a letter to Rebecca would be best, and I would craft the letter so they would believe she was my sister.

*December 10, 1862*
*Miss Rebecca Thatcher*
*305 Elk Street*
*Galena, Illinois*
*Dearest Sister:*

*I miss you so much these days and wish you were here so you could give me some comfort. I hope the store is doing well, and business is brisk. Will you be so kind as to tell George that he should use the following order for the store supplies: 27 Bushels of wheat, 34 Bales of hay, 50 canning jars, 52 lids in case some are lost, 56 sack ties, 25 lantern wicks, 40 barrel stays, 17 bales of cotton if you can get it these days, 56 sharpening tools for the plows, 34 barrels of beans, 25 barrels of sunflower seeds, 21 cigar clips, 40 packs of hard ball candy, 19 bundles of tobacco, 27 horse collars and 29 leather belts of various sizes. That should be enough to carry you through the winter and into spring. I do not know if you will receive this in time, so I hope you will take action on this order as soon as you receive it. Be well.*

*Tom*

If Rebecca received this letter, I knew with every confidence she would figure out what I was doing. In the meantime, I would rely on my wits to keep me alive. A Union guard began collecting letters. As I saw him round the corner, I prayed for God to guide the letter to delivery. Later on, I heard what I hoped was the mail wagon leaving the front of the prison.

Several days passed since the letter was sent and my health was declining. I tried to keep my mind sharp by playing mental games. I would imagine tactical drill formations of the troops. Attention, Shoulder Arms, Present Arms, Shoulder Arms, Order Arms, and so on repeating the drills in my head. Images of the troops moved through my head, forming battle lines and maneuvering in the field. It helped to fight the boredom. Some southern sympathizers would come by the prison occasionally and hand us bread and other baked goods. These were welcome treats. Daily rations consisted mostly of bacon or some bad salt pork with water or coffee and occasionally a bite of bread or a vegetable.

I took to conducting an analysis of the battlefield situation at Bull Run and what I could have done differently. Self-doubt began to run rampant in my mind. I got some aid from a kindly guard who was new to the prison. He scrounged up an extra bit of clothing so I could double up on pants and a shirt. Christmas came and went, and while my body healed somewhat, my spirit did not.

Then one cold day in January, my cell prison swung open, and I was escorted to the front of the prison. I was taken into a small room with a warm stove in the corner. This was the most welcoming thing I experienced in this prison, and I stood as close to the stove as I could. It was sheer bliss. After a few minutes, another door opened, and a group of officers and enlisted men entered. I thought this was the answer to my letter I sent to Rebecca. I was sure she figured out the code and sent a rescue party to finally get things right.

"Major Blake, be seated," commanded the officer at the door. I chose to remain standing.

One officer sat down at a desk in the room and spoke, "Sir, I am Commandant William Wood, and I am in charge of all military prisons. I will choose my words carefully because information has reached me that you may not be Major Blake but someone who looks remarkably like Major Blake."

He motioned toward the door, it opened, and two armed guards entered with a prisoner in tow. The man was dressed in Confederate butternut clothes that were terribly ragged and dirty. He held his head down so I couldn't see his face, but I knew who it must be. He lifted his head and was placed in a seat across the room from me. There was the same reaction in the room as that night in Mound City. Commandant Wood waved his hand, and the prisoner was removed from the room.

He rose and crossed the room with his face inches from mine and asked his question, "Can you offer us any proof you are not James Blake?"

"Sir, I was an aid to General Grant. I was an officer in charge of a company of men at Bull Run. I was selected by General Grant for a special mission to infiltrate the Rebel south as Major James Blake. I am really Colonel Thomas Sawyer, US Army."

There was a long silence in the room. Commandant Wood had a stern look come over him as he went back to his chair.

He sat leaning back, fingertips touching each other, contemplating what I was said. "Sir, I have a prison where some of the population are Confederate sympathizers from the north and have aided the enemy in many respects. I have a few Confederate spies held in this prison well versed in pretending to be Yankees. I believe I need something more."

A guard approached the Commandant and whispered something in his ear. A quizzical look came over his face. He looked at me and said, "Guards, take off his shirts."

Two guards approached me, stood me up, and unceremoniously removed my jacket and shirts.

The Commandant looked at my left shoulder and said, "Private, you are correct, this must be Colonel Sawyer."

I hadn't noticed, but the private standing in the room was from the 13th New York. This company was closest to mine when we were overrun at Bull Run. He must have seen me get shot during the battle and knew exactly where I was wounded.

He smiled at me and came forward, "Welcome back to the Union army, Colonel Sawyer." We hugged, and this time I smiled warmly.

They immediately got me a new shirt and a Union uniform. I asked if I could have the Confederate uniform I was imprisoned with, and permission was granted. They gave me a warm coat and helped me to my feet.

"Thank you all for releasing me from this place and especially Private Collins for his quick thinking. I am grateful that you finally recognize me as Colonel Sawyer."

After tucking the packaged uniform under my arm, I slowly walked toward the prison doors with an escort. I entertained a brief thought about the real Major Blake and wondered what they had done with him.

As I stepped out into the cold January air, an indescribable sense of freedom overcame me. I was no longer hiding from anyone. I was no longer in prison. I accomplished as much of my mission as allowed and managed to survive. It was indeed a joyous day for me. But then it got even better, for walking toward me was Rebecca. She began running and leaped into my arms.

"Oh Thomas, I was on my way to the prison, and I would have torn the place down with my bare hands to get you out. I managed to decode your message but was delayed. I have so much to tell you."

We hugged for the longest time. We kissed and hugged again.

"I really want to hear about your journey, but I do need to get cleaned up and get something to eat."

"Of course," she said.

"Oh my, how I missed you, Rebecca. I have so much to tell you as well."

We reached the front of the hotel, and I had to stop and rest for a bit. I held her hand, looked into her loving eyes, and started to cry. She wiped away my tears with her fingers. "Thomas, Thomas, I thought you were dead. I hurried to Washington as fast as I could, but the train delays were horrendous."

As she held my hands, I closed my eyes and slipped into a state of drowsiness.

"You poor dear," she said. "I don't know if you should eat or sleep first. I have made arrangements for a room at the Willard."

The last thing I remember was her warm and gentle touch on my forehead, bidding me rest. I slept soundly. When I awoke, Rebecca was sitting beside me in a chair.

"Good morning Colonel Sawyer! She cheerily exclaimed."

"How long have I been asleep?"

"Almost a full day," she said.

"I am famished."

"I expected that."

She crossed the room and grabbed a tray from the dresser, placing it on my lap.

"Here you are, Colonel." She tucked a napkin under my nightshirt collar, and I chuckled.

"You needn't put up such a fuss over me." She smiled.

"I will have a hot bath drawn for you as soon as you finish eating."

As I ate, she began to tell me her trials in reaching Washington.

"At first, when I read your letter, it didn't make any sense. I showed Father, and he thought it strange. We knew it was you from the handwriting, but we were hard-pressed by the content. We didn't have a store of any kind, so I began to think about the content. Then it suddenly came to me the numbers were the most important thing. I separated the numbers and discovered you were using that Confederate cipher we worked out. The trip was an adventure in itself."

I took a deep breath through my nose and caught a whiff of myself.

"Hold that thought. I really think I need that bath."

Rebecca walked me down the hall and left me at the door of the bathing room. Once in the tub, I began to wallow in the water. It had been months since I had bathed, and it did much to ease both my aching body and my nose. After some time passed, I heard a knock at the door.

"Thomas, are you all right?"

"Yes, I am fine. I just need a few more days in here, and I will come out a new man."

She giggled and went back down the hall. It did indeed take me over an hour in the bath. I saw that Rebecca gathered some civilian clothes for me to wear and left them in the bath. They were too large, but when I returned we used a bit of tucking here and there to make them work. They were fresh, laundered, and made me feel more human.

We settled back into my room. Later that afternoon, there was a knock at the door. I didn't recognize him at first, but when he took off his hat, I could see that he was General Halleck.

I slowly rose to my feet and saluted him. "General," I said. "I tried to get someone to listen to me, but no one would."

General Halleck shook his head. "I know, I know, we were operating in the strictest secrecy and until we knew where you were, and your circumstances, we had to maintain that secrecy. I did bring you two new uniforms."

He laid a package on the end of the bed.

"General, I suppose you know I was almost done in by our own troops more than once."

"Yes, Colonel, once we realized your situation, we made every effort to obtain your freedom. You just beat us to it . . . so to speak. You need to rest a few days here, and we will talk again. In the meantime, do not worry about your bills as the army will take care of them. You have performed valiantly, and the army thanks you. As for the real James Blake, he is once again in the Old Capitol Prison."

With that, he turned and left the room.

"Well," I said. "It's good to know the army finally caught up with me."

Rebecca smiled, "At least they didn't have to give you a military funeral."

"Rebecca, I couldn't bear to part with Major Blake's old uniform. I have this strange feeling that someday I would want to return it to him or his family."

Over the next few days, I spent time getting my strength back. During that time, I received a telegram of thanks from General Grant. He made arrangements for me to have an extended furlough. General Halleck came by to visit again and tell me he approved General Grant's request. He encouraged me to recharge over the rest of the winter at home. I also received a telegram from Judge Thatcher, wishing me a complete recovery.

The army gave us train tickets for passage from Washington to Chicago and from there on to Galena. I learned of the bloody mess at Stones River in Tennessee. It seems our army can't catch a break on any front. I made an inquiry through General Halleck as to the condition and whereabouts of George Washington and Daniel Blake. He promised to look into the matter regarding George. As for Daniel Blake, he informed me he took ill with pneumonia and died a few weeks ago. Rebecca spent this time telling me I was pretty grouchy and needed to improve my attitude before we started for home.

It was time to write the letter I was thinking about:

*12 February 1863*
*Major James Blake*
*Old Capitol Prison*
*1st and A Streets NE*
*Washington, D.C.*
*Dear Major Blake:*

*I write this knowing it is in God's hands that all things are possible. How I came by the knowledge I wish to impart is not essential, but I feel I must tell you because it weighs on me. If your stepbrother has not already told you, by now, you will have become a father. Sally Turner was with child at your leaving for the war. I know she would still be in the Clarksville area. If you have an ounce of love and care for this woman, I suggest you seek her out if you are paroled.*

*With Sincerest Regards*

I didn't sign the letter as I didn't want the least hint of animosity to color the truth. I was up and around now and reading the papers. I saw some of those troops were heading east as I was about to head west. This war was far from over. And, in spite of all I had been through, I still felt a strong desire to see it through to the end. I was granted a furlough for two months to recover, and Rebecca suggested we remove ourselves to Galena as soon as possible. It would be far from gun powder, death, and destruction.

The steam whistle sounded, and the cars lurched forward as we began the journey home. Rebecca and I were content to settle into our seats. I was lucky to be traveling by train as most of the train passages were only for military purposes. Mostly soldiers on board this train, but there were a few civilians. There were three gentlemen near the front of the car that caught my eye. They were animated and talking when we first boarded but became subdued when we entered. I was fixated on them for the longest time.

"Quit staring Thomas, you are making me nervous," Rebecca said.

"Oh, sorry, you know those men up there may be up to no good. I am going to walk past them and see if I can pick up on their conversation."

"Do be careful."

"Good morning gentlemen, are you traveling together?"

One of them spoke up. "No, sir, we just met on the train. We are all in the sales field, and we were discussing the current business climate."

"Very well then, have a good day," I said, and returned to my seat.

"Rebecca, they said they were salesmen, but I don't believe it. They possessed no baggage under the seats. And no salesmen are traveling as well-armed as these men are. We must be on our guard."

"Oh Thomas, you are probably imagining things. Just relax and enjoy the trip."

I settled back in my seat, and Rebecca laid her head on my shoulder. I fell into a dream state with the steady clickety-clack of the rails beneath us. Most of the passengers were Union troops on furlough. Some with amputations of limbs were going home for good. I thought about the old woman and the farmhouse where I visited. I prayed she would get help with her farm. I was brought out of this prayer when the train suddenly lurched to a stop. Passengers began to tumble about with sacks and baskets flying around. You could hear the screeching of the cars as the engine reversed. The conductor came through the car.

"Please remain calm; we have an emergency in front of the train. There are military on board seeing to the situation. Please remain in your seats."

I opened the window and looked out into the wintry landscape. Many of the soldiers that were capable grabbed their weapons and waited for the train to stop. Soon there was the clatter of guns firing.

"Rebecca," I said. "I need to see what is happening."

"Oh no, you don't, Thomas Sawyer, sit back down in this seat right now."

A report flowed back through the train that a group of outlaws piled logs on the track and set them ablaze in an attempt to liberate the government payroll money. Three of them were killed in the incident, and two of our soldiers were wounded, but not seriously. They were met with such ferocity of gunfire by our veteran soldiers on board that they turned tail and ran. I thought; what idiots would try and rob a train with veteran soldiers on board. All that remained was to clear the tracks. Rebecca relented for this duty. We settled back into the car when I noticed the three suspicious characters were gone. I made my way forward to the payroll car.

"Captain, I am Colonel Sawyer. I wish to inform you that three men who were on board the train prior to this stop were missing afterward. I think you should be extra diligent in your security precautions regarding the payroll."

"Yes sir, Colonel, we have already added security due to the robbery attempt. And thank you for being so watchful."

We reached Philadelphia without further incident. The warning about the three strangers must have worked. We spent the night at a hotel and then boarded a train for Pittsburgh the following morning. There was a long ride across Pennsylvania, which allowed for some extended conversation with Rebecca about my tribulations. Despite changing trains in Pittsburgh to our train to Chicago and several delays due to an engine breaking down, we made it to Chicago. By late the next night, we finally arrived in Galena. We hired a wagon to take us to Judge Thatcher's house, where we were greeted warmly.

"Tom, it is really good to see you. Ida and I were so worried about you. It must have been traumatic being locked up in prison. I hope Rebecca has taken good care of you. Come sit down and relax."

"Tom," Ida said. "You are welcome to stay with us for a while. At least, until you decide what you are going to do."

"I appreciate your kindness."

We sat in the parlor for just an hour before I found myself nodding off.

"You need to rest," Rebecca said. "Let's get you to bed."

I crawled into bed and slept through the night and into most of the next day. The next few weeks would be filled with reflection on what happened and what I would do. After what I went through, no one would blame me for resigning my commission. In any case, it was good to be back in Galena.

# 11

## Settling the Unsettled

By the first half of March, I was my old self again, and the awful Bull
Run dream was occurring less frequently. The trees were beginning to leaf out in fragile miniatures of what was to come. The storefront
I used as both home and office, changed hands a few days after I left for
war, so the judge was kind enough to let me stay with him. The beauti-
fully painted law office window was now clear glass. Although my name
was erased, I was around to see it. The end of the month would bring
an end to my initial leave. I applied for another sixty days, and it was
granted. I fully expected to hear from someone in Washington, but at this
point, nothing came.

The Thatcher's gave me permission to use their address as my contact. Receiving letters from the men in my former command was mostly
positive. Some were expressing well wishes and hope for my return.
Other letters informed me of battlefield losses. It was as if each letter was
a battle with an outcome. My heart went out to the families of those lost.
I responded to each letter with encouragement and scripture to try and
appease their anxiety. I didn't realize how many men I influenced in my
brief period of leadership. It was both sad to think some were gone and
gratifying that those who survived cared enough to contact me.

I finally received a letter from General Halleck.

*Colonel Sawyer:*

*I am writing to inform you that I will now be the contact for any
scout activity. I will not go into detail, but Mr. Allen Pinkerton has
returned to service with the railroad. I wish to thank you again for*

*what you have done for the Army and wish you a speedy recovery.*
*As to your request, Mister GW has been located in a hospital here*
*in Washington. Doctors say he will make a full recovery from his*
*wound. He expressed the sentiment that he has never served with*
*a finer man and will look forward to meeting you again.*

*Henry Halleck*
*General in Chief*

As my healing progressed, Rebecca and I began to walk about the streets of Galena. I met old clients from my law practice, and we exchanged pleasantries. One evening we stopped on the same bench where Rebecca solved the Confederate cipher.

"Thomas," Rebecca said. "Do you remember when we were children, and we met after school? Do you remember what we said to each other?"

I paused to gather my thoughts.

"Yes, I remember, we pledged our love to each other."

"And what was the other part?"

"Let me see now, as I recall it was something about Amy Lawrence."

"No, silly, you know better. It was about us pledging to marry, and we sealed it with a kiss."

"Oh, Rebecca, that was long ago. So much has happened to us both."

"Do you still feel the same way now?"

I paused a moment to let the question sink in. I had grown a lot since then. I had taken many chances with my life hanging in the balance. I was thinking about an opportune time to ask the question, and this did seem right. I turned to her, so our knees were touching. I took her hands in mine and looked into her eyes.

"Rebecca," I said. "Will you marry me?"

She paused for a moment and replied, "Oh Thomas, I do love you with all my heart, but do you think it wise while you are still in the army. I don't know if I could bear the thought of marrying you and then . . ."

As she said this, she lowered her head, and when she raised it again, there were tears in her eyes.

I continued, "I have already asked for your hand from your father, and he has consented. You have been and always will be the only woman for me. I would sooner die as your husband than to live without our joining as one. Please, say yes, Rebecca?"

We stood, and she hugged me tightly, pulled her head away from my shoulder, and smiled. "Colonel Sawyer, you have stolen my heart. I will marry you."

With those words, I produced a simple gold band and placed it on her finger.

"This is all I can afford for now, but someday I will get you a better ring."

"But we must hurry and make the arrangements. You may be called away at any moment." She broke away from the embrace and spun around. "Dance with me, Colonel, for we may not get another chance."

"But," I protested, "There is no music."

"Yes, there is, you just need to listen with your heart."

We embraced, and we began to sway back and forth. The pace quickened, and we began to twirl around in the manner of a waltz. We made our way out into the street, where we were watched by all. We slowly and gracefully made our way across the street and toward her house dancing all the way.

When we reached the front door, we were greeted by my future father and mother in law with open arms. We fell in a heap on the parlor settee, laughing and giggling like children.

"I take it she said yes?" said the judge.

"She did indeed, sir," I replied.

"Then, we must celebrate. Hanna, bring us some brandy."

"Thomas," the judge began, "I wish to welcome you most heartily into the family. You and Rebecca have known each other since childhood and I know you have your ups and downs. From your beginning back in Missouri, I felt sure you would grow to appreciate each other. I recognized your courage early on when you saved Rebecca from that cave and Injun Joe. It is altogether fitting that it has blossomed into love. My wish is that you and Rebecca have a wonderful life together."

"Thank you, Father," Rebecca said.

"Your mother and I will retire for the evening, as I know you to will have much to talk about."

We spent an hour talking about buying a house, children, our money supply, and our dreams. Rebecca said she would continue to help her mother and father until my return. She was bubbling over with excitement. At a little past nine, the conversation took a more serious tone.

"Thomas, forgive me for saying this because I think I know the answer . . . but I want you to resign your commission and stay here in Galena with me."

I was silent for a moment and then realized what she might be trying to do. Was she promising her hand in marriage so I would stay with her in Galena? I began to feel anger boiling up but I suppressed it.

"Rebecca, I have said to you before that I cannot resign my commission. I made a commitment to the army for three years, and I need to know my sacrifice to this point has not been in vain. I hope you understand and didn't consent to marriage just to keep me here in Galena."

"No, No, Thomas, I want to marry you regardless of your decision, but I am so fearful you won't return."

"Then let's do it now," I said. "With haste, so this war and my service won't be a deterrent to anything from here on. I promise you when I return from the war, we will have a grand wedding. I will get you a good ring, a fancy dress, a bouquet of flowers, and we will do it up right and proper."

She looked at me, hesitated for just a moment, as though I might not be serious. Then she left me and ran up the stairway to her father's room.

"Father, Father, come down to the parlor; we are going to be married tonight."

Her father opened the door, took one look at his daughter's face and then said,

"Very well, just give us a moment."

"Ida," he said. "Please go to the Grant's and tell Julia we would like for her to be a witness to the ceremony."

It was not long before she returned with Julia bearing an additional surprise. Mrs. Grant brought with her a set of wedding rings. She said the rings were handed down from a relative in the family and received after she and the General were already married. We should consider the rings a wedding gift from the General and his family. Rebecca's ring was a diamond and blue enamel ring with a single diamond in the middle and four smaller ones on each of the corners. My ring was a thick gold band that suited me well. We gathered in the parlor, and the judge proceeded with the ceremony.

I heard him say, "Thomas Sawyer, wilt thou . . ." all the while, I kept my focus on Rebecca's eyes until she elbowed me, and I responded, "I will."

He then turned to Rebecca repeating the vow, and she responded, "I will."

We completed the vows, and the judge pronounced us man and wife. He gave the command, but before he finished, I was kissing her. We held hands and prayed that God would protect us now and in the days to come. Once again, the brandy flowed as we celebrated for more than an hour in the parlor. We talked about our future and laughed our way into the night. As the evening wound down, we bid good night to Mrs. Grant. She said she would send her husband a telegram about the joyous event in the morning.

Despite our long train trip together, I did not tell Rebecca about everything I experienced as a scout. I felt it was too risky for her to know. There were still spies in the north who would take any opportunity to strike at me through her. Tonight was our wedding night. I wanted to make it special, but there was not enough time. Passion overtook us three times during the night. Each time was like a huge ocean wave with a crescendo that broke against the shore. We finally fell to sleep in blissful exhaustion. I began dreaming about my new bride and the life we would live together after the war. I recall having another, more fitful dream.

> *An explosion tore a big hole in the wall and threw us all into the air. The judge was bleeding—fatally injured. Ida was thrown back against the china cabinet and lay unconscious on the floor. Mrs. Grant had what looked like a broken leg, but worst of all, my precious Rebecca was killed instantly. I looked around in shock at what had happened.*

"Thomas," Rebecca said, "You were screaming. Are you all right?"

"Yes, I think so." The judge and Ida came into the room.

Ida poured me a glass of water. I recounted the nightmare to them, and they attempted to comfort me. The next morning, I awoke with my bride at my side, clothed in her nightgown and robe. As I tried to get out of bed gently, she stirred.

She smiled, said, "I love you," and fell back to sleep.

I washed my hands and face, dressed, and went down to breakfast. Hanna placed some hard boiled eggs, fried ham, biscuits, and honey on the table.

"You had a hard night Thomas," Ida said. "Do you want some cold buttermilk to go with your breakfast?"

I eagerly accepted, then sat and ate in silence. I was still contemplating the night when the judge walked in the door.

"Thomas . . . you have a telegram here."

*25 March 1863*
*Colonel Thomas Sawyer*

*Colonel Sawyer, Hope you are well. I require your assistance immediately. More when you arrive. Sending courier Lieutenant Davidson to guide you. Be ready to leave when he arrives.*

*US Grant,*
*Major General*

As I finished reading the telegram, Rebecca entered the dining room. She looked at me holding the telegram and started to cry. I took her in my arms and tried to console her by kissing her tears away.

"You will be careful and come back to me, won't you?" she pleaded.

"Rebecca, you are the smartest, bravest, most beautiful, most intelligent girl I have ever met, or ever will meet. I will always do my very best to return to you."

We made a pact to spend every minute together until the time came for me to leave. That time would turn out to be very short, for early the next morning, Lieutenant Davidson arrived. He said he traveled through the night to get to Galena.

"Colonel Sawyer," he began, "I was lucky to be nearby when I received orders from General Grant to come and escort you. I have here your orders from General Grant. You are to accompany me to his headquarters. It won't be an easy journey, and I can't divulge the location yet, as maintaining secrecy is a priority. I am sure you understand."

"Yes, but you must give me some time with my new wife. Would it be all right if we leave this afternoon? We want to have a picture made before I leave. It will be a remembrance of our love for each other."

"Very good, sir, I will check the steamer schedule and be back at 2:00 this afternoon. I could use some rest myself before we start back. But, if the schedule requires it, you must be ready to go immediately after, as the general wants us to start back today. Congratulations on your marriage sir"

Rebecca and I headed down to the photographer's shop. She asked me to wear my dress uniform. She wore the dress she had on when we were married. It took so long for us to get the picture made it was nearly 1:00 before we finished. At precisely 2:00, Lieutenant Davidson returned.

"I beg your pardon Mrs. Sawyer, but Colonel Sawyer and I must be going. I have secured passage for us, and the boat leaves at 2:30 sharp."

"Lieutenant, I have a small trunk and some personal items I wish to take with me."

"Very good, sir, I have an army wagon waiting outside to take us to the terminal."

The Lieutenant was very resourceful about getting things done, partially because he knew the magic words in Galena "General Grant." I began to have doubts about my decision to leave. I held Rebecca close to me for what might be the last time. A surprise gift from General Grant came aboard the steamer. It was my horse, Ares. He seemed in good spirits and, although skittish at first, warmed to my touch. The steam whistle blew. Rebecca began to cry as I boarded the steamer. My trunk arrived just minutes before we pulled away from the dock.

"Well, Lieutenant, is there a cabin where we can talk?"

"Certainly, sir. Please follow me." He escorted me to a cabin below deck.

"Colonel, the general has a major offensive underway to attempt to take Vicksburg. He is ordering you to take part in it. You will be briefed on the specifics of your duties when we reach the general, but for now, it is enough for you to prepare yourself."

The steamer sped its way south, picking up supplies and troops. We passed St Louis and continued south as night fell. The river changed to a placid ribbon of water with dark shadows on the banks. Lantern lights and bonfires along the shoreline served as markers for our journey south. Once we reached the Tennessee border, we transferred to a Union tinclad vessel, the USS Rattler. The darkness which served to hide us was also good cover for Rebels or sympathizers to take shots at us. At last, and after three days travel, we pulled into the port of Memphis. Lieutenant Davis requested another meeting.

Once we were alone, he began, "Sir, I was authorized by General Grant to brief you on our mission, once we reached Memphis. Upon our departure, we will be joining a flotilla that will make a run past the Confederate batteries at Vicksburg, Mississippi. Admiral Porter's fleet has attempted this once before and took heavy losses. I would suggest you take a good breakfast here in Memphis and be prepared to leave at dawn."

An ironclad, well equipped to return fire, was our next means of transportation. It took several hours to transfer all the men, freight, and supplies to her. Every inch of space onboard was used. I went below deck, began to look around, and saw a face I thought I recognized. I carefully stepped over soldiers already fast asleep to get a closer look. He was dressed in a sergeant's uniform from a company out of Minnesota. I didn't believe he was with me at Bull Run, but where had I seen him? It's funny how your mind can become consumed with this sort of thing, and I was now deep in thought. Then, like a bolt of lightning, it came to me. He was one of the three men I saw on the train to Galena, vanishing after the attempted robbery.

"Say, sergeant . . . don't I know you?"

"Colonel, I do not recall our meeting," he said. His manner indicated to me he was lying.

"Well, sergeant, I believe we have met."

He began to back away from me slowly. He turned and began to slowly walk with his head down as if he were invisible to me. I pulled my pistol.

"You, sergeant, are a liar, and I mean to know the truth."

He turned back toward me, lunged forward, and tried to wrestle the gun from my hand. I pulled it away and struck him with the barrel, causing him to hit the floor. He got up slowly, wiping the blood from his cheek.

I said, "Now, let us try this again, sergeant. You need to start telling the truth."

"Well, Colonel—" He sprang for the hatch and leaped onto the deck.

"Stop him!" I shouted.

Just as I got onto the deck, he jumped overboard and was swimming away. I took careful aim, fired one shot, and he rolled over and floated motionless in the river. The astonished group of men who observed looked at me in disbelief. I knew this kind of thing would spread among the men and foster a sense of distrust.

"Men, you must understand the man who leapt from this vessel was a conspirator and possibly a Confederate spy, I recognized from a previous encounter. He would surely have been hung for his deeds had he not met this end."

"Lieutenant, please fish this saboteur out of the water and see to his burial wherever appropriate."

He returned a few minutes later.

"Sir, the Confederate has been interred. He possessed papers written in cipher. It will take us a while to decode them."

"Thank you, Lieutenant. I hope the information turns out to be valuable. I happen to know a cipher that the Confederates have used and I will write it out for you. It may not help in this case, but it is worth a try."

The Mississippi River was difficult enough to navigate in daylight, but we would have to cross the batteries at Vicksburg in the dark. Once we finally got underway, you could feel the tension on board as men found ways to divert their nervous energy. Some whittled, others played cards or wrote letters. The heat below deck was like a steam bath, but coming out on deck meant exposure to Confederate snipers. It made for a constant movement to the deck for short intervals just to get some fresh air. The sun began to set on the river, and streaks of gold reflected across the water. It reminded me of the scripture, "Bless the Lord, O my soul: and all that is within me bless his holy name." I prayed for God to be with us as we made this journey.

At around one in the morning, we rounded the bend just north of Vicksburg. The lead ships were just into the turn when Confederate guns began to blaze from the bluff above. We were initially out of range, and most of the shots splashed harmlessly into the water, but then they seemed to adjust their range, and fused shells began to explode near our waterline.

"We need all you Army men below deck. Take her about, Captain, and hug the eastern shore. Man the guns and be ready for action. You there, Colonel, I could use you as we round this bend."

"Yes, Admiral, what is it you need?"

"See to it that ammunition is kept flowing to the guns off the port quarter."

I selected a place along the ammunition line so that I could see most of the men in this dark environment. Firing was now almost continuous from the lead ships. Once I saw that the men were ready, I tried to view the scene from a gun port. There was a corporal there overseeing that portion of the line, so I returned to my initial spot, speaking words of encouragement to the men along the way.

I would likely never get this chance again so I ventured onto the deck for just for a moment. It was quite a sight. The red orange flame of the muzzle flashes on the lead boats indicated their return fire. Then the cannon on our ship opened up. The deafening noise reverberated through the iron ship again and again as they fired. Smoke swept through the ship and obscured our vision at every discharge.

Scurrying back down, I noticed a man pausing to lean up against the bulkhead for a moment to wipe his brow.

"You there, keep the ammunition moving."

The young man looked at me fearfully and said, "Yes, Colonel."

There was an explosion that rattled the deck where we were. A piece of shrapnel struck the sailor manning the gun port next to me, and he went down with an apparent chest wound.

"Keep ammunition coming," I screamed. Doctor, I have a man down here."

"Colonel, can you man that gun port and return fire?"

"Yes, Admiral."

I took up his musket and began shooting. It was so dark the only thing I could shoot at was the muzzle flashes on the shore. These became obscured at times by the choking smoke from the guns. Shells slammed against the iron hull without much effect. An hour passed, and we were finally clear of Vicksburg and the deadly guns. We arrived safely at Bruinsburg, Mississippi, just as the first hints of sunrise were beginning to lighten the sky. Two of the ironclads sustained damaged, and one of the tin-clads went down soon after we made Vicksburg. Six of the tin-clad crew members survived the sinking and were picked up. They reported that most aboard were killed when the ship exploded, and the rest were presumed missing or captured. We had run the gauntlet and survived.

# 12

## Catching Up on the Spy Business

For the first time in a long while, we were operating behind enemy lines, and the excitement showed itself on the faces of the men. I looked around to see if there was an escort to headquarters. From a distance, I saw an officer walking amongst the men and checking uniforms. He stopped and hailed me.

"Colonel Sawyer!" he exclaimed.

I nodded, and he made his way to me through the crowd.

He saluted crisply and said, "Sir, I am Major Hawhe, 49th Indiana. I have been sent to escort you to General Grant."

"Very good, Major," I replied, "but I must see to my horse first."

"Lieutenant Davidson, I want to thank you for your service. You can return to your company now. You are dismissed."

"Thank you, sir. And sir, the way you flushed out that Confederate spy was something I will never forget."

Major Hawhe spoke up, "Sir, I will have a sergeant take charge of preparing your horse. You look as though you need to get some rest. I will wake you when we are ready to move out."

He was right. I was bone-tired and evidently looked it. I joined a group of officers taking rest in a grove of trees. It turned out to only be a short one-hour rest, but it helped. Some of the Regimental flags from McClernand's XIII Corps could be seen in the distance marching away from us, so we were playing catch up. We rode on with a tide of men and equipment. Major Hawhe led the way past several brigades, and he slowed to acknowledge some of the men in his company. Soon we came upon the General Grant and his staff. After hailing him, he wheeled his horse, and we made eye contact. An ever so slight smile came across the General's face, and I knew this was about all I would get. As we got closer, we came to a stop and saluted one another.

"Colonel Sawyer, it is so good to see you again."

"Yes, General, I have looked forward to this moment,"

"We have our work cut out for us, Colonel."

"I understand, sir, and I am assuming we will be marching to take Vicksburg."

"Yes, but not directly. For now, we must press onward with all haste. The enemy knows we are here. We must execute my plan before they can react. With the taking of Port Gibson and the surrender of Grand Gulf, we have created our best opportunity yet. Why don't you and Major . . ."

"Major Hawhe, General" came the reply avoiding an awkward moment.

"Yes, Major Hawhe," the general said. "The 49th Indiana I believe."

"Yes, sir," came the reply, and he glowed at this mention.

"Major Hawhe, you have my gratitude and are dismissed to return to your regiment. Colonel, you remember Lt. Colonel Rollins of my staff?"

"Yes, General," I replied . . . as we rode, the conversation turned toward many topics.

"Well, Tom, I hear you and Rebecca are married now."

"That's right, sir."

"Julia sent a telegraph message to me the day after the ceremony. I was fortunate to receive it so quickly. There are some things I do not understand. It sometimes takes five days to get a message for approval of military operations from Washington and only two to get word of your marriage." He managed a brief smile, and so did I.

We rode silently for some time, and then he began again,

"Colonel, we have already fought to secure our line in Mississippi. The army is heading toward Vicksburg but by a different route. I intend to have the army stay east of the Big Black River and watch for the response by Pimberton in Vicksburg. I also need to keep an eye on Joe Johnston at the same time. I would like for you to be part of General McPherson's Corps and stick by him. Follow his instruction: support any battle as they might progress but use your special undercover skills. I have information that they will be necessary. Your orders will reflect this request."

We ended the day's march at Haskins Ferry.

"Colonel Sawyer, you have your assignment. Read these orders carefully. I bid you good night."

General Grant arranged for me to have a tent nearby. It was good to be in service again, and my heart swelled with pride at the sight of the blue-clad columns. I also knew how lucky I was to be near General Grant. Most men would never get to share any time with him. I felt the freedom to write about my current situation while not giving away any military information:

*My Darling Wife:*

*I deplore being away from you again, especially since we have now been joined by God. I hope all is well with you and your parents. You mean so much to me, and it now becomes imperative I return to you after this war is over. Have I mentioned that I love you? Here it is again. I love you more than the width of the largest ocean or height of the highest mountain. I know death hangs on my doorstep while I am here. If I were to die, know that I will always be with you and you with me as our love is eternal. The thought of you and your loving arms gives me purpose for today and hope for tomorrow.*

*I have met with my old friend General Grant today. I can tell the war is beginning to wear on him. He was pleased to see me, but we couldn't tarry long as the entire army is on the move. I feel as though things are about to be turned toward our side, and I pray the war will be over soon. I am well for now, but my shoulder does bother me on occasion. I feel somewhat reluctant to command again, but if called upon, I will do so. Morale with the army seems high, and there is much hope we will be victorious. Pray for me. All I have been through pales in comparison to what I may be called upon to do.*

*Thomas*

The quartermaster supplied me with a new pistol, ammunition, and a special gift from General Grant. In his last meeting with Admiral Porter, he was given a Spencer repeating rifle and 100 rounds of ammunition. It was brought to my tent by Lt. Colonel Rollins with a note.

*I will have no use for the weapon, but perhaps you can see to it a few Rebels will feel its fire.*

As I lay down to sleep, it occurred to me that other than the command with the 79th New York and Smith's Second Division, I had never been in a leadership role. I wouldn't let my friend down. In fact, I looked forward to it. A few moments later, came a fitful remembrance of Bull Run. It soon passed, and I fell asleep. The next morning was a flurry of activity. I drew three days rations and was told to make it last six as we couldn't count on being regularly resupplied. A quick stop to send my letter to Rebecca, and then it was on to find General McPherson. His third division was just coming up from crossing the Mississippi at Hard Times, Louisiana. I met briefly with Major General Logan and showed him my orders. He seemed perturbed with the idea of having me assigned to General McPherson, but when he saw General Grant's signature, his manner changed. We proceeded to march northeast to join the rest of the XVII Corps. By evening we were camped just outside Rocky Springs.

"General, it is good to see you again," I said.

"Colonel Sawyer, I do not recall our having met. You must refresh my memory."

"Fort Henry, sir, I was with a detachment under your command. I thought you might remember."

"Sorry, Colonel, I do not. Regardless, what brings you to me?"

He took a moment to read my orders, looked up at me and scowled.

"What makes General Grant think I need someone to watch over me?"

"It's not like that at all; I am unattached and have been in service since Bull Run. I was wounded and have been undercover working for Major Allen. General Grant hopes my experience behind enemy lines and knowledge of the Confederates would be of special use to you." His scowl became more relaxed.

"Sorry, Colonel, the burdens of command are weighing on me presently, and I didn't mean to be ungracious. Welcome to XVII Corps. For now, you will stick with my headquarters staff, dismissed."

The troops were allowed a four-hour rest on hard ground and were on the move again at 4 a.m. We kept moving northeast along the Big Black River. We were repositioning our forces, and the XVII Corps was to lead the way past Utica toward a place called Fourteen Mile Creek. The advance brigade made contact with the enemy just outside Raymond. Cannon fire erupted, and rifles began to pop and crack as our men deployed in battle lines. I came up with General McPherson and requested permission to ride the brigade formations to see if I could be of assistance. He granted permission. I mounted my horse, pulled the reins, and headed north around the rear of our lines. I passed the 80th Ohio of Holmes's Division and 124th Illinois of Smith's Brigade. They seemed to be holding up well. I met Brigadier General Smith in the field and asked where I could help.

He just pointed north and shouted, "20th Illinois."

The battle continued to heat up, and as I reached the 20th, they were attempting a push forward. They were heavily engaged with the Rebel's 7th Texas regiment. Fighting was fierce, and minié balls whizzed all around us. I dismounted and ran to the line firing and struck one Rebel in the chest. Our cannon battery on the left of the line let loose with a volley of canister shot. Two men of the 20th went down beside me, with one taking a direct shot to the head. He twisted, fell sideways, and landed near my feet. To my left, a Lieutenant Colonel was directing fire. It was an attempt to protect part of his brigade stranded in a creek bed. He was felled by two minié balls at once. This happened just as three Confederate infantrymen overran our line and were coming fast. I raised my rifle and fired one, two, three times, each time striking one of the Confederates. Number three was only wounded and raised his musket at me. I froze for a half second and then let him have two rounds. I pulled even with the rest of the line and fired my last round, hitting one Rebel. I didn't take time to reload. I believed that the tide could swing our way with a good charge. I went back to my horse, drew my sword, and rode to the end of the line.

"Forward men . . . forward, 20th Illinois charrrrrge!"

The rest of the 20th moved forward with me. They fought hard and made some progress pushing the Rebel line back. Just then, a break came in the center, and the whole of the Rebel line began to retreat. The 20th captured several prisoners and some Rebel artillery as we moved forward. The fighting slowed and sputtered out.

Some members of the 20th were surrounding the body of their Lieutenant Colonel. I rode back, dismounted, and helped the men carry their leader's body to a shaded area. The captured cannons and prisoners flowing past us now seemed less important than the loss of their leader. I felt a little out of place, not having known him, but I offered my condolences. I asked them if I could offer a word of prayer, and they consented.

"Dear God, I and the men of the 20th would ask that you watch over the sole of this brave Lieutenant Colonel. I entreat you to open the gates of heaven for him. Bless those who knew him and especially his family and loved ones. What he gave can't be replaced by man, but we know he is now being lifted up by angels. Blessings on the other members of the

20th both killed, wounded and captured. We thank you, God, for their lives and their service to the cause, Amen."

Members of the 20th gathered to thank me for my leadership. They wanted a look at the repeating rifle. Most of them had never seen one before and were impressed by its firepower. I felt as though I was accepted by the men of the 20th.

I returned to General McPherson's headquarters to add my report to the record. In the command tent, I came across Brigadier General Smith, Commander of First Brigade.

He said, "Colonel, where did you come from? I would like to thank you for helping my boys in the 20th today. I am grateful for the way you picked up the fight and carried it forward. What is your name?"

"Sawyer, sir, Thomas Sawyer, I am on special assignment to General McPherson."

"Well, Colonel Sawyer, I will certainly speak favorably of you in my report to General McPherson."

"Thank you, sir."

After getting several hours sleep, I was again facing General McPherson, this time, at my request.

"Colonel, I have reviewed General Grant's orders in detail and understand why he wanted to place you with my corps. It seems he has evidence of some Confederate spies among us, and they are getting information to the Rebel lines about our position. I take it from your earlier statement you have some experience in this business.

"Yes sir."

"Well, Colonel, I won't stand for such activity under my command. The penalty for any such treasonous action is death. As this campaign continues, you will look into this matter and report to me with your findings. It is obvious General Grant trusts you, and I will give you the same trust unless you give me reason not to. Whatever you glean in this task must not be rumor, false accusations, or innuendo but facts. I will expect nothing less. You won't act independently of me in any cases, as I fear as much for your safety as for our men. Is that understood?"

"Yes sir."

"I have read General Smith's report of what you did today on the battlefield. I commend you for those actions. I am sure when General Grant reads my report, it will have a favorable light on your service. You are dismissed."

I knew General Grant was placing a lot of trust in me to root out the spies. I was hoping to leave the spy business behind. Instead, I was being plunged back into the shady, cut-throat business again. What I needed was a cover story that was believable and would allow me to be everywhere in the XVII Corps without arousing suspicion. I went back to General McPherson.

"General, could you write an order stating I will be evaluating the logistics of the corps. I believe this will give me cover for free movement among the men."

This he did, and the order went out the next day along with subsequent orders indicating a move toward the Mississippi capitol of Jackson. We marched until we came near Clinton and fell out to camp. It was a comfortable night until the rain came. At first, it was just a drizzle, then it began raining harder. The dust on the roads turned to mud. The weather seemed as much an enemy as the Confederates when it came to maneuvers.

> The enormity of the task hit me. I was to glean through thousands of men to try to find an undercover operation. But where do I begin? After some quiet time in prayer it came to me that in Matthew chapter 25 it says, "Then shall he answer them, saying, 'Verily I say unto you, In as much as ye did it not to one of the least of these, ye did it not to me.'" Who would have the least amount of knowledge about military service and still travel with the corps? The mule drivers of the supply wagons would be a place to start. However, there was every conceivable type of conveyance in this corps. They foraged from the farms surrounding the route north. This made things a bit more difficult. I needed a way to shorten the task.

We moved out just before dawn the next morning in the direction of Jackson. I learned from General McPherson that we were going to attack Jackson along with Sherman's Corp. I informed the General I would be in the rear observing the supply line. He looked at me as though I was crazy.

"Colonel, I understand your assignment, but I can use a man of your caliber on the line as we engage the enemy. This request is against my better judgement."

He paused then and reconsidered.

"On second thought, you might be right, you may proceed."

"Thank you, sir. I sincerely believe it is necessary to find the Confederate spies among us. You won't regret this, sir."

"I hope not, Colonel."

I mounted my horse and began to drift back down the long procession of soldiers. I got some puzzling looks from some of the men as I passed. But as I passed the 20th Illinois, they cheered and waved their hats. As I came upon the supply train, I knew there was one thing I couldn't do. I couldn't stop the progress of this long and winding procession of wagons, carriages, buckboards, and such. There were six-mule teams with skilled drivers. There were one-horse buggies with a single driver. Other drivers occasionally lost control of their animals and their wagons. I decided that I would do interviewing on the move.

I rode up to a six-mule supply wagon.

"Say there, Corporal, do you mind if I ride along for a while? I have a few questions for you."

"Begging your pardon, sir, but I suppose the Colonel can do whatever he likes."

"What is your name?" I inquired.

"My name is Crooks, sir, Mason Crooks."

"Corporal Crooks, I am Colonel Sawyer, have you seen the order about my assignment?"

"Yes, sir, I did. I don't know how you're going to speed up this damn mess. I can't imagine what old Unconditional Surrender is thinking. He will probably have to send half his army out for forage if he wants to keep up this pace. I been with the XVII Corp since before we crossed the Mississippi, and I tell you I never seen such men. They can whip a whole heard of charging elephants with just one company."

"Well, Corporal, thank you for the conversation."

This man seemed genuine enough, so I moved on down the line making eye contact with each driver as we traveled. When one refused to make eye contact with me, I pulled alongside to chat. This went on for over an hour, and I didn't see or hear anything suspicious. We passed Clinton, and engineers began directing the destruction of the railroad. Soon, all along the rail lines, bonfires appeared, and rails were being heated, twisted, and turned into steel pretzels.

———— ⌇ ————

As we approached Jackson, the sound of gunfire indicated skirmishers contact with the enemy. The Corps began to deploy with each division forming in multiple lines of battle. They set up reserves and sent two divisions to the front. Supply teams halted as they got closer to the action. Mules don't do well under fire, so they needed to stay in the rear. Drivers began to pull over to feed the animals. One private pulled out of line and took his team of mules around a large bluff where he was hidden from the rest of the line. I followed him, staying some distance back. He took a small tree branch, bend it around and tie it in a knot. This aroused my suspicions, and I went to investigate.

"I am Colonel Sawyer, and who might you be?"

"Muller, sir, Private Muller."

"Well private, which is your regiment?"

"It's the 20th Ohio," he said with his head down.

"I noticed you tying that small branch. Would you care to explain?"

He paused for a moment and said, "Well sir, it's," again, he hesitated, "It's a signpost."

"And what or whom are you signaling?" My hand began moving slowly toward the butt of my pistol.

"It's my girl, sir. She is following this train with some sutlers. She says she loves me and wants to marry me. But the General, he don't allow us to see any of the folks that follows us. So, I am leaving her a sign to let her know she is on the right road. She promised me she would follow us, sir."

"Private, we are deep in enemy territory without a rear guard, so there are no sutlers or camp ladies. Would you care to try again?"

He said nothing, so I walked to the tree and began looking closely at its branches. Wedged in a fork was a small folded piece of paper. I opened it to discover a ciphered message. Then everything went black.

When I awoke, my vision was blurry and faded in and out. When I could see somewhat, it was dark, and the smell of horse manure was nearly overpowering. My eyes began to get used to the darkness, and I saw moonlight streaming through cracks in walls. The dust floated in the air like a gentle, unyielding fog. My uniform was gone, and I was dressed only in my undergarments. My hands were tied behind me with a second rope securing me to one of the stall posts. A stiff gag was in my mouth. I tried pulling on the ropes, but they were securely tied and the harder I pulled the tighter they became. I listened intently and didn't hear any animals. There were also no noises from the outside. Someone must have taken all the horses, including mine. I lay there with my head throbbing and my mouth hurting from the gag. There was a rattle at the barn door, and I heard someone enter. The lantern light they carried exposed three men. I recognized one of them right away as Nate Wilson. I didn't recognize the other two immediately as they stayed in the shadows. Nate was first to speak.

"Well, Colonel Sawyer, I see you are awake. Don't worry about your being tied up. In a few days, we will turn you loose, and you can go where ever you like. You see, we have been watching General Grant for months now, and he didn't even know it. You and your friend were the only ones who even got close to doing us in. Oh . . . I thought you would like to know that some friends of yours are here for a visit."

Appearing from the shadows was James Blake wearing my Union uniform. Along with him was Lieutenant Johnson, the very cavalry officer who requested a meeting with General Grant on that train trip to Galena so long ago.

"By the time we are finished," Nate said. "You will be the most wanted man in the Union army."

They turned and walked out of the barn. I heard them leave but curiously no sound of horses. They left one man behind, and he chained and padlocked the door. I wiggled around to where I could get to my knees. Then, with a great deal of effort, I jumped up to my feet. The rope to which I was tethered was just long enough for me to stand up and maybe take one hop. I watched silently as the guard blocked the moonlight between the barn slats as he walked.

I sat back down and, to my surprise, got a sharp pain in my rear. I managed to scoot around and found a wooden handle buried in the hay. I shuffled the hay with my legs and uncovered an old hoe. I squirmed around and began to methodically rub the rope on the blade. My arms were starting to ache, and my old shoulder wound was causing me some grief. I was just about to quit, for a moment, to relieve the pain, when the rope gave way, freeing my hands. The guard was still pacing around the barn, but he would stop every few revolutions. I waited till the guard stopped, took the hoe, and quietly climbed into the loft. Fortunately, the loft floor was solid and made no noise. I cracked the loft door and saw the guard lazily drinking from a flask. When I opened the door, he looked up, I swung the hoe hard and struck him in the head. He went down, but he was not out. I landed square on his chest with my knee, struck him in the head again with the blade of the hoe, and he was dead.

I unlocked the barn with his key and drug him in. Then I borrowed his clothes and pistol. There was a farmhouse about fifty yards away, and a lantern light glowed from one of the front windows. I crept up to the window, peeked in, and saw a table and a large oil lamp. In the back part of the room, the three conspirators were seated at a small table. I ducked under the window and went to the front corner of the house. There were four saddled horses tied to the porch rail. I noticed an old dough trough. Creeping onto the porch, I carefully placed it upside down directly in front of the doorway. I crept back to the open window. I aimed the hoe like a spear and hurled it.

The hoe struck the lamp. Coal oil spewed from its base, igniting the table and part of the floor. I rushed to the corner near the doorway just in time to see Lieutenant Johnson fall head over heels over the dough trough. The second man through kicked the trough to one side, and in the growing firelight, I could tell this was James. I took aim and fired one shot striking him in the left side, and he doubled over. Lieutenant Johnson picked himself up and drew a bead on me with his pistol while I did the same toward him. He fired and missed, I didn't. But there was no sign of Nate Wilson. I turned back to the side of the house and saw him climbing out a back window, gun in hand. I shot just as he got his right leg over the sill, hitting him in the left leg. He struggled free of the window, raised his pistol, fired, and missed. He limped behind the back corner of the house. I chased him around the house, and he mounted one of the horses.

"You ain't got enough to catch me, Sawyer, Sic Semper Tyrannis." And he rode off.

All was quiet then except for the fire consuming the house. In the firelight, I could see a steady trail of blood back around the house and knew his wound was pretty severe. If he didn't get help soon, he would probably die. That's when I heard banging and screaming. I went in through the back door and found a back stair to the upper floor.

I hollered, "Where are you?"

The banging and hollering came again from the end of the hall.

"Stand back!" and I let fly a kick to open the door.

Inside the room, there was a terrified farmer, his wife, and two small children. Together we raced out the back door and around to the front of the house. In the firelight, I saw James move. I drug him away from the fire. The farmer and I untied the horses just as the porch began to collapse. We all sat in stunned silence, watching the fire consume the house. Dawn was beginning to break, and with it came a realization. If I wanted to save James, I must move quickly. He would have a lot of valuable information on the Confederacy.

"Sir," the farmer said. "I thank God you came when you did. Otherwise, I am sure we wouldn't have survived. I have two sons who are fighting for the Union. This war has already brought us great sorrow and the loss of one son, and now it has also cost us our home."

"You have my deepest sympathy for your loss. The men who died tonight were Rebel sympathizers. The one still alive will have information for my command, and I need to get him back to headquarters alive. He has a clean wound and is not bleeding badly."

"My wife will patch him up as best she can," said the farmer.

"I will report this to my command and ask for reparations on your behalf."

He had two, possibly three dead bodies to bury and a house to rebuild. He helped me put James on a horse and tie him to the saddle. It was the only way to get him there quickly. The farmer's wife brought me some ham and honey from their cellar.

"How far are we from Clinton?"

"About two miles, just follow this road till you come to the rail tracks and follow them west. They run right through Clinton."

"Thank you again for your kindness."

I had now been up for nearly twenty-four hours and was feeling the fatigue. I kept thinking about Rebecca as I turned west along the railroad. We traveled until I could travel no longer and stopped for a short rest. I left James tied to his horse, but by giving him water, he roused up slightly. I covered his bandage as best I could with scraps from my shirt. Around 10:30 am, I could make out the faint noise of cannon firing in the distance. This meant our boys were engaged at Jackson. Unless I missed my guess, we would soon be coming up on the rear of the Union lines. I checked on James, and he was still alive, although unconscious. By 3:30 or so in the afternoon, I approached the rear guard, and as it happened were men from the 20th Illinois. At first halt, they didn't recognize me in civilian clothes. I cut the cordialities short and asked where the field hospital was. As I lead the horse along to the hospital, there were peculiar looks from the men when they got a glimpse of James. I slid him down off the horse and, with some assistance, brought him into a hospital tent.

"Do what you can for him and get that uniform off him and return it to me," I said.

They took him to an open area and lay him down. He was still alive, but barely.

I am still puzzled as to why they didn't question if I was Colonel Sawyer. I guess sometimes it's good to be lucky. I needed to get to General McPherson and report on the conspiracy. The Confederates had broken off the attack, and fighting sputtered to a stop. I found the General's tent and asked to see him.

"Well, Sawyer, what happened to you? You're dressed like a cowhand," he said in an angry voice. "I could have used you today. You were ordered to report to me with your findings each day. I am beginning to think I made a mistake in my report to General Grant. Explain yourself, sir."

I did the best I could to review the events since yesterday and what happened with Private Muller. As I did, the general's persona began to change. He looked at me and then to his aid.

"See that Private Muller and anyone else in his presence are brought to me immediately."

They were shocked to see me when they entered headquarters. Under intense questioning, they confessed to attacking me but insisted they were not Confederate spies. After hearing my report, the General ordered them to be kept under guard and executed in front of the Corps in the morning. I put in a request to bring Major Blake's old uniform from his saddlebags to me. It would be more difficult for him to rejoin the Confederacy without it. I had grown attached to the rags. A sergeant brought my uniform from the hospital area and sent a new shirt to go with it.

The next morning, I ate a good breakfast and wrapped up James' Confederate uniform for travel. I went to see if I could talk to him. There were so many wounded I wasn't sure what they had done with him. In my search, I spotted a doctor.

"Major, I am Colonel Sawyer, have you seen a man who looks like me among the wounded?"

He paused for a moment and responded, "Yes, he was taken back to one of the rear tents. I don't think you will be able to see him, though. I heard General Smith has ordered him held under guard in a restricted area. Only doctors are permitted.

"Thank you, sir."

As I walked toward the tents, I saw the dead and dying along the road. This gave me pause to think of Rebecca and my going home again someday. It could have been me lying dead outside that farmhouse. I began writing my report on the events of the day. Things never are ordinary in my service to the army. I liked it that way. It gave me a sense of autonomy. After finishing my report, I lay down to sleep.

## 13

# Home Again, Home Again, Market Is Done

At the next sunrise, McClernand's Corps engaged the enemy. A breakthrough on the Confederate flank caused Pimberton's men to spend the rest of the day retreating to the Big Black River. The XVII Corps didn't have much action, and I was grateful. I still hadn't recovered fully from the blow to my head. The Army of the Tennessee kept pressing forward, and as darkness fell, they encamped. I went to see General McPherson to give him my formal report on what transpired and to see what my additional responsibilities would be.

"Colonel Sawyer, I am grateful to you for getting those Rebel spies out of my corps. While I can use you in the XVII Corps, I am leaving the decision on your duties to General Grant. For now, it seems you have made a home for yourself with the 20th Illinois. Until I have word directing me otherwise, I am ordering you to work with the command of the 20th. Is that understood, Colonel?"

"Yes, sir."

As I was leaving the tent, he grinned. "Oh Colonel, if you run across any more Rebel spies, please let me know."

"Yes, sir, I will sir." I left the general feeling vindicated, but not endeared.

I caught up with the boys of the 20th on their way to the Bakers Creek Bridge.

"Hello Colonel, it's good to have you back."

"Thank you, Major."

"Say, Colonel, did you hear that Uncle Billy Sherman has split off his corps to flank the Rebels? I think we may have a shot at capturing the whole of Pemberton's army."

"I hope you're right. But the defenses of Vicksburg are very stout."

"The XVII Corps is being held in reserve now, Colonel. The Rebels are just the other side of the Big Black. We have been ordered to make a showing in the morning so Uncle Billy can get behind them Rebels."

At first light, the cannon batteries cut loose. This was repeated time and again down the line. Per orders, no one moved forward. Then there was action by the 9th and 12th divisions of McClernand's XIII Corps. This was considerably more than the "showing" that was ordered. They engaged the Rebels and were pushing forward. The command came down for First Brigade to assemble. The drums rolled as the 20th took their positions. As we advanced, the Confederates began to fall back. Soon they were in full retreat and on their way to the fortifications at Vicksburg.

At dusk, we made camp for the night. I went to General McPherson to see if he received any news from General Grant and to file my report. When I arrived, I was told the General was attending an extended meeting with the other staff officers. At this point, I was glad I was not a general. I don't think they sleep. I returned to the 20th and got ready to bed down. Laughter and singing were coming from many of the campfires. General Logan stuck his head into my tent and invited me to a meeting of the brigade commanders.

Once we arrived at the meeting, he announced, "Gentlemen, I have ordered that ammunition and food be brought up tonight. We need to ensure that each brigade is in a state of readiness. You have performed well today, but we plan to establish new lines against the Confederates in the morning. Our brigade will be moving out just after breakfast, so be ready. Draw supplies and clean arms tonight."

Establishing new lines meant only one thing. There would be an advance against the enemy works.

The day dawned, and troops began to busy themselves with breakfast. I thought it might be a good time to try visiting General McPherson again. I was wrong. The General was in preparation for the assault on Vicksburg. Supplies from the river fortifications at Hanes Bluff continued to pour into the camp. As I was returning to my tent, I was hailed by a sergeant, "Sir, you were not around for the mail. You received this letter, sir." I recognized the writing and tore the envelope open.

*Dearest Husband:*

*I long so much to be in your loving arms. I miss you every second you are away, and I am so empty without you. I long to hear your laughter and feel the spirit you bring to my life. Thomas, I worry so much and pray God will return you to me after the dreadful war is over. I spend the hours volunteering to help keep the books for Father's business but can't help pausing every few minutes to think of you. There is much we have to be thankful for, but that thankfulness is tempered by our being apart. Father and mother try their best to console me and bolster my spirit, but it does not compare to your being here with me. When I walk the streets of Galena, people always enquire about you, and I do not know what to tell them. I say you are fine and pray that is the case. I want you to know you are much admired by the citizens here.*

*I did have one rather odd experience, and I think you should know about it. A man called to our house and asked for your whereabouts. He had a bandage on his leg and was limping. I told him you were in service with General Grant and gone south by riverboat. He seemed to regard this as not surprising and left. I am assuming he must have been someone from your command. Mother and Father send their regards. Father wants you to know he has made some contacts with members of the former Underground Railroad. He seems insistent on helping Negroes, and once his mind is made up, he is like a dog on a fresh ham bone. I do support its purpose but deplore its necessity.*

*Be well darling, have I told you I miss you terribly.*

*Rebecca*

It was getting to be late afternoon, and I went off to see if I could locate James. I was told that the Confederate wounded were held at the back of the tents. Finding a medical tent that was under guard, I approached the sentries and asked for permission to enter. A doctor met with me and after I explained my relationship he let me enter. I found James. He was pale from loss of blood but still very much alive. It was like looking in a mirror to see him.

I came close and whispered, "James, James." He opened his eyes. He saw me, and then his gaze turned away.

"How are you feeling?" I asked. His head turned back to me.

"You!" he exclaimed, "It would have worked if it hadn't been for you. I aimed to get Grant, but you—damn you—you ruined the whole thing. Why don't you get the hell out of my life?" He turned his head away from me.

"Did you get a letter about Sally Turner?" His face slowly turned.

"You sent that letter?"

"Yes, I sent it to you. I wanted you to know about the baby and that you were a father."

"Why? You can stay out of my life. I assume you got the information by going to my home. How dare you go to my family and pretend to be me. I thought I had cause to hate Yankees, but you . . . you are the vilest of all. Get out of my sight." He winced in pain and turned away.

Our conversation ended as he refused to even look at me again. Night was beginning to fall, and I was bone-tired. My head was aching again when I reached my tent. I collapsed on my bed and slept fully clothed.

The next morning the sun rose, and with it the temperature. Orders came down to Sherman, McPherson, and McClernand to get as close to the enemy works as we could and be ready to attack. I moved with the 20th into position in the center of the line. We were told three cannon blasts would signal the assault. There was an air of anticipation and tension that was almost unbearable. Men whittled wooden sticks while resting beside their weapons. Some sat in silence, reflecting on what was to come. Others pinned their names to the inside of their uniforms so they could be identified if killed. The order came down to ready for battle and then suddenly, boom, boom, boom, and we poured from our positions marching toward the Confederate entrenchments. I immediately sensed trouble as the Rebel batteries rained down a murderous fire on us. Stalks of cane tore at my clothes. I stopped, staggered, and then continued forward under a hellish rain of enemy fire. Armed as I was with the repeating rifle, I was firing shots as we went. The soldier next to me got hit with a solid shot that took off his arm. He took two more steps and then went down hard. One of his comrades stopped briefly to apply a tourniquet but left his companion on the field and moved forward.

Some of us reached a small ravine just in front of the Rebel works. I reloaded my rifle. From this position, we couldn't be fired upon, but neither could we make it up and over the embankment. We were trapped with a continuous fire being poured over our head from directly above. The embankment was too steep and thick to shoot straight down on us. I thought about leading the men back across the open ground, but that would be suicide. It was the ground from hell with bullets and cannon fire flying in both directions. A hand grenade was lobbed over the wall. It exploded about six feet away from me and instantly killed one of our men. I was on the receiving end of some of its metal fragments ripping gashes in my left arm and leg. We stayed that way, pinned down for hours. Finely, darkness came, and we managed to hobble our way back to our lines.

I found myself back in the hospital again. This time, when I awoke, I sat up and found my wounds freshly washed and bound.

"You, Colonel, are a very lucky man. Those grenade fragments managed to cause only minor wounds, and you will heal with some rest."

"Nonsense," I said. "As long as I can march and hold a rifle, I'm good."

I hopped down from the table, took one step, and the pain stopped me cold.

"I said, with some rest, Colonel! You will be reported on sick call until you are cleared for duty."

"Yes, doctor," I said begrudgingly.

I was handed a tree limb to use as a cane and became one of the walking wounded moving to the rear. I passed some of the men from the 20th, and they began to congratulate me.

"Are you kidding me?"

"No, sir, Colonel," one private said. "If it were not for you and that repeating rifle, more of us would be dead. You killed two Rebels from that cannon crew right in front of our charge. They were about to fire canister directly into us. We figure you saved at least six of us, maybe more."

"Thank you for your kind words, but like you, I was just trying to stay alive."

"Just the same Colonel, we will report this to General Smith."

At this point, my left leg and arm began to throb. I found my way back to the camp, and by now, tents were being brought up. Two of the privates from the 20th put one up for me and managed to procure a blanket.

The next morning, after a skimpy breakfast, I got in line to see the doctor and was pronounced unfit for duty. Perhaps the cane gave it away, or perhaps it was my insistence that I was fit for duty. At any rate, I was not going to see any action. I spent the next day in my tent writing letters to Rebecca and brooding about not being able to fight. When word came down, there would be another assault on Friday the 22nd of May, I was willing to try again. The bleeding stopped from both my wounds. That morning I lined up for medical review and was once again denied. I wished the men from the 20th good luck and said I would pray for them all the while they were in action.

The battlefront was much larger this day, and there was a tremendous roar as things got underway. The cannon barrage lasted for about an hour, and then I heard the small arms fire pick up. For another two hours, the battle raged. Finally, at around 6:00 pm, the fighting died down. A flag of truce was waved by both sides to collect the wounded and to bury the dead. The wounded poured into camp. The struggle picked back up again only to end as darkness fell.

Evidently, God saw fit to let my prayers for protections of the men go unheeded. The 20th took heavy losses. General Grant ordered the digging of trenches close to the enemy works. The feeling was that the General was settling in for a siege. As the days passed, cannon fired day and night from our lines and the gunboats on the Mississippi. Sharpshooters continually made life in the trenches both annoying and deadly. My wounds were progressing nicely and healed to the point where I could serve as a camp messenger for General McPherson. On July 3rd, we awoke to a strange sound, silence. I dressed quickly and went to General McPherson's headquarters. Word reached us that an appeal for terms of surrender was being discussed. On July 4th, General Pemberton and the Confederates of Vicksburg surrendered to General Grant. That afternoon I received another letter from Rebecca written just a week ago:

*Dearest Husband:*

*Please know I love you very much. I wanted you to know my mother is very sick and the doctor says she may die. Father is in an unfit state and can't take care of his affairs although he tries. There is much gloom in the house right now, and it affects all of us. This has burdened the house staff and me considerably. I will continue to serve as best I can as proxy for my father's interests. I do wish you were here. Remember, dearest, I love you and am eagerly anticipating your return.*

*Rebecca*

I took the letter to General McPherson and asked if I could have thirty days of leave to go home and help with the situation there.

"Colonel, I have spoken to General Grant about your service to the army. You have done more than can be expected of any man. I am granting you 60 days leave. But leave can be suspended at any time. In your current physical condition, you would be a marginally effective officer regardless. Go home, take time to heal, and return to us refreshed and ready."

This was all I needed. I packed light for the trip home. It was only a short distance to Port Gibson on the Mississippi River, and with luck, I could catch a steamer or conveyance of any kind going north. The prospect of seeing my wife again made my wounds less painful. Hopefully, I could lift everyone's spirits. I didn't even stop to send Rebecca the news as I wanted to surprise her.

"Welcome to Port Gibson, Colonel. The next boat heading north is not due here for two days. You might as well relax and make yourself at home. I am sure the supply sergeant can round you up a tent."

"Thank you, Lieutenant. Are you sure there is nothing available to get me upstream?"

"No, sir, not scheduled anyway."

"Then what is the ship in the distance?"

He looked in his spyglass.

"That would be the Blackhawk. It is Admiral Porter's flagship. She probably will pull in here to refuel. She looks to have some damage, but we are not equipped for repairs here."

As soon she was docked, her men began quickly loading fuel on board. I inquired from one of the cargo hands where she was bound. She was on her way to Memphis for repairs. I hung around as cargo was loaded, and soon a lieutenant came ashore to sign off.

We exchanged salutes and I said, "Sir, I am Colonel Sawyer. I am a special aid to General Grant and request permission to come aboard for a secret mission to Memphis."

"Can I see your orders, sir," was the reply.

I looked him squarely in the eye, "I have no orders to that effect as to carry them would risk certain death, were I to be captured. Regardless, I said sternly, it is that imperative I reach Memphis. Otherwise, my mission will end in failure. Admiral Porter can check with General Grant if he wishes but also advise him that this mission has been approved by

General Halleck. I do have papers here saying I am on leave, but this is to cover my movements."

"Yes, sir, I will check with the Admiral." was the response.

The Admiral accommodated me. I assume it was the mention of General Grant and General Halleck. The Black Hawk plowed northward on the Mississippi at full speed. We were occasionally fired upon by Confederates on the bank, but it was nothing like before Vicksburg fell. Men on the boat spoke of General Sherman's encountering the Rebels at the Big Black River but knew nothing more about the issue. We arrived in Memphis, and I thanked the Admiral for his attention to my mission. I made connections by train and arrived in Galena at 10:00 the next night, giddy with anticipation. No one in town knew I was coming. When I left the train station, I first sought some medical attention for my wounds. Having gotten them redressed, I swore the doctor to secrecy and continued on to the judge's house. I lay down my bag and softly knocked on the door. The judge opened the door. As the pail light reflected my features, he sprang forward and gave me a hug.

"Not too tight, sir," I said. "I have been wounded again."

"Tom, Tom, It is so good to see you, my boy," his eyes began to well up. "I can't tell you what it means to see you here. You must tell me your story, but before you do, we should go and collect Rebecca. She is volunteering at the mining office." He lowered his head and continued. "She realized work needed to be done, work I'm afraid, I should be doing. She considers it her contribution to the war effort. This will be a wonderful surprise, so let us go and get her."

We walked toward the mine office where lantern lights made a warm glow on the dark street. As we approached, the judge stopped me.

"Tom, let me take the lead on this."

"Rebecca," he said softly, "It is late, and time for you to come home."

"Yes, Father, I am just finishing here."

"Whatever you have left, I promise you, it can wait."

I peeked through the window and saw her long, graceful fingers slowly close the ledger. Her golden hair and lovely complexion gave my heart a sorely-needed lift. She made her way to the doorway where her father stood. He took her by the arm, and together they rounded the door frame. She looked up, saw me, gave a small squeal of delight, and leapt into my arms. I held her in my arms until I could stand the pain no longer. The judge patiently watched and smiled.

As we walked back toward the house, I explained how I received my wounds and my leave. Rebecca said her mother was improving slightly. The judge interposed.

"Say, I have an idea, why don't you both spend the night at the hotel tonight. It would be my welcome home gift."

When we reached the house, Rebecca hurriedly gathered some overnight things, and we left for the hotel. Childlike joy overtook us as we walked down the streets of Galena. Rebecca and I bid good night to the judge. I remarked, "Why is it always my left side? I guess it's because I am right-handed, and God is watching out for me."

"Well, Colonel Sawyer, I hope to make you forget all about those wounds tonight."

"Let us say a prayer before we retire. Oh God of all creation, guide us to a higher place in our relationship. Let our spirits soar as our physical love soars as well."

"God knows what is in our hearts," She said. And we sat back on the bed.

Rebecca helped me undress, and I felt a little awkward having to deal with the bandages. She was indeed wonderful in every respect. Our passion took hold again, as on our wedding night, and we enjoyed our intimacy into the wee hours of the morning. We cemented our lives together to the fullest. Both of us slept well into the afternoon. We ordered food brought to the room and a copy of the morning paper. I fully expected the headlines to be about General Grant and the victory at Vicksburg. Instead, the headlines were about General Meade and the victory at Gettysburg. Rebecca carefully settled into my arms in a chair. Together we read the accounts of the battle. We did find some mention of Vicksburg in another article.

Rebecca could tell I was disheartened, and she laid her head against my chest, gently rubbing my good arm and said, "Don't worry, Thomas, the Union will prevail. So what if General Meade gets the glory today. General Grant will have his day." When Rebecca and I left the hotel, we walked straight to her father's house. We discovered her mother was getting better after the doctor changed her medicine.

"She is upstairs resting," the judge said, "But she may come down and join us for our evening meal. Well, Tom, tell us what your military experience has been like so far?"

For the first time, I felt free to explain not only what happened in Vicksburg, but what happened in Virginia. This was my wife and father-in-law, whom I trusted implicitly. It took the better part of two hours, and I am sure I left out details. They were, in a word, dumbfounded. Hanna called us to the dinner table, and we were all delighted when Mrs. Thatcher came down to join us.

"You missed out on a very descriptive tale of Tom's adventures Ida," the judge said.

Ida Thatcher smiled politely. The evening passed into night, and we adjourned to the sitting room with Mrs. Thatcher excused herself to return to her room. That is when I broke the news that I was only on a sixty-day leave, and I could be recalled at any time. There was a brief period of silence.

"Tom," the judge spoke up, "What date does your volunteer period end?"

"June of next year, sir."

"Well then, you won't have too much longer to be in service. After our conversation about your accomplishments, I think you have done enough for the cause. You could resign, stay in Galena, re-establish your practice, and settle down with Rebecca. No one could fault you with your military record."

"Judge, I have appreciated your advice and counsel all these years. But, I made a promise to the army to finish my commitment and see this country re-united. I couldn't, in good conscience, resign now."

"I know, son, I was just testing to see if you really felt the same way today as you did when you left. After all, you are a married man now."

He excused himself, and this left Rebecca and me alone.

"Thomas, I placed my trust in you and want you to do what you feel is right. I won't like your returning to war. But I know you, and you wouldn't be able to live with yourself if you didn't return and see it through."

The judge re-entered the room with some papers in his hands.

"Thomas, I had some papers drawn up to make you half owner in my mining operation. While the war continues, my business is becoming very lucrative. I am already fairly well off with my salary and other investments. Having this business in the family should guarantee you and Rebecca a good income for the foreseeable future. In time, you will receive our other assets, but I feel you should begin sharing now."

"Judge, are you sure you want to do this? It is very generous," I said.

"You, Tom, are now a member of this family, and I can think of no one more fitting to receive this."

Rebecca was close beside me, reading the documents as well.

"Oh, Thomas, this is truly unexpected and would benefit us greatly. I think we should take advantage of the opportunity it presents, thank you daddy."

She smiled, and I looked into her beautiful blue eyes. I put pen to paper, and the deal was done. I was now part owner in the mining business.

"I will file these papers at the courthouse tomorrow," the judge said. "You realize, of course, that for the remainder of your time here, it would benefit both of you to learn all you can about the business."

"Yes, sir," I replied, "it would be my pleasure."

I spent the next two weeks going to the mining office daily with Rebecca to learn all I could about the business. I had two excellent teachers because Rebecca knew the financial end of the company, and the judge knew the operational end. If we were to own a business in Galena, it was time we found a house to live in. Rebecca forbade me to use Mr. Blackwell to find a house. She thought he was a cheat. I managed to find a small, two-story brick house for sale at 113 South Dodge Street. I started the process, and things moved along rather quickly. By the end of the following week, we secured the house and moved in. Friends of ours and friends of Mr. and Mrs. Thatcher gave us some furnishings; they included a large wooden bed with a massive carved headboard, a dresser, a dining room table and chairs, Rebecca's bedroom set and a lovely set of dishes that was Rebecca's grandmother's. Rebecca turned out to be quite the homemaker and immediately began decorating to suit her taste. I wanted her to have this freedom. She should be happy and comfortable while I would be away from home. I felt that my wounds were healed now, and I was continually trying to help with the moving of furniture. Rebecca was just as continually setting me down and urging me not to reinjure myself.

In early August, she and I spent most evenings in front of the house snuggling, laughing, drinking lemonade, and greeting passersby. The war seemed a million miles away, and I never felt so relaxed.

As everyone expected and no one but me wanted, I received a letter from the Army. As they didn't yet know my new address, it came to the judge's house.

25 July 1863
Colonel Thomas Sawyer
305 Elk Street
Galena, Illinois
Colonel Sawyer:

*As of your receipt of this letter, you are returned to active duty. You
will report to me for duties as I see fit. I have again sent Lieutenant
Davidson to escort you. He will be arriving by train on August 11
with your travel papers. The army has kept all your belongings
and will have them here when you arrive.*

US Grant Commanding

When I gathered myself, we stood and formed a circle linking arms.
We prayed for us all to be protected and for God to guide me in whatever
endeavors were brought my way. It would only be two days until Lieutenant Davidson would arrive. Two days filled with anxiety and a rush getting things in shape before our parting. Rebecca and I had our own going
away party. We invited several friends and former clients to our home.
There was music and laughter for at least one night. I prepared as best
I could for the journey ahead. It was good to know Ida was improving
every day and looked close to being her old self again. This brightened
the judge's demeanor considerably. Of course, I needed to see Rebecca
was taken care of as well. With the mine being lucrative so far, this money
plus my allowance from the judge would see her through. As the next
two days flew by, Rebecca and I took the time to take evening walks and
shared the desires of our hearts together. When Lieutenant Davidson
showed up at the judge's house, we walked over to meet him.

"I am beginning to think, Lieutenant, you are bad luck for me.
Whenever you show up, I must leave my loved ones."

He just smiled and said, "Yes, sir, I can see how you would feel that
way, sir."

Leaving time was again filled with hugs, tears, well wishes, and
prayers. As I boarded the steamer, I waved good-bye to my new family.
I felt a melancholy come over me I had not experienced before. Once
again, we traveled south on the Mississippi, but this time it was different.
We could steam full ahead and only stopped for fuel. When we reached
Vicksburg, Lieutenant Davidson and I had but a short journey to Grant's
Headquarters. I found the General in good spirits as we saluted each other.

"Well, Colonel Sawyer, General McPherson has reported you have again succeeded in breaking up a Confederate operation to have me killed. That, sir, is worth celebrating, but I have word of something even better. Colonel, due to your meritorious service to me, and to the United States Army, I have here documents making you a Brevet Brigadier General. I wish to personally thank you for your efforts."

"Sir, I wish to continue to serve this Army in any way I can. But I cannot accept the promotion you honor me with." He paused for a moment and looked at me.

"Colonel, I have never had one of my officers turn down a promotion. Are you sure about this?"

"Sir, I want to be the best soldier I can be, and having command of a division wouldn't allow me to be free to conduct myself in my, shall we say, customarily unorthodox manner. If I accept the promotion, I will be thrust into a role of command of a regiment or possibly an army. I believe I am at my best when I can freely go where the problems are. If you would pardon my brashness, sir, I wish to serve as an aid in your command. You have realized the fruits of my labor, and I will continue to serve you in a similar role until the end of my enlistment. I would consider it a privilege if you would grant me this single request."

"Very well then, if you are sure about this, Rawlins will see to it."

I was overjoyed at the idea of serving with General Grant. I was proud and humbled by the offer of the promotion, but times and events have changed the way I felt. For now, being in command didn't suit me. After being dismissed, I sat down to write Rebecca telling her what I had done.

## 14

---

# Quit Your Coffin

My fellow soldiers and I fought through Chattanooga and Lookout Mountain with hard-won victories. I acted as both a courier for General Grant and as a part-time spy catcher. I was getting a reputation amongst the troops as someone to be avoided at all costs. A man with nine lives was the word amongst the soldiers. This was not what I was hoping for when I volunteered for the General's staff. General Grant was called away to Washington and made Lieutenant General in charge of all US Army Forces. Serving under General Grant's command, I knew that if they gave him control he would take it . . . and he did. Then the telegram came:

> Colonel Thomas Sawyer
> Army of the Tennessee
> US Army Field Command

> With the permission of General Grant, we are requesting you re-
> port to the War Department Headquarters in Washington D C.,
> 17th Street and Pennsylvania Avenue NW. You are to report to
> Edward M. Stanton's office, Secretary of War. At the time of your
> arrival, you will be briefed on how you may be of service to the
> Army. Arrangements have been made for your travel to Washing-
> ton via train. Please depart at once. Your horse and other personal
> items may be transferred, if necessary, should you choose to accept
> this assignment. Otherwise, they will be quartered by the army.

> Peter Watson, Assistant Secretary

These mysterious assignments were beginning to get to me, but I supposed if the General approved, it must be important. I wrote to Rebecca regarding the new developments and started packing. The trip to Washington was rather uneventful with the usual break downs and re-routs. People clogged the streets of Washington from wounded soldiers to politicians to businessmen. Almost all the public buildings had now been pressed into use as hospitals. I made my way to a series of buildings that was the War Department and entered what appeared to be the main entrance.

"Can I help you, Colonel?" the receptionist said.

"Yes," I replied, "I am here to see Secretary Stanton."

"Please have a seat, sir, and I will let him know you are here. And what is your name?" "Sawyer, Colonel Thomas Sawyer."

I sat down to wait, but I didn't realize how long the wait would be.

Finally, the receptionist came over to address me, "Colonel, Secretary Stanton won't be able to meet with you until this evening. He suggested you get a bite to eat and come back at 6:00."

With that bit of news, I left the building and sought out some food at the Willard hotel. I was a bit irritated at having waited almost four hours only to be told to come back later. Whatever this assignment was, it wasn't getting off to a good start. After my meal, I returned to the War Department building precisely at 6:00.

"Can I help you, sir?" a different receptionist said.

"Yes," I said, "I am Colonel Sawyer, and I am here to see Secretary Stanton."

"Please have a seat, sir, and I will let him know you are here."

As I sat there wondering about how long I would sit here this time when the front door opened. In walked the Commander in Chief himself. I sprang to my feet and saluted. He stopped in front of me, returned my salute, and then shook my hand warmly.

"Nice to meet you, Colonel," he said, "And what is your name?"

"Mr. President, I am Colonel Thomas Sawyer from Galena, Illinois. It is a real honor to meet you, sir."

He smiled, "Well . . . we meet for the first time Colonel Sawyer. But, your reputation precedes you, and we are indeed fortunate to have you in a Union uniform. It is truly a pleasure, and I wish I could afford you more time, but I can't tarry. I have some pressing matters to attend to."

"It is my pleasure as well, sir," I stammered.

He stepped quickly through security and into a door marked Communications. I thought myself very fortunate to have been here long enough to meet the President. I couldn't wait to tell Rebecca about meeting him. It put at ease my frustration at the delay. Finally, a door opened, and I was escorted in. The room contained desks, chairs, and some large windows with the curtains pulled. The men present rose to greet me.

General Halleck opened the conversation. "Colonel Sawyer it is very good to see you again. This is Secretary Stanton and Assistant Secretary Watson. I am grateful you have recovered from your wounds."

"Well enough," I said.

"I have briefed Secretary Stanton on your previous experiences on both the Union and Confederate sides. I want to provide you with some information and will explain our request for your services as we continue. Major Blake remains in our custody and has been moved to facilities in Cincinnati, but as far as the Confederacy is concerned, Major Blake is to be exchanged again soon. As far as General Lee is concerned, his headquarters is expecting him to return. Of course, this information has been planted by our scout network."

The room was quiet for a moment as if they were judging my reaction.

"Perhaps, if I were to describe to you the mission we have in mind, it might influence your thinking. You have the right to refuse this mission, of course, but it will necessitate your resigning your commission with the Army. We believe that while maintaining Major Blake's identity, you can travel across Confederate lines and return for a short mission. Our scout network has obtained a copy of Jefferson Davis' protection plan for the entire Confederacy. It is a tricky situation because the scout who has the plans is currently being held in Libby Prison in Richmond, and only he knows where the plans are. He is being detained by suspicion alone as he didn't have the plans on his person when captured. Otherwise, he probably would already have been executed. We need someone to get into Libby Prison on some pretense, learn the plan location, and get that information to our scout network. You know most of the members of the network. You, sir, are the only logical choice for this mission. I have here the plans to make this mission a success if you care to look at them?"

I stood up abruptly and verbally exploded, "General Halleck, Mr. Stanton, Mr. Watson, I am not sure you know what you are asking. I don't think I have the fortitude to go behind enemy lines again. It took every ounce of my energy and courage to do this the last time. I can't count the number of times I was almost compromised on that assignment. I am a married man now and have obligations to my wife. I can't believe you would even propose such a thing."

With that statement, I picked up my hat and turned to leave.

Then General Halleck spoke up, "Colonel, before you go, would it help you to know who the operative is? It is the man you know as George Washington."

I stood frozen as if hit by some mysterious power. To think of George in that horrendous situation and his potential execution gave me pause. I couldn't easily dismiss this.

"Gentlemen, I owe George my life. I can't believe I am even considering this, and if it were anyone else, I wouldn't do it. But I can't bear the thought of his execution at the hands of the Confederates. You have me."

"We thought you might feel that way, Colonel," General Halleck said.

They all stood, and each shook my hand thanking me profusely. They talked about shortening the war, patriotism, heroism, and the like, but I heard none of it. Obtaining the plans would be a bonus if it occurred. My goal was to get George out of that prison. I told the General I still had Major Blake's old uniform in a parcel amongst my things. It seemed as if God was divining me to do this. I reviewed the plans that were given to me. At least I wouldn't be subjected to the Akens Landing again. I was to leave by steamer the next morning and be transported as far as feasible along with a horse and a Confederate saddle. The rest would be up to me. I wrote Rebecca saying she wouldn't be hearing from me for a few days and not to worry. I knew she would worry even more.

After a quick but sumptuous breakfast, I readied myself. I put on my Union uniform and rode south with an escort as far as Port Tobacco. There I switched uniforms and became Major Blake. There was a tugboat at the docks to take me to Nomini Bay. From there, I went by land crossing the Rappahannock River at the Jones Plantation by ferry. I took back roads avoiding Confederate patrols until I reached the outer fortifications for Richmond. There I was stopped by pickets.

"Halt or I will fire." was the command, "What business do you have?"

"I am Major James Blake, and I have served on General Lee's staff. I have just been released in exchange for a Yankee major. Here are my papers."

I presented my forged documents to the sergeant on duty. He looked them over carefully and then asked, "What, sir, is the password for today?"

I responded immediately, "Sergeant, how am I supposed to know that? I told you I have just been exchanged and am reporting for duty. If you wish, I can wait right here while you contact General Lee's headquarters."

"Very well, sir." And he left me.

Two hours later, he came back.

"Sir, we checked, and you have been ordered to report to Colonel Stevens at the headquarters of the Richmond defenses."

I was in. The scout network had done their job. Richmond was awash with hospitals set up in every available large facility and Union prisoners being escorted to and from different locations. There were preparations continually being upgraded on the outer defenses of the city. According to the instructions I memorized, I was to go directly to Elizabeth Van Lew's home and check in with her. Darkness was beginning to fall as I approached her mansion.

"Major Blake to see Miss Van Lew," I said.

"Come right in Major, Miss Van Lew has been expecting you."

I entered the parlor and sat patiently for her to arrive. She came flowing gracefully into the room. She wore a brown silk and lace dress with a full hoop skirt and matching fan.

"Well, Major, do you bring me good news?"

"Yes," I said, "My dog is dying a slow and painful death."

"Very good," she said.

She began pulling the drapes around the room, glanced at me once this was done, and motioned to come to her parlor table. She reached under the table and pulled a lever. The entire center of the table flipped over, revealing a map and correspondence held in wooden slats.

"Colonel, it is good to see you again. I remember the night on the ironclad vividly and wish to thank you for your service. This mission can be crucial to a Union victory, so listen carefully. Mr. Washington is being held on the second floor of Libby Prison in solitary confinement, and my operative within the prison can't get to him. This won't be easy, but I propose for you to take him out right under the noses of the guards.

Mind you, they have heightened security since the mass escape and are more watchful than ever."

She paused to look at me and my reaction.

"You will have precious little time before they discover you haven't reported for duty, so speed is essential. You will go to the prison and request Mr. Washington be remanded to your custody. Prisoners are being moved regularly now, so hopefully, this won't attract much attention. You must give every impression that you represent Lee's staff and want Mr. Washington for questioning. I have here his forged release documents."

She pulled the documents and a small map from amongst the papers.

"Once you have obtained Mr. Washington, you both will proceed three blocks east down the street and turn into this alley between two warehouses. There you will wait until my carriage stops at the alley and blocks the entrance. You and Mr. Washington will board the carriage, and it will bring you here. Once Mr. Washington gives us the location of the plans, someone in the scout network can retrieve them. It will be too dangerous for either of you to be seen on the streets again for some time. After a few weeks here, we can smuggle you out of Richmond. I can promise you, we will get the plans if they are still where Mr. Washington left them. All we need is to know where they are located. You must watch to be sure you are not seen boarding the carriage by anyone."

"Well, Miss Van Lew, I owe George my life. I will do everything I can to set him free."

She reset the table, handed me the documents, and I followed her up the stairs and down the hall.

"My servants will attend to your horse."

I was left alone with my thoughts about what was transpiring. I looked over the documents, and they were masterfully done right down to Robert E. Lee's signature. After freshening up as best I could, I was greeted by Miss Van Lew.

"Colonel Sawyer, are you ready?"

"Yes."

"Please sit and have something to eat. I am sorry there is not more food, but it is getting difficult to find sustenance with deliveries that are intermittent."

After quickly finishing the meal, I stood up and walked out the front door. A moonless night would make for good cover. As I approached the prison, it seemed as if there were guards everywhere.

I addressed one of the guards and said, "I am Major James Blake. I am here to see Lieutenant Emack regarding one of your prisoners."

I presented the fake documents to the guard, and he entered the prison. He returned and motioned me to enter. So far, so good, I said to myself. Lieutenant Emack looked up from his desk. He was a stern-looking man with a black mustache.

"Major Blake, I will remand this Washington fellow over to you with one stipulation. As soon as General Lee is done with his questioning, he is returned to this prison. How long do you anticipate this will be?"

"Sir, I can return the prisoner by the day after tomorrow. I am sure that will be enough time to get out of him what the General requires."

He looked at me, gave a grunting noise, and made a motion to one of his guards. There was a pause of several minutes and in walked George with his hands bound. My heart sank to see him. His clothes were almost in rags. He was looking down at the floor but managed to raise his head. He clearly saw me, but his expression didn't change.

"Very well, sir," I said, Lieutenant Emack saluted, I returned the salute, and we left.

George and I walked slowly out of the prison and turned down the street. We said nothing to each other, and when we reached the alley, we immediately turned in. There were a few people on the opposite side of the street, but no one seemed to notice us. There were some barrels stacked along one side that came out far enough for us to hide behind them. I turned to George, cut the ropes from his wrists, and we hugged each other.

"We can talk later," I said. "Just follow my lead."

The carriage appeared presently, stopped, and blocked the view from the street. We moved cautiously from behind the barrels and unobtrusively through the door of the carriage. The interior was big enough we could lie down on the floor and slither under the seats. Anyone seeing the carriage from the outside would take it for empty. It was not too long until we were at the Van Lew estate and pulling into the carriage house. George and I rolled out from under the seats and found two servants waiting for us. We were given water and some biscuits, but I gave mine to George. The servants brought us civilian clothes. We didn't know if we could trust the servants, so we said nothing. We slipped into the back door of the mansion, and Miss Van Lew met us in the parlor.

George said, "Let me start by saying how grateful I am to you both for getting me out of prison. I was beginning to think I wouldn't make it out alive,"

A servant interrupted, asking what should be done with our old clothes.

Miss Van Lew spoke up, "Burn them."

"Just a moment," I said. "I want you to know I am officially saying good-bye to Major James Blake's uniform."

There was a pause, and Miss Van Lew motioned the servant to leave the room. A commotion soon ensued outside, and one of the servants came back. She whispered something to Miss Van Lew, and she left us for about half an hour. When she returned, she appeared somewhat distraught.

"Gentlemen, a small incident has occurred, and one of my servants has been wounded. I will take care of this issue, but you must be on your guard."

"Now about the plans," George continued, "They are on the second floor of the Masons' Hall just behind the Worshipful Master's chair in a tube marked wallpaper samples. They got there by my hand as I knew the hall location was its best chance for survival. Unless they are retrieved quickly, they will be discovered. I was caught soon after I placed them there, but they had no proof I took anything. It is my fault that I received solitary confinement. I made an escape attempt."

There was a knock at the front door. George and I looked at each other, wondering what we should do. Miss Van Lew gave us direction.

"Stay right here and get behind the settee. I will see who it is."

"Relax gentlemen: it was just one of my acquaintances bringing me information. Let me take you upstairs so you can see your accommodations."

We moved upstairs and down a long hallway to an end room. She opened the door to reveal a room with two beds, a pitcher, wash basin, chamber pot, small desk, lamp, two chairs, and some essentials. There was one small window to the outside world on the far wall covered by a heavy curtain.

"You will need to confine yourselves to this room for the immediate future. No lantern lights after dark and no smoking or drinking except what is provided. There is a small bell in the corner with a rope descending through the floor. If this bell rings, you must hide until it rings again."

She pulled one bed from the wall slightly and stuck a knife into a small seam in the wall. It opened a portion of the wall just big enough to squeeze through into a blind room. It was possible to reach out, pull the bed back, and then close the panel from the inside.

"I hope you will find the accommodations acceptable. Your meals will be brought to your room, and your chamber pot will be emptied by my servants daily. We will arrange for you to bathe once a week during the night. Good night, gentlemen."

She left and closed the door behind her. I was expecting a short stay in this house, but we would have to rely on Miss Van Lew for our safekeeping. Apparently, it was used to harbor others as well. It was now time to catch up on things.

"George, what happened to you?"

"After my wound healed, I took some time to heal my soul as well. You know how lonely the scout business can be. I wrote a letter of retirement to General Halleck. I thought a trip might do me good, you know, relax a bit, so I took the train to Galena to see you. You weren't at home, so I traveled back across Pennsylvania and eventually back to Washington. I met up with General Halleck again, and he offered me a sizable sum of money to get those plans. With a little ingenuity, I had time to copy them right off old Jeff Davis' desk," he said with a sly grin. "It is amazing what you can do with enough hustle. After some dodging in and out of various alleys, I was able to find an open door in the back of the Masons' Hall. I found the wallpaper tube and hid the plans. The next day someone identified me as being around the government buildings. A suspicious character they called me. I was arrested, but they were not able to prove I took anything. I was confined in the Libby rat hole for what I assumed was an indefinite stay. Thanks to you it was shortened. What about you, Tom?"

"Oh, just bagged a few Confederate spies and got myself married to the most beautiful girl in the world. I was hoping to get back home in a few days, but it looks like that won't happen."

George shook his head in agreement.

"Say, George, what is your real name?"

He looked up to answer, and the little bell rang. We quietly scrambled to get the bed aside and slip into the dark cavern in the wall. We maintained our silence. The room had two stools and was just big enough for two people. It was oppressively hot as there was no other door or window. When the bell sounded again, we cautiously and quietly slipped back out again. Fortunately for us, the bell didn't sound very often. I didn't ask George what his real name was again. I figured every time I asked, something bad happened so, I gave it up. I passed Miss Van Lew a message for Rebecca. She sent it to General Grant, hoping it would be forwarded. She gave us a newspaper every week to keep us informed. A month passed, and the war raged on. Evidently, General Grant was pressing Robert E. Lee to his fullest. The local militia was still looking for us. Miss Van Lew suggested we wait until this aggressiveness decreased. The days dragged on into May. Eventually, we met with Miss Van Lew to discuss an attempt to leave.

"Let me begin by saying Jeff Davis' plan for the defense of the entire Confederacy made its way safely into Union hands." Miss Van Lew said, "I have been in touch with several authorities who tell me more pressure is being put on General Lee and the Army of Northern Virginia to defend Richmond. As I am sure you have surmised by the delay, it is becoming more difficult to get anyone in or out of the city unnoticed. I believe it would be safer for you to attempt to leave individually rather than together. We shouldn't risk both of you being caught as it would serve no purpose and may expose our network. One man will have a greater chance of evading capture."

This was not what either George or I wanted to hear.

"George," she began again, "I believe we will attempt your escape tomorrow night. A major battle has begun near Spotsylvania, and it has taken some troops from the perimeter of Richmond. You will dress as an undertaker, and take with you a wagon and coffin. The team and wagon will be here tomorrow night at 9:00 p.m. If all goes well, forged papers will let you cross into Union territory by feigning the return of a body to Bermuda Hundred. This is the current location of General Butler and the Union army.

You will say, "This is the body of a young man who bravely fought and died defending Richmond and is being returned to his father, Mr. W.T. Johnson."

Mr. Johnson is an actual merchant in Bermuda Hundred and has a son in the service. This should be enough of a ruse to make it to General Butler's lines."

George and I looked at each other, and he gave a nod of agreement. We had been cooped up far too long. We went to bed, having formulated our own plan for this escape. The next day we ate our meals in our room as we had always done. We passed the time playing cards and waiting for the appointed hour. At 9:00 p.m., we looked out the window to see the promised wagon pull into the back of the mansion. We waited for the signal that the coast was clear and went gingerly down the stairs. Miss Van Lew, ever cautious, had most of the lanterns extinguished.

"George, you look really good in that undertaker suit. You might think of taking up a new occupation," I said.

"Yea," he said. "I put enough people in the ground to make it a permanent position."

"Miss Van Lew, George and I have a slight variation on your plan. I am going along with George. Only I will be riding in the coffin."

"You will what? I don't think it advisable. I thought we had this whole thing planned out for you to leave separately. It is taking a great chance, and I am against the idea. Who's to say what could happen to you in that box?"

I said, "Look, George and I have been through a lot together from being shot at to risking our lives to make getaways. We trust each other and know one of us will make the ultimate sacrifice to see the other makes it through. There is no one I would rather travel with than George. I appreciate all you have done for us. You have done a magnificent job. Please don't ask us to separate."

"Well, it's up to you, but I feel you are making a mistake."

She backed away, called one of her servants to bore holes in the end of the coffin, and remove the bags of sand. The lid was rigged with a rope to a release pin from the inside, so I could get out easily. Straw was used to line the coffin. Some cut nails were used on the lid to give the appearance of a sealed coffin. We again thanked Miss Van Lew for her hospitality and set out. We traveled but five miles when we ran into a scouting party from General Beauregard's troops.

"Halt, what business is this?" George pulled the papers from his pocket.

"I am travelin' on an errand of mercy for a merchant Johnson. His poor son has sacrificed his life for the cause of the Confederacy, and I am returning him to Bermuda Hundred for a proper burial."

The sergeant spoke up, "what are you doin' traveling at night?"

I really like George because he thinks so quickly.

"This here body has been dead for three days now, and we wrapped it as best we could, too late for embalmin' you understand. It's cooler out here in the night, and I don't want him to smell any worse than he already does. I can open the coffin up if you care to, look, but he is already startin' to turn black."

"Shoot, we seen enough o' them dead bodies. You can move your wagon, Mr. Taker."

The wagon began to jostle its way east. The hay to soften the ride in the coffin did little for the side to side banging. As we moved along, George began singing old Irish folk songs. The sun was just peaking over the hills when I felt the wagon slow to a stop.

"I need a break," George said as he climbed down off the wagon.

I opened the coffin, and we proceeded to eat what food we had left.

"George, I am guessing it is fifteen miles or so to Bermuda Hundred, and we should have seen Union troops by now, what say you?"

"I believe you are right, sir."

"I can't stand it anymore in the box. I'm going to ride in the open now."

We neared Swift Creek when we heard the sounds of battle. We moved south cautiously toward the firing using Harrowgate road and came up on the pickets of General Gillmore's X Corps.

"Halt. Where are you bound?"

"Fixed Bayonets," George said.

"Very well, you may pass," was the reply.

We looked at each other, and both of us breathed a sigh of relief. Thankfully Miss Van Lew supplied us with the correct Union password. We reached a series of log structures being used as headquarters. We were told General Butler was too busy to see us.

"George, I need to get back into uniform, so I am going to find the quartermaster."

"Well sir," the quartermaster said, "I need some proof you are a Colonel. So far, all you have given me is a story I can scarcely believe."

"Then, I will do just that."

I went back to headquarters again so I could get a wire to Washington regarding my status. I received a rapid reply. Soon I got a new Colonel's uniform slightly too tight, but it would do. I also received a pistol, ammunition, and sword. Meanwhile, George needed to shed his undertaker suit, so he wandered off to find some sutlers. He bartered well and got some black pants, boots, rope belt, white shirt, gray vest, and a black bowler hat. General Grant wasted no time in wiring George and I a pass to Washington by steamer. I wrote a letter to Rebecca telling her I was once again safe and missed her ever so much. Things sometime happen slowly in the course of a war, and we spent the next three weeks in Bermuda Hundred awaiting transport. On the third of June, we finally traveled to Washington, happy to be alive and well.

# 15

## Washington DC

### *The End of the Road . . . Almost*

It took another three days to reach Washington. Our captain maneuvered his vessel to avoid a Confederate warship and ran us aground. There we waited for the tide to lift us into a navigable position. We finally made it to the Capitol and found a room at the Willard. It was discouraging to read the newspapers about Spotsylvania and so many dying. I knew General Grant well enough to know the loss wouldn't stop him. He kept moving south and east, engaging General Lee's forces every time it was possible and practical. We met with General Halleck, and I gave them my full report on our actions and the escape to Bermuda Hundred. I mentioned my consideration to resign my commission. He granted me leave time to make that decision.

"Colonel Sawyer, I want you to know the army is very grateful to you and Mr. Washington for your actions in Richmond. You have both performed magnificently."

"I thank you, General," I said. "But if anyone deserves praise, it's George."

"We need to show our gratitude for what you both have done. I am asking the President to write a letter of commendation for each of you."

"Very well, General, Please give my thanks to the President."

"And mine also," said George.

After the meeting, George and I left the War Department and headed toward the Willard.

"George, my commission is up on June 30th, and I can't see me staying in the army. I am weary, and it is time for me to go home."

"I understand. I believe this will be my last assignment, as well. I spoke to Allen Pinkerton, and he mentioned my working security for the railroad. This last assignment has left me with enough money to consider my options regarding employment or retirement."

We looked at each other and smiled.

"The evening is waning. Let's go to our rooms and get some rest." I said.

I slept well into the afternoon of the next day and was awakened by a knock at the door.

"Room Service," the voice said. I opened the door, and there stood Rebecca. My heart leaped for joy, we embraced and kissed.

"My dearest, why did you come east?"

"I received your letter, and when you mentioned you were trying to get back to Washington, I couldn't resist the trip. I knew it was only a matter of time till you arrived. I have been useful, though. I looked at all the wounded when I arrived, and my heart went out to them. I volunteered to help and was told I could write letters for those who couldn't write. It was so rewarding to know I was making a difference in their lives. I met Walt Whitman, the famous poet, doing the same thing. But now you are here, and we are together . . . that is my reward. And what pray tell have you been up too?"

"Well . . . I have kept myself busy. I helped rescue George from a Confederate prison, got important maps back to the Union troops, and have been recommended for a commendation from the President. I did have a happenstance meeting with President Lincoln."

"Really . . . you met the President?"

"Yes, it was only a brief encounter. He was gracious and humble but, at the same time, exuded an aura of authority."

We gathered George from his room, and the three of us went to the hotel dining room. "You are both my guests for dinner," I said. "We are celebrating our triumphant return to Washington and my retirement as an Army Colonel. Rebecca and I will return to our beautiful little house in Galena and have seven children."

With that statement, Rebecca blushed.

"Oh, Thomas," she said. "You needn't broadcast such private thoughts. Besides, I may want more than seven . . . and a bigger house."

Then it was my turn to blush, George snickered and slapped me on the back, and we all laughed hardily.

After dining, we sat and talked for a few minutes before George excused himself. He was to meet with Allen Pinkerton to discuss his job situation. Rebecca and I went to the front lobby and sat looking into each other's eyes. We talked about our future together and how things were going back home.

"Father is investing in the Bank of Galena. There are plenty of profits from the mining operations. He believes returning soldiers will help businesses prosper. Men will need capital for all kinds of businesses, and he wants to be in on the ground floor. I believe it will be a good move, and we could be a part of the banking business in the future."

"I could never see myself as a banker. Honestly, could you?"

"Well . . . no . . . I guess you are right about that. You are too much of a free spirit."

"What our future holds, I do not know, but I promise you we won't become your mother and father."

"As long as I am with you and my parents are doing well, I will abide by the life God grants us."

We smiled, hugged, and then kissed a long and passionate kiss. I stopped at the desk to let them know Mrs. Sawyer would be staying in my room.

The next morning, I awoke to a thump as the newspaper was dropped outside our door. My lovely wife was still sleeping, so I perused the headlines quietly. General Grant was, once again, face to face with General Lee across the Chickahominy River. His dogged determination was ever-present. There was a production of Faust tomorrow at the Grover's Theater with a preshow at 6:00 pm. I thought it would be wonderful if Rebecca and I could attend, so I planned on surprising her. We made no particular plans for our return to Galena, and this would be a good night out for us. She slowly awakened, and her eyes met mine.

"Come here," She said playfully, and I lay down beside her on the bed. We snuggled together and held each other close. We didn't leave the room until around noon, then taking a bite to eat at the hotel dining room.

"Thomas, I was hailed by the desk clerk on our way into the dining room, and I have received a telegram from Father wanting to know about our return. What do you think?"

"I think we should spend the weekend and leave on Monday. If it is agreeable with you, I will book our train tickets today."

We spent the rest of the day lounging around the hotel lobby. We enjoyed a lively and hard-fought game of chess, which Rebecca won. I checked at the front desk for messages. The hotel clerk handed me a small, folded piece of paper. "Be careful, you are being watched—GW." This sent an ominous shiver through my body. I walked to the train station and obtained our tickets to Philadelphia. From there, we would take a connecting train to Indianapolis and then Galena. I looked closely at them to be sure of the time and date, 7:00 AM, Monday, June 13, 1864, Washington to Philadelphia.

"If anyone asks about our destination, please keep it confidential," I said to the Ticketmaster and he assured me he would do so.

Stopping by the Grover, I picked up two front row seats for Foust. I went back to the hotel and found Rebecca sitting in the lobby waiting for me.

"Shall we retire for the evening? I have three new dresses to try on, and you can tell me which looks best."

We went to our room, and she began pulling dresses from her trunk.

"I have this blue one, a pink one and an all-white one. Please be a dear and sit while I model them for you."

She went behind a large mirrored screen and began to change. She came out with the blue dress on.

"Well . . . ?"

"Very nice,"

She changed into the white one.

"Too bright," I exclaimed.

She retreated behind the screen for the third dress, but before she could get changed, I peeked around the corner and exclaimed,

"I like you better like this!" She threw the dress at me.

I caught it and said, "Dearest, although any of them would be fine, I like the blue one best."

"Of course, you would silly, it matches your eyes."

She did try on the last dress, but we settled on the blue one.

"I have a surprise for you. Tomorrow night, we are going to see Foust at the Grover Theater. It will give you a chance to wear that blue dress." She grabbed my arms and kissed me.

I said, "Well if we are going to the Grover's Theater tomorrow night, we need to get some rest."

The next morning, we began some preliminary packing with the clothes we wouldn't need right away. I packed a change of civilian clothes, my pistol, belt, and ammunition in a travel bag to carry with me. We finished packing what we could and went down to breakfast. On the way through the lobby, I stopped at the desk, asked for messages, and was told there were none. I paid the bill through Sunday night and told the clerk we would be checking out early on Monday. The discussion at breakfast consisted of how we might redecorate our house in Galena. We again spent the day playing chess and relaxing. It was soon time to get ready for the evening. I wore a new black suit that Rebecca purchased for me. I told her it made me look like a banker, and that made her laugh. We didn't want to be late for the show, so we came down the stairs at 5:30 to make the walk to the theater.

We were passing by a group of four men when they grabbed both of us and forced us into an alley. I was punched in the chest several times, and it was hard for me to breathe.

"Okay, Colonel, where is it? Come on, where is it?"

Rebecca bit the hand holding her mouth, and when the evildoer let go, she screamed and gouged his eyes with her newly freed hands. She spun around and kicked the other man hard in the groin. Both her captors ran off down the ally. While she was taking care of her captors, I head-butted one of the men attacking me. This move had enough effect on the assailant to make him let go. I grabbed him by the throat and used his body as an anchor to kick the other man in the chest, sending him reeling backward. Just then, George came around the corner. The two men attacking me ran down the alley.

"Colonel, are you all right!" George exclaimed.

I didn't answer as I was too concerned about Rebecca. I went to her and held her closely for a few moments.

"Darling, are you all right? Did they hurt you?"

"Yes, I think I am okay, but you've got blood running down the side of your face. Let's go back to the hotel and get you patched up,"

We made our way back to the hotel and up to our room. The police and a doctor were summoned. I continued holding a kerchief on my forehead while we told our story to the police. Fortunately, or unfortunately, depending on your view, Washington was flush with doctors. When the doctor arrived, I recognized him as one of the doctors that served my company at Bull Run.

Rebecca insisted that she was fine and that an examination by a doctor wasn't necessary. The doctor bandaged the cut on my forehead. I knew the evening would be spent in our room, so I handed our tickets to the doctor.

"Colonel Sawyer," he said, acknowledging his recognition of me. "This is not necessary, sir. There is no charge for treatment."

I responded, "Major, this is a gift for your quick response. Please keep the tickets."

"But I can't use them as I have duty this evening at a hospital."

"Then give them to a deserving patient," I said. He smiled.

"Very good, sir, I will do so."

George accompanied the two of us up to our room and arranged for food to be brought up.

I said, "George, do you have any idea what is this all about? I got your note, but someone watching you is different than being jumped in an alley."

Rebecca had a confused look on her face.

"Well," George began, we think it's about the uniform."

"The uniform! What uniform?"

"Major James Blake's uniform," he said.

"But, I thought it was destroyed at Miss Van Lew's house?"

"I did, too," George continued, "but evidently, it was stolen. I was contacted by General Halleck today. You remember Miss Van Lew's servant was injured by a stranger outside the house. Whoever it was, assaulted the servant, and made off with the uniform. Miss Van Lew did not put any importance to it at the time as she thought the uniform burned. Scout sources found the Rebels wanted the uniform and were willing to kill for it. Miss Van Lew had her servants sift through the ashes of the fire to be sure it was not burned. This was all information given to General Halleck in a cipher message. I was just notified of it this morning by one of my scout connections. Those people in the alley must have thought you still had the uniform. But, since your commission is up at the end of this month, I suppose this would be of no interest to you."

"Wait a minute. First, you tell me we are being watched, then we get attacked on our way to the theater, and you think I am not interested?"

Rebecca finally could contain herself no longer.

"Hold on both of you. You need to fill me in on this little adventure of yours? I was a part of this attack, too, and I deserve to know what's going on."

George and I filled her in on all the details of Richmond and the Bermuda Hundred. This took some time, and when we were finally finished, she looked at me with a degree of disdain.

"Thomas, were you not going to tell me about this?"

"Of course, I was my dear: I just didn't want to worry you." Rebecca became enraged.

"Well, from now on, you need to share everything with me, or you will be worrying more about me than about Rebels," she said crossly. "Is that clear?"

"Absolutely," I responded, "From now on, you will be the first to know—everything. So, George, what is it about this uniform that makes it so valuable?"

"That's just it," he responded, "I don't know. I do know I spotted some suspicious-looking characters watching you two at a discrete distance. This is why I wrote the note. I followed you from the hotel, and when I heard Rebecca scream, I came running."

"I don't believe Major Blake's uniform was retrieved by the Rebels," I said. "The men who attacked us repeated to me, 'Okay, where is it?' twice. This leads me to believe they are still searching."

George was kind enough to send one of his rail agent friends to the train station to get a refund on the tickets and send a telegram to the judge that our return would be delayed. George moved his room at the hotel to the same hallway as ours. Until we knew for sure what was happening, we felt it safer to spend some time at the hotel. George and I were used to being cooped up for days on end, but not so Rebecca. She became nervous and fidgety.

"Thomas, I can't do this anymore. I need to get out of this hotel. When you fight your battles, do you have patience with the Rebels? No, you shoot them. If we are going to be shot, then let it be so, I can't stay in this room any longer."

At that moment, there was a knock at the door.

I opened it and, to my surprise, there stood General Halleck.

"General Halleck, how are you, sir?" I said.

"Fine, Colonel, and yourself?"

"Good General, but I am afraid my wife is a bit weary of being cooped up here. Do you bring us any news?"

"Yes, I have a report from the scouts. They discovered Major Blake's coat may contain some sort of coded message. It is important enough the Rebels want it back. As long as Major Blake was around, or at least you portraying him, they felt the information secure. I must leave as I have business to attend to, but I wanted you to know what we learned and tell you that we will try to keep you informed."

Rebecca and I were alone again. There was a long silence as we both were thinking about what the General said. I decided to risk setting her off again with another issue.

"You know, darling, it would be like looking for a grain of rice in a wheat field."

"Thomas, you are not seriously thinking of searching for the uniform, are you? You might need to travel back into the South and be confronted by who knows what. You couldn't do it without the support of the scouts. There is far too much risk, and you have risked enough already. You need to return to Galena with me and give up all this running about. I want my husband back with me. I need you with me, Thomas. It is as simple as that."

"Okay, I see your point, and I want you to feel safe. But, as long as someone is looking for this uniform, none of us can feel safe, not even in Galena."

She thought for a long time and then suggested we get some sleep and discuss it again tomorrow. On this point, I heartily agreed. We prayed together that God would provide us direction in this matter.

The next morning, we dressed and went down to breakfast in the dining room. We found George munching on an apple and drinking coffee. After we greeted him, he insisted that we join him.

"How was your evening, George?" I enquired.

"Quite well," he said as he asked for another cup from the waiter. "And yours?"

"Very good," I said. "Rebecca and I would like coffee, please, as a starter."

He was reading the paper and seemed relaxed as though the events of the past few days never happened. Then he came across an article in the paper.

"Great Scott, Thomas, look at this."

It was the first time he ever called me Thomas. He showed me the paper, and there was a very brief advertisement at an end column. It read: "Limited Time Only, Confederate and Union Military Uniforms Wanted, Will pay top U.S. dollars, Uniform Shop, West 9th and South G Street." I showed the article to Rebecca, and she read it and looked up.

"Well," she said, "it seems as though God has given us an answer, and we need to investigate."

"We?" I said.

"Yes, we," she said. "I believe if the answer to this problem lies in Washington, we must take the bull by the horns and look into it ourselves. Otherwise, I will have a husband who can't leave it alone, and I will have no peace."

After a moment's thoughtful consideration, I said, "Listen, we must act carefully, so let's formulate a plan."

"I would think the army has seen this ad also," George said. "It could be an enterprising person wanting to cash in on war souvenirs, but it doesn't seem feasible for uniforms?"

"It could also be a trap," I said. "They know we know about the uniform. On the other hand, army scouts may be trying to recover the uniform from someone who may not know the value of what they have. I suggest we send a note to General Halleck."

About an hour after sending our message, we received a return message from the General. The note said it appeared as though this was a privateer looking to cash in on uniforms and resell them for a profit. While this was frowned upon, it was not illegal. We could hardly believe this message, but there were many things in Washington to occupy the army's time. We decided it would be a good idea for us to pay this shop a visit. It was now late afternoon, and we thought it best to wait until tomorrow to present our masquerade. George was in charge of costuming and formulating our exit from the hotel. We met George downstairs for breakfast the next morning. We needed to discuss his efforts at disguise and a plan for our outing. George left and returned after an hour, handing Rebecca and me packages.

"Here is how I think this should go. You and Rebecca leave separately and meet me down the block by the Grover's Theater. I will be wearing my old backwoods clothes and stationed across the street. You two need to avoid attention by using the servant's entrance at the back of the hotel. Play your roles well, but be alert at all times. Take notice of anything suspicious and return as we discussed."

I had to chuckle as Rebecca changed into men's clothes, bundled her blond hair on top of her head, and placed a slouch hat over it. She looked up at me and smiled.

"This will be proof of my acting ability."

I opened my package and found a full suit of black clothes, complete with a ruffled shirt and tie. I didn't know where George came up with this stuff, and I didn't want to ask. Rebecca laughed, telling me I looked like a real banker.

"You see, you are now fit for Father's venture into the banking world. Colonel Sawyer, you look fantastic."

"Thank you, my dear, you look like my long-lost cousin or something."

She hit my arm hard. I reminded myself never to get into a physical altercation with her.

We walked toward the waterfront until we came in sight of the store. George was there on the street, attempting to get passersby interested in little bird whistles he was selling. I entered the store with Rebecca or Reb as I was now calling her. The inside of the store appeared to be a quickly converted blank canvas. Nothing seemed to be where it should be in a proper store. There was a small desk in the far corner, and behind it sat a little, squeamish looking character in a black suit. The shelves on both walls were lined with uniforms, both Union and Confederate, with care taken to separate sizes. Near the desk, there were trunks marked for shipment to Philadelphia, Nashville, Petersburg, and Atlanta. Reb kept her head low and looked along the shelves at the opposite side of the room. I walked up to the desk and got a rise out of the attendant.

"Can I help you, sir?"

"Yes," I said in my most impressive banker's voice, "I would like to speak to the manager of the store if you please."

"Just a moment, sir," was the reply.

He got up slowly and didn't break eye contact with me. He moved in a sideways shuffle and went through a doorway. He returned with a man I thought I recognized. While I couldn't place him, the only thing I was hoping for was that he did not recognize me.

"Sir, my name is Reginald Barranger, and I am interested in purchasing uniforms, Union to be precise, but they must be in fair to good condition. They are for a new company that is organizing in upstate New York. I need thirty or so uniforms twenty-five privates, three corporals, one sergeant, and one major. This is on short notice as the men have already signed papers. Can you accommodate me, sir?" There was a short pause while he eyed me carefully.

"I am Mr. Allison. I do not believe we can accomplish so large an order at this time. Perhaps, if you return in two weeks, we will be able to do so."

"I wish to look at your stock just the same to see what I would be purchasing."

He asked his assistant to get a selection of Union uniforms laid out for viewing. I led him away to the front windows pretending to have better daylight for viewing. While this was going on, Reb was near the desk, collecting information.

"I believe these will do nicely if you can deliver in two weeks," I said. "But I will want to see the merchandise before I give you any kind of payment."

"I understand, sir," was his reply. "We will do our best to accommodate you."

I bid him good-bye, and Reb and I left the store. I gave a scratch of my head to signal George, and we returned to the hotel. When we got to our room, I changed back into my officer's uniform, and Rebecca changed into riding clothes. We packaged up our costumes and returned to the real world. We were waiting in the lobby when George came in.

"Let's go up to your room so we can talk in private," he said.

"Well, Reb, what did you find out?"

She smiled, and then her look turned more serious.

"I took a close look at the desk. At first, I didn't see anything that would appear incriminating, but then I noticed a partially opened drawer. I caught a glimpse of a cipher wheel for writing code. I have been looking into this sort of thing in Galena since you sent the prison letter. I am sure it was a cipher wheel. I also noticed something else that struck me as odd. There was a pile of receipts on the desk. The ones on top were printed receipts, but the edges of those underneath appeared to be blank. Why would they go to that trouble except to convince people they were doing a lot of business? It could be for marketing purposes, or it could be something more sinister. What about you, Colonel Sawyer?"

"I noticed the man at the front desk seemed nervous about my presence, but his partner was even more so. I don't know if they recognized me, but I have seen the partner before. He was one of the three men on the train to Galena that disappeared after the botched robbery attempt.

I ended up shooting one of them. There is definitely a Rebel connection with this man. George, what do you have to offer?"

"I sold three bird whistles while you two were messing around in the store."

Rebecca hit him several times with a pillow.

"Wait," he said smiling, "I also noticed an alley entrance to the shop with several riding horses saddled and a delivery wagon with a team hitched. No one leaves animals in that condition unless they plan on making a hasty exit. Listen, if we are serious about this, then time is of the essence. We need to start surveillance of the place now. Colonel will take the first watch and let us know if there is any activity. We can rotate surveillance at odd times, so we won't draw suspicion. There is a restaurant with a storefront bench across the street, giving a partial view of the alley. There is also a barrel and another chair outside with a checkerboard. Try and engage someone in a game of checkers and make a small wager on the game. If something does happen, whoever is on duty comes straight back to the hotel to get the others. In the meantime, I will make arrangements for travel, and we can be on their tail fairly quickly. Remember, someone could still be watching us, so only use the back entrance to the hotel."

"I will head over there right now," I said.

Rebecca and George stayed behind to work on other details. I reached the store across from the shop in just a few minutes. I settled down onto the bench, and the barrel next to it had the checkerboard. I tried to engage several passersby in a game with no success. I pulled out a newspaper I had taken from the hotel lobby. For the first two hours, no one entered or left the establishment, and I became bored. At around 6:00 p.m., Mr. Allison left and came back with a bag, which I presumed was his dinner. At 7:30, he and his attendant came out, locked the shop, and went away. It was getting too dark to read, so I tried the checker game again. This time a passerby agreed to a game for the sum of one dollar. I purposefully lost the game, thinking he might tell others they could earn an easy dollar.

Gas lanterns were lit along the street, and traffic continued into the night but nothing from the darkened shop. At 9:00 Rebecca came with a sandwich and a canteen of water. I refused to leave her alone to stand watch in the dark, so we sat for a while, as the street traffic began to dwindle to just a few passersby. Around 11:00, we noticed someone coming down the street. He entered the uniform shop and lit a lantern. The light revealed that it was Mr. Allison, and he sat down at the desk and began writing. Two other men came down the street, one carrying a parcel and the other nervously looking up and down the street as they walked.

"This is it," I whispered to Rebecca. Go get George and meet me back here as quickly as you can."

In the dark, it was difficult to tell who the men were, but it didn't matter. This was not a typical visit to a uniform shop. I watched as they entered the store and spoke with Mr. Allison. The discussion seemed to become heated for a few seconds when one of the men pulled out a pistol and aimed it at Mr. Allison. He opened a cash box and started to pay them. They pushed him back, took cash from the box, and left without taking the package. Mr. Allison didn't move from the desk. I moved across the street and positioned myself at the edge of the store window. From here, I could get a clearer view of what he was doing. I was fairly certain that the package contained our missing uniform. He looked around nervously and then pulled a cipher wheel from the desk. He wrote two coded messages using the wheel. Oddly, he didn't seem perturbed that he had just been robbed. Coding messages takes time, and this helped us immensely. George and Rebecca arrived and stationed in an ally just across the street. George blew a short tweet on one of his bird whistles to let me know they were there. I moved back across the street to join them. Two other men came from the back of the shop and talked with Mr. Allison. He passed the messages to one of the other men and blew out the lantern.

The moon was shining brightly enough to give us a nearly clear view of the alley. The two men exited the shop, mounted the horses in the alley, and rode off through town. Neither of the men appeared to be bearing a package. We watched Mr. Allison as he, package in hand, locked the rear door to the shop, and walked to the wagon in the alley. He untied the team and came out of the alley at such a good rate of speed, that dirt was sent flying as he rounded the corner. We mounted our horses and followed the wagon at a discrete distance. The wagon continued south through the streets of Washington. We took turns falling back and riding within sight to try to avoid the appearance of followed him. He traveled south until he reached the fortifications on the outskirts of the city where sentries stopped him. We stayed back while he handed them some papers.

Before the sentries could approve him for passage, I rode up to the sentries and said, "I am Colonel Sawyer, US Army. I believe there may be reason to detain this man."

While I was doing this, George and Rebecca rode up.

One of the sentries asked, "What proof do you have that this man should be detained?"

"Search him," I said. "And you will find a coded message regarding Confederate communications."

They asked Mr. Allison to get down from the wagon, and they began to search him from head to toe. Then one of the sentries turned back to me. "Colonel, we can find nothing on this man. His papers seem to be in order for travel, and they are signed by General Halleck."

"Very good, sergeant, I must have been mistaken, and you may let him proceed."

The sun was just beginning to light the sky. We rode back to the Willard and turned the horses in at the livery. We hurried to the Sawyer room, closed and locked the door.

I turned to George and asked, "Did you get it?"

He smiled and pulled the package out from under his coat.

"Imagine Mr. Allison's surprise when they open their package and discover a gentlemen's suit fit for a banker. His spying days will probably be numbered."

We all gathered around the bed, and George laid the package in the middle.

"Who wants to do the honors?" he asked.

"I think Rebecca should open it. She deserves it after what she has been through."

We all watched as her deft fingers pulled the knots away from the package.

"There it is," I said. "Major Blake's uniform stained, soiled, and worn but still intact. Careful dear, we need to preserve any clue."

"It looks just like any other Confederate uniform," Rebecca said.

We searched the uniform without any sign of anything indicating a code. We looked at each other with a great deal of disappointment.

"There must be something," said George, "Why was this smuggled into Washington? Why was this valuable enough to kill for?"

George tried everything he knew from tests for secret invisible writing to ciphers or codes anywhere on the garment. We looked at the seams, the lining, turning the sleeves inside out. We stretched it, we pulled it, and still, there was nothing. Disappointed, we decided to sleep on it for the night and see what we could do in the morning.

# 16

## The Great Discovery

"General Halleck, we have looked this uniform over very carefully and found nothing," I said.

"Do you mind Colonel, if I call in some of my army experts for examination?"

"No, not at all, that is the reason we brought it to you."

Several hours went by as the army experts examined the uniform. We went to get some lunch and returned in the afternoon.

"My men have examined the uniform and have the same result. They could have switched uniforms?" the General said.

"Not possible, sir," I replied, "I have worn this uniform and am familiar with every stain. This is Major Blake's uniform."

"Well, it appears we must concede this one to the Confederates. I don't know what else we can do."

"General, if you don't mind, I would like to keep this uniform. It has been a part of me for years now, and I hate to give it up."

Rebecca spoke up. "Thomas, you know the uniform has brought you nothing but grief. Why would you want it? What good could it possibly serve except to remind you of a terrible time?"

"I think we could someday return it to his family. After all, I did spend some time with them under the pretense of being James. I knew I couldn't tell them, but I felt so guilty. If he is killed in battle or dies in prison, the least I could do is to give them his uniform."

"You can take the uniform," the General said. "I do appreciate your effort in this matter. Colonel Sawyer, would you want to consider extending your commission with the Army? This fight is not over, and we could certainly use your skills."

"No, thank you, General. I believe my soldiering days are behind me."

I repackaged the uniform carefully, and we left his office.

A week passed while the three of us stayed at the hotel. We did occasional excursions out to be certain we were no longer being watched. Confederate forces moved near to Washington, and there was restricted travel in and out of the city.

One evening, Rebecca and I played chess with a bet that the loser would do the household dishes for a week when we returned home. It was a Spartan contest, but she won.

George would venture out on occasion. We eventually discovered that he had a lady friend he was visiting. We began to tease him into giving us an introduction. He finally agreed and asked us to lunch so we could meet her. We met in the lobby of the hotel, and George greeted us with hugs and handshakes. He said, "This is Miss Mary Anna Henry. She is the daughter of Joseph Henry of the Smithsonian. She is, in my opinion, one of the brightest women I have ever met.

"Very nice to make your acquaintance," I said. "This is my wife, Rebecca."

We exchanged handshakes and walked into the dining room, where we were seated for lunch. Miss Henry began chatting with Rebecca about her interest in the Smithsonian while George and I began to discuss my leaving or staying in the military.

"If I were you," George said, "I would get out now, go back home to Galena. You have been through enough and have been a great asset to the cause. Take my advice. You have a wife that loves you and a home to go back to."

After lunch, Rebecca and I retired to our room.

"George seems to be a bit smitten with Miss Henry," Rebecca said.

"Yes, it does seem a bit serious, but we shall see."

On Tuesday, an article appeared in the National Intelligencer announcing the closing of the uniform store. It seems the proprietor didn't return from an extended trip. In a separate report, there was a story about the capture of two spies and their subsequent imprisonment in the Old Capitol Prison.

"Maybe . . . if we can't find anything out by using the uniform, we might be able to question the two Confederate spies about why the uniform or the correspondence was so important," Rebecca said.

I liked the idea and went to ask George what he thought of it.

"Hmm," he said thoughtfully. I don't expect we would get a straight answer from either of them. They are likely both professional spies and know how to lie with a straight face. However, a look at the correspondence could lead to something. I will see what I can do on both counts."

Rebecca and I had a serious discussion to attend to. I pulled the commission papers from my bag to check the date. There it was, "The commission of Major Thomas Sawyer ending June 30, 1864." As I reread, I think my heart skipped a beat. My commission was to expire in six days, and I needed to decide what I would do.

"You know," Rebecca said, "I don't want you to continue for another second in this business. But I also know you have always wanted to see this war to its conclusion. I believe the way things are going now it will soon be over. Although it pains me to say this, I can accept whatever decision you make regarding your volunteering."

"Rebecca, I am still torn."

We sat quietly for a few moments. I reached out and took her hands, and we prayed together for God to guide us in whatever decision we would make. The next morning, we met with George for breakfast.

"Thomas," George said. "We have been given permission to examine the correspondence of the two spies. General Halleck said it would do no good to interview them as they were not cooperating under intense questioning. Let's go have a look at what they were carrying. Mrs. Sawyer, will you be joining us?"

"Of course," she responded, "Someone needs to keep you two out of trouble."

We finished breakfast and left for the War Department. When we arrived, we were presented with the documents. We were informed that the cipher was not yet broken, and if we wanted to try, we were welcome to. The War Department was using a cipher square to attempt to break the code. It was the most likely choice for a code using letters. I explained to Rebecca how the square was built by sketching one on a large piece of paper.

"The alphabet is written across the top of a page in a row from A to Z, like this. Starting with the letter A, the alphabet is repeated down the left side forming a column from A to Z. The letter A becomes the intersection of the row and column. At the B on the column, the alphabet is repeated down the row with the next consecutive letter. When the letter Z is reached, the row continues repeating the letter A again. Each letter in the row is placed under the letter above. The same process is used for the other rows moving down the left-hand column. The result is a twenty-six-letter square." When I finished, George began his cipher lesson.

"A key phrase is used to translate any message. Without the key phrase, the message would be virtually impossible to decode. Let me give you an example. Say I want to write a cipher message to Thomas saying, 'Bring More Grenades.' Thomas and I would come up with a key phrase such as 'Union Army Forever.' To encrypt the message, I would write the message 'Bring More Grenades' on a piece of paper, including a space between each word. Below that line, I would write our key phrase 'UnionArmyForeverUnionArmy . . .' without any spaces, aligning the letters with our message, and repeat it as necessary. Then we move to the cipher square. To make the cipher message, you find the letter B in the word 'bring' in the top row of the square. Then find the first letter of the key phrase, in this case, U, in the column. From the letter B on the row, go down, and from the letter U on the column, go across. Where the two intersect is the first encrypted letter of the message. In our case, it is the letter V."

"Oh, I get it," Rebecca said. "Using the R in word, bring and the N in union, the next ciphered letter would be E."

"Correct," George said. "Assuming they used an alphabet square to write the document. The only thing we need to come up with is the key phrase, and as I just said, it is nearly impossible. In the Confederate document, 'ZBZDEJKVBCE MZGPSCMMUBRVLN' appears to be the title. This may add a new wrinkle because there are usually spaces between the words."

The three of us worked into the night trying key phrases, but nothing seemed to make a translation appear. We tried everything we could think of, "Confederacy forever," "Secession or die," "God is with the South," and "Blessed be the South," even to the point where it got ridiculous. We were trying hymn titles and advertising slogans. It was clear we wouldn't succeed tonight or maybe ever. The General allowed us to have a copy of the correspondence. We were to contact him immediately if we were able to solve the cipher.

By next morning I reached a decision about my army career. I would let my commission expire and return to Galena with Rebecca. I told Rebecca, and her reaction was one of subdued joy.

"Are you sure, Thomas?" She asked, "I don't want you to regret this decision."

"Yes, I am sure. We need to make arrangements for passage back to Galena, and I need to inform George, the army, and General Grant."

We went to the telegraph office and sent a telegram to the Governor of Illinois informing him.

> *June 26, 1864*
> *Governor Richard Yates*
> *Springfield, Illinois*
>
> *It is my honor to tender my resignation as Colonel, United States Army effective at the end of my three-year term of volunteer service on June 30, 1864.*
>
> *Your obedient servant*
> *Thomas Sawyer, Colonel*

I also sent a copy of this to General Grant with a personal note:

> *"It has been an honor to serve with you, my friend. I wish you God speed in your quest and hope we can meet again in Galena when this war is over. I will give Julia your regards when we return."*

Rebecca took the opportunity to wire her father and let him know we would be coming home. George happened to be coming out of the hotel as we were returning. I informed him of my decision.

"This is a big decision, Thomas, and I fully respect it. I hope you and Rebecca have a happy life in Galena. I will tell General Halleck about your decision, and I assume you will inform the army in writing."

"Yes, I already have. Look, George, it is nearing noon. Why don't the three of us have lunch together?"

We sat down at a window table looking out over the street.

"This calls for a celebration," I said and signaled to the waiter. "Waiter, bring us some of your best wine."

We had an excellent meal and talked the afternoon away, sipping wine and telling stories. We put the cipher in the back of our minds. After all, the military code breakers were very good at their jobs. It was approaching dinnertime, but none of us were hungry, so we moved to the lobby. I suggested we all get a good night's sleep, and Rebecca and I would make travel arrangements in the morning. George bid us a good evening, and we retired to our respective rooms.

The sunset was spectacular, making the clouds glow with a pinkish hue. Rebecca had the water pitcher replenished for the evening, and then she and I got ready for bed. As darkness fell, we slipped into bed.

"Thomas," she said. "I think it is wonderful you and I are finely coming home to Galena. Our house is so comfortable, and I can't wait to start a new life. I am assuming you will start up your law practice again, is that correct?"

"That my good woman, I haven't said. Don't cross the bridge till you come to it, is a proverb old, and of excellent wit."

"Oh . . . so now you are quoting Longfellow? What do you really mean?"

"The mining business is doing well for now, but I can foresee a time when it won't. Until then, we'll have enough income that I can take my time in deciding what I want to do."

"Very well," she said. She turned on her side and went to sleep.

My eyes were willing to close, but the darkness brought me no solace. Again, the dream came back, the Confederate soldier, the shots, the smoke, the wound it was still haunting me. But this time, I was in a half state of sleep and consciousness, and I managed to fight off the images. I made no sound, and the stillness was broken only by Rebecca's soft breathing. I prayed for direction and kept repeating this prayer until, at last, I drifted off to sleep.

We awoke to a steady rain that drowned out the sounds of the wagons traveling up and down the street. The life of the great city continued unabated, but so also continued the hauling of the wounded to and from locations around Washington. After breakfast, the rain began to diminish, and we took a walk to the B&O Station. We purchased two fares to Chicago, and the train was to leave at 10:00 am. This left us very little time to pack and say our good-byes. We stopped at George's room to tell him we were leaving today, and he said he would see us to the station. I put on my Union uniform figuring I would wear it one last time for the trip home.

"You look very handsome in your uniform," Rebecca said. "I am so fortunate to have married you." I smiled, held her close, and kissed her.

"Ready?" George said.

"Yes, I think we are," I replied.

Upon our arrival at the station, we had but a few moments to wait prior to boarding, George took my hand and said, "I've made arrangements to get your horse and other equipment sent to Galena as I knew you wouldn't have time. I am sure the army has more important concerns than keeping track of your things."

"Thank you, George, you have been a good friend to me. Hopefully, we will see you again soon."

"Be careful, my friend," I said.

He nodded, we hugged, and I climbed aboard.

We prepared for the trip this time by bringing books to read. We arrived in Philadelphia, and both of us got off the train to stretch our legs a bit. After some short delays and layovers, we reached Galena in a record two days. We were met by Rebecca's father and mother, and hugs were exchanged all around.

It felt good to be home again. The community arranged for us to have a return celebration at the judge's house on July 4th. This would work out well as it gave us a few days to open our little house on Dodge Street and clean things up a bit. The judge hired a wagon, and all my stored possessions, plus some additional furniture, were delivered to our front door. He made arrangements for boarding my horse and riding equipment. Rebecca found some second-hand rugs at a Galena dry goods store. There was nothing extravagant about my wife. While she was finishing the details of setting up our house, I went on to explore Galena for a place to set up my law office. Finding nothing suitable, I decided to practice from our home in the interim. Rebecca was not thrilled with the idea of using our parlor as my office but relented when I agreed to find somewhere else quickly.

I learned that some of my runner boys were taken by the army to fight in the war. In three years, Jimmy Miller grew into a strapping young man, was nearly six feet tall and muscular.

"Hello, Major," he said with a smile, "I really missed you around here."

"Jimmy, I am now Colonel Sawyer. I am starting my law practice again and am looking for an apprentice. How old are you now?"

"Almost sixteen, and I am near graduating from school."

"Jimmy, how would your parents feel about you having a full-time position?"

"Paw got killed at Gettysburg, and to tell you the truth, I thought about enlisting myself. But, Ma . . . she wants me to help her around the farm. We are raising chickens and have quite a few laying hens now." I interrupted him.

"I am asking if you would be interested in the job."

"Would I," he replied, "That would really be something special, but I don't think I can. I couldn't leave Ma to tend to the work at home. She is a bit frail and needs me right now, but thanks for the offer, Colonel."

"I understand Jimmy, but if there are any special projects that come up, would you like for me to call on you?"

"Yes, sir, Colonel, I would be happy to help."

"I will, of course, pay you for your services."

The fourth of July celebration in Galena was one to behold. There was a parade in the streets with many veterans from various Illinois militias. There was a fireworks display along the river, with many people uplifted by political speeches and word of victories on the battlefield. The war was looking more and more like the Union would have the upper hand, and this lifted the spirits of some. The loss of life at Cold Harbor in June, tragic as it was, now belonged to the past. Rebecca and I took a stroll to the waterfront to watch the activity. More young men in uniform were being carted down to Cairo, and we assumed to get transported east. Some looked like they were not even out of puberty.

"Rebecca," I said. "These boys do not know what they are volunteering to do. They think like I thought, the war to be all glory and honor. Some of this is true, but it is also true that mingled with that glory and honor is a host of death and destruction. I pray God will help them by putting an end to this conflict. How ironic this is the nation's birthday, and they are celebrating by departing for war."

I found a vacant store in town just two weeks after I promised to remove the practice from our parlor. I paid to have a sign hung across the width of the boardwalk. It was not as fancy as the window but more noticeable. Cases came to me slowly at first but then picked up to the point where my time was running long on the law and short on my family. I spent a lot of time at the Jo Daviess county courthouse filing routine paperwork when I should have been dealing with essential case details. I couldn't find time to focus on serving my clients, and it was upsetting me. Rebecca could see the change in my attitude.

"Whatever happened to the idea of hiring an apprentice?" she said.

"I guess I had forgotten about it," I responded.

I began interviewing prospective candidates some veterans of the war, like myself. I just didn't feel any of them were suitable. I did eventually hire an apprentice, one Jimmy Miller. Luckily he had not been conscripted into the army. His mother remarried, and the farm was now secure. I got Jimmy started doing the clerical work at the courthouse, and I continued to serve my clientele. I began teaching Jimmy law two nights a week. The rest of the summer and fall went by, with the war still raging. General Sherman marched his army across the face of the south with devastation in his wake, and by early December, reached Savannah, Georgia.

The pace of my practice picked up to the point where Rebecca could tell I was a little stressed. She suggested we take an early Christmas holiday and go to Chicago. I left the practice in Jimmy's hands and told him not to accept any new clients. He was instructed to contact Judge Thatcher should something come up he felt he couldn't handle. It was a short train trip to Chicago, and we would be gone for ten days. When we boarded the train, I was not in any way relaxed. I was unsure of leaving the practice, the house, and Galena. Rebecca did her best to calm me down.

"You have taught Jimmy well, and I am sure he can handle any situation with the practice. Mother and Father will keep an eye on the house for us. Quit worrying, silly. This will be a fun trip for both of us. You need this time to rest and relax."

She laid her head on my shoulder, and we held hands. She prayed aloud God would calm my nerves and settle my disposition. I, on the other hand, didn't think there was much wrong with my disposition, but if God was going to fix it, who was I to argue.

The conductor came by our seats and checked our tickets.

"Sir, I think there is a problem with your passage to Chicago. If you would come with me, sir, I think we can straighten this out."

"What problem?" I said in a rather loud voice, "I paid our fares and resent being treated in this manner."

Rebecca touched my arm to try to calm me down. The conductor began again.

"Sir, if you will just come with me to the rear car, I am sure this will all become clear. You will need to come also, he said to Rebecca, as this involves your seat too."

Reluctantly we followed the conductor to the rear of the train. He stopped short of the last car and said he was instructed to go no farther. I opened the door for my wife, and we entered the car. It was elaborately decorated with fancy curtains, luxuriously appointed seats, a large settee, tables, and a silver coffee service. A man was standing pouring coffee for three. He turned. It was George.

"Ah . . . you have arrived," he said.

I was aghast.

"What . . . how . . . ?"

I couldn't contain myself. We hugged, Rebecca hugged him, and we sat down to coffee. "When I saw you two come aboard the train," he said, "I couldn't resist a little fun. I have the duty of escorting this car and its cargo back to Pittsburgh from Galena, but I didn't have the chance to say anything about my arrival or departure. We are indeed lucky chance has brought us together again."

Having a luxurious train car all to ourselves for the balance of the trip to Chicago was wonderful. George was now head of rail security for the Baltimore and Ohio Railroad.

"Say, George," I asked, "Do you know if they ever solved the cipher?"

"No. I have been gone for a while, but as far as I know, they are still working on a key phrase."

"How are things with you and Miss Henry?" I asked.

"Very well, in fact, I plan on proposing to her soon."

"Well, congratulations!" Rebecca said. "I hope you have a happy future together."

We relaxed with drinks and some lunch in our private oasis. All too soon, the train reached Chicago, and we had to say good-bye again. George promised to stay in touch, and the next time he came through Galena, he would certainly stop by and see us. I gave him our new address on Dodge Street and said he better keep in touch, or I would be finding him. Rebecca and I spent the next three days taking in the sights of Chicago. The city was in a Christmas mood even with the war on, and it lightened both our spirits. Rebecca went shopping and bought some new dresses while I tried to catch up on the latest news from the war. Sightseeing in Chicago was something we never had the opportunity to do while traveling to and from Washington. We stopped in at C. Strobel and Brothers to look at desks. Giles Brothers to look for a watch. And we attended a Grand Carnival at Ogden Skating Park. The nine days passed much too quickly, and we boarded the train for the return trip, this time without George.

When we reached Galena on the next evening, there was a cold wind blowing, and snow started to fall. As Rebecca and I left the station, it began snowing hard. We didn't take the time to let the Thatcher's know we returned but went straight to our house. The Thatcher's had provisions waiting for us, which was providential because the snow began to pile up outside and traffic around Galena ground to a halt. I kept busy going through some of my things. I pulled out the Spencer rifle and cleaned it thoroughly. Rebecca was putting things away when she discovered the package containing Major Blake's uniform. She carried it into the parlor and suggested she would try to clean it so it wouldn't deteriorate further. She sat in her rocker and held up the jacket examining the dirt and stains.

"This really needs a gentle washing," she said.

Just then, one of the buttons popped off the jacket and rolled under her rocking chair. She was not quick enough to react, and when she rocked forward, it came down on the button, smashing it.

"Oh no!" she exclaimed and bent down to pick up the pieces.

It was then that she noticed a very tiny piece of paper. It must have come from inside the button. I was standing by her side now, concerned we would never get the uniform back to the family in one piece.

With great care, we unfolded the paper and held it up to the lamplight. There was one letter written on it "u." We looked at each other and began to get very excited.

"Do you know what this means?" I exclaimed, "This must be it."

We began to move quickly. We tapped the buttons and found eleven more were hollow. By working with a knife and being very patient, we pried the buttons apart. After several minutes of work, we discovered each one contained a letter. There were twelve in all, but they needed to be arranged in a combination that made sense. There was u, y, c, t, r, o, o, i, i, n, n, and v. We began writing down every word that came to mind containing these letters.

"Let's see," I said. "There is unicorn."

"Don't be ridiculous, Thomas. No Confederate would use unicorn."

"How about 'Ivory'?"

"That could be."

"Yes, but ivory what?"

"Ivory Country,"

"That's Africa."

We tried it on the cipher square with negative results. This went on for several hours, trying different words in combination. We took a break, had a cup of tea, and resumed the search. I came up with Runt Onion, no good. Rebecca came up with Tiny Corn. A negative also. Then I hit upon the word Union. But Union what, or what Union I thought? We looked at each other.

Then I said, "What would be the worst thing that could happen to the Confederacy?" "That easy," she said. "For it to fall and the north would win. That's it, who would have ever thought. A victory, and here it is. The key is Union Victory."

We quickly went to work, trying to decode the copies of the Confederate documents. The title was the first thing, and it translated "For the Protection of the President." As we translated, it became clear what we were dealing with.

"Rebecca, this is a security plan for the Confederate Government. It details the plans for the fortifications at Richmond and contingencies should Richmond fall. We need to get this to the Army right away."

There was an army presence in Galena, but it was also dangerous to give the code to just anyone. The telegraph was unsafe as a message could be intercepted. The safe thing to do was to telegraph General Halleck we broken the cipher and to ask for instructions. I returned to the house and found Rebecca busy translating more of the document.

"This is fascinating; it details what is to take place, and the timing of events, should the Confederacy fall. I can see why it was so important a document and why the Confederates wanted its return."

"Don't be so sure about that. As long as there is a Confederacy, there will be spies among us. Who is to say this was not meant as a decoy?"

Soon a telegram arrived from General Halleck. He would be sending an emissary to pick up the code. His name was Lafayette Baker. This was a name I recognized as being in the army scout network, and I knew I would recognize his face.

The next day was Christmas Eve, and Mr. Baker arrived. I presented him with the information about the code and what we translated.

"Colonel Sawyer," he began, "I can't thank you enough for what you have done here. By uncovering the code, you have given us a window into the Confederate plans. I will leave for Washington at once and get this information to the army. It may be of great value in the coming days."

We invited him to dinner, but he graciously declined. The snow was melting now, and the roads were mud pits. He stepped gingerly into a hired carriage, wished us Merry Christmas, and he was off. Rebecca and I held each other close and sighed almost simultaneously.

"Well, darling," I whispered, "I believe this closes the final chapter."

We kissed a long and embracing kiss. We were looking forward to a Christmas Day celebration with Rebecca's parents. The night wrapped its darkness around the town. We joked about seeing who would be the first one into bed.

I said. "When I blow out the lantern, we will race through the parlor to the stairs."

Just as I blew out the lantern, a musket shot sounded, and a minié ball pierced our parlor window. It was clear having spies as friends, has its risks.

# 17

## Chasing Rebecca

I grabbed my Spencer rifle and plunged out into the darkness. Everything was quiet, and I could see no one. There were shadows from the moonlight playing along the ground as the cold winter breeze blew the trees. I told Rebecca to stay in the house and keep the lanterns off. I went to fetch the sheriff. The sheriff seemed quick to disclose there was little he could do. The minié ball lodged in a door frame opposite the parlor window. Judge Thatcher and Jimmy came to the house to give us moral support and help temporarily patch the window.

"You know," Rebecca said. "It was probably meant for you. I am sure with all your exploits the Confederates would want you out of the picture."

"I have placed us in danger in our own home. We are not safe until we know for certain who is behind this. I will go over things again in the daylight to see what I can find."

"Oh Thomas, I was so afraid for you to go away to war and never return. Now I am afraid for both of us and my family."

The sheriff did post a guard at our house for our protection. He was relieved by another guard at daybreak. After a bit of breakfast, I put on my coat went outside to scout around the neighborhood for possible evidence. When I reached the neighbor's yard, I went between the houses and spotted something on the ground. It was a cigar band from an expensive Cuban cigar. The soil was softer in that area, and I found footprints leading to the site between the houses and exiting back the same way. At the end of the tracks, was a small area with bits of cigar ash in the footprints. I tucked the band into my jacket pocket. I had a reasonable repair job on the window and door frame done by the afternoon.

The Christmas celebration came and went at the Thatcher household. There was a feast for dinner and good company in the parlor. Rebecca and I gave the judge his new watch and her mother a bracelet. We got a new stove for our house. 1865 was celebrated at the Sawyer household with a toast to the New Year, and a prayer for an end to the dreadful conflict was still before us.

Jimmy and I spent January and February immersed in law cases. Jimmy's knowledge of the law was increasing. I felt like he might be able to practice as my partner. This New Year seemed to have brought peace to the household. Rebecca arrived home from the doctor one evening with some unexpected news. We were going to have a baby. I experienced many joys in my life, but this . . . this was the best news yet. A little Sawyer would soon be gracing our home. The grandparents were thrilled with the announcement and made immediate plans on how they would begin spoiling their new grandchild. One of the bedrooms in the house would now need a complete makeover as a nursery. The estimated delivery date was around the end of August.

Despite the loss of life on both sides, General Grant's plan of standing and fighting as long as it takes was beginning to tell on General Lee and the Army of Northern Virginia. Things were looking up for the Sawyer family as well. We just finished decorating the nursery, and I was carving a small wooden horse for my new child. There was no more thought of the minié ball from months ago. One afternoon the judge came to the house.

"Tom," he said breathlessly, "I am afraid I have some bad news . . . Rebecca . . . she, she is . . . missing. She left the bank this afternoon after getting some cash for the household expenses and never returned. I have notified the sheriff, and everyone in Galena is looking for her. No one seems to know where she is."

"Oh, my God."

I immediately locked the house and went to join the search. The judge and I searched all day without any leads. I kept going despite the fact that a cold rain had come upon us. Exhausted, I returned home at around 2:00 in the morning to try and rest. I could not sleep at all. As the sun rose, the rain departed. I met the judge at his residence, and we went over plans to widen the search. Flyers were printed up asking for information, and we offered a fifty-dollar reward for any information that could be validated as authentic and lead us to Rebecca.

It was clear I needed help, so I sent a telegram to George asking if he could spare some time and come to Galena. I wired General Halleck and asked for any possible assistance from the army and the army scouts. I was going crazy with the thought of losing Rebecca and our child at the same time. What little sleep I was getting was marred by dreams of her suffering in some deep dark hole. Two more days passed without a word from anyone. Finally, George arrived. I met him at the train station, and he had a few suggestions that had not entered my mind.

"I am guessing no one has seen Rebecca because they hid her somehow. We need to check the train station and the docks and ask the right questions."

I approached one of the station employees, "May we speak to the station master?" I enquired.

When he approached, George introduced himself and asked, "Sir, have you noticed anyone boarding a train that might have been unusual or seemed out of place? Was there anyone with their face covered so you couldn't recognize them?"

"Not that I know of," he responded, "Wait a minute, the day before yesterday there were two men who boarded the train with an invalid aunt. They dressed her in black from head to toe and put a veil across her face. They got tickets for Pittsburgh via Indianapolis. I didn't think nothin' of it till you said somethin' just now. She didn't walk like no invalid, and they stuck mighty close to her side." George and I looked at each other.

"When is the next train to Pittsburgh?" I said.

"Tomorrow morning," came the response.

"We'll take two tickets, please."

The next morning, we boarded the train with preparation for an extended journey. George sent a message to General Halleck asking for any help the army could give and told him the particulars. We arrived in Pittsburgh the next afternoon. George and I immediately began questioning all of the agents and baggage handlers, asking if they had seen this threesome arrive. We found a rig driver who said he took them to the Monongahela House Hotel.

"We're understaffed," the clerk said. "The manager isn't here right now. It's hard for us to keep the place clean, let alone keep track of the guests."

I stepped closer to the desk clerk, covered both of the clerk's hands with my own, and pulled them toward me. I then leaned in to within an inch of his face speaking quietly and forcefully,

"Well, sir, I am going to ask you this again, and I expect a clearer response. Did you see the three people I described to you?"

"You see this badge," George said, "I am an inspector for the railroad, and this is official business. You might want to consider giving us a straight answer."

The man's face went white, and he said, "I *really* don't recall, sir, but you can check the register."

We did and came across two men and one woman registering as Mr. John Smith, Mr. Allen Smith, and Aunt. No name for the aunt pointed to this being her captors.

"Are the Smith's still here?" I asked.

"No, they checked out yesterday."

"Do you know where they went?"

"No, but I do remember this now. It was strange because they arrived in suits and when they left, they changed into riding clothes. Funny thing, though, that woman was still covered completely in black."

We took the opportunity to change clothes and grab some food for the trip. I checked the telegraph office, and there was no news from home. We went back to the hotel to rest a bit before continuing and sat in the lobby. That's when I noticed the cigar band on a table. I pulled the one from my jacket pocket, and they matched. We arrived at the livery and began to question the proprietor.

"Yes, sir, they were here all right. Got the three mounts they boarded here last week. They left in a hurry."

"What direction did they go?" I asked.

"They went south out of town toward the border."

"How much would you charge for two of your best horses, saddles, and gear?" I said.

He was about to say something when George showed him his badge and said this was official railroad business, and he wouldn't be cheated. Before leaving town, George sent a wire meant for some of the scouts asking for assistance. He was going around General Halleck, but he knew they would do what they could. I wired the judge we were leaving

Pittsburgh and wouldn't be in touch for some time. We started south with a guess and a prayer.

After some hours journey, we came across a farmer with a wagon full of barrel staves. He said the trio passed him only a few hours ago headed south. We were both weary of being in the saddle, but indications were that we were gaining on our quarry rapidly.

George spoke up, "You know this could be a trap, don't you? You were shot at, and they may be using Rebecca as bait to get you where they want you."

"I know, but it is a chance I am willing to take. At any rate, they have gone progressively slower, and unless I miss my guess, Rebecca is slowing their progress in every way she can. I also think she will take the opportunity to escape if it becomes available."

We rode from Pittsburgh to just outside Cannonsburgh. We made camp for the night in a small grove of trees about a half mile off the road. The trees were sparse, but we were hoping it would be cover enough. We ate some apples, bread, and honey and settled in for some rest.

We slept for about six hours and were on our way again. The sun was just beginning to show light on the horizon as we pushed on southward. We stopped in Washington, Pennsylvania, to get supplies and question some of the locals. We could find no one who saw the trio which concerned me. I prayed we were still going the right direction. The sun was soon fully up as we passed through Waynesburg and pushed on to Newton. Suddenly we saw riders coming from the east toward us. Just to be safe, I drew my rifle out of my saddle sling and loaded the first shell. As they came closer, George recognized one of them.

"There's no need for that rifle, one of them shouted, we're on your side, and we bring you news."

"Greetings, Harry," George replied, "Harry Troutman, this is Colonel Thomas Sawyer."

"Nice to meet you, Colonel Sawyer, your reputation precedes you. This is my partner Doc Buckner. We heard from the network you were headed this way from Pittsburgh and hoped we would meet up with you."

"You have news of Rebecca and her captors?" I said.

Their faces turned glum, and they looked at each other.

"Well, no sir, I wish we did, but we have contacts south of here, and they are looking. We do have other important news. Just four days ago, Petersburg and Richmond fell to General Grant, and Richmond has been evacuated. The Confederacy is in turmoil, and no one knows what will happen now."

"Well, George," I said. "We hoped for this news but not in our current situation. I want to thank you for riding out to intercept us. This is indeed what we all have been working for these years."

"You are welcome, Colonel Sawyer," Harry said. "We will continue to search for your wife, Colonel, and do what we can."

"Thank you, Harry."

We pushed on passing through Newton, crossed into West Virginia through Greenville, crossed the Monongalia River on a ferry, and stopped in Morgantown. I asked the ferry driver if he had seen a party of three, and he said yes, just a few hours earlier. We pushed on south out of Morgantown, knowing we were getting close. It was getting dark and we had to stop for the night. For the next two days we followed them into Virginia. We became more suspicious of a trap when the time interval between when we reached a location and their passing through was always the same. They were leading us on. This was most likely an attempt to wear us out.

We came to a place where the road passed through a grove of tall pines on both sides. My gut was telling me this was not a good situation. George pulled his horse to a stop. I gave him a sign to go right and skirt the wood, and I would go left. He nodded in agreement and signaled we would meet on the other side. I started my horse slowly around and immediately ran into some fencing, but there was a narrow path along the fence row. I quietly reined my horse to a stop. There, through the trees, I saw a man with a musket aimed at the road. Just as we suspected, it was a perfect ambush.

I quietly watched the man from about 30 yards away. He was puffing on a cigar. The pine needle carpet made my foot approach almost silent. There was gunfire from the opposite side of the wood, and my target went sprinting through the trees. I gave chase, overtook him, and wrestled him to the ground. Two strikes to the head with my pistol butt, and he was out cold. I kept on going and reached the road. There, standing in the road, was Rebecca, dressed in men's clothing. She came running to me, and I pulled her into the woods for cover. We huddled down to watch the road, and I held her close. We soon saw movement through the trees. I gave my pistol to Rebecca and moved to get a better vantage point. There emerged a man walking slowing with his arms raised as if in surrender. He was followed closely by George carrying a musket and a pistol. We stood up and walked out onto the road.

"I found this one waiting for us, and we exchanged a few shots," George said. "I convinced him it would be better to surrender than to die."

The man before him was small in stature and wore a large floppy hat on his head.

"Well," I said. "Let's get a better look at our captive."

George took the hat off his head, long hair fell down, and the face of Mary Blake was revealed. She looked up at me, her face red with anger.

"You monster," she cried, "James never came home, you killed Daniel, and you killed my father. I wanted to hurt you . . . hurt you bad . . . and then kill you for what you have done."

She lunged toward me, but George managed to corral her before she reached me. At that moment, her partner came staggering from the wood with blood streaming from his forehead. He fell at my feet. Rebecca took my knife and cut some material from his shirt to bandage his forehead.

George piped up, "Let's get off this road before someone else comes along that may have heard the shots."

We moved into the shade of the trees where I turned toward Mary and spoke in quiet, even tones, "First of all, let me set the record straight. Yes, I did shoot James, but I also did everything I could to save him, including riding very hard for several hours to a doctor. He was still alive when we reached the hospital, and I know he has been transferred to a prison in Cincinnati. I suspect he is still there. Second, Daniel was where he wanted to be and not where you wanted him to be. He contracted pneumonia and died at his home. There was nothing any of us could have done to save him. But, for the life of me, I don't understand how you can blame me for your father's death." Mary looked up.

"He died from a bad heart, all because his boys never came home. You were the one that caused him to worry himself to death. I hired this man to track you down and kill you. Unfortunately, he missed. So, we took your wife instead. It still won't be easy for you to get out of Virginia alive. I have friends here."

There was a moment of uneasy silence. I asked George to keep an eye on them while Rebecca and I talked.

"Dearest," I began, "How did you manage to get away from them?"

"I took my time knowing there would be an opening at some point. They kept me tied up most of the time, but when we arrived here, they began preparing for the ambush. I knew it was now or never, so I began working at the ropes while they were concentrating on how their plan would be executed. When they split up to set up for the ambush, Mary took charge of me. I managed to work free, and just as I did, George came up behind us. That's when I made my breakout through the woods."

"It was fortunate George was able to get her to surrender," I said. "Otherwise we could have wounded on our hands or worse."

Rebecca and I gathered all the horses and supplies and moved them into the woods. We chose a spot where we were out of sight of the road with a small clearing for the horses. We tied up and gagged Mary and her accomplice. It was near dark now, and it seemed best that we stayed where we were for the night. I looked at Rebecca, and for the first time, I realized how tired she was.

"How are you feeling, darling?"

"I do feel exhausted. I need to lie down."

"It's getting dark now, dear. George made a bed out of pine straw for you and put your bedroll on top. I think this will help."

"Thank you, dear."

I went to check on our charges when I heard the sounds of other horses and riders on the road. The riders were in a hurry and moving north. It was too dark to tell who they were or what side they were on as they came thundering past. Our cover was enough, and they didn't see us. I guessed around twenty riders, maybe more. They passed down the road, and I went back to George and Rebecca.

"We need to decide what to do with them. We can't just release them. They might just go to their friends and re-arm themselves. We need to think about this tonight and decide what to do in the morning. I will take the first watch." Things settled down, and George relieved me around midnight. I slept for about six hours, and after checking our prisoner's bonds took his place. I was watching the darkness give way to the slightest hint of dawn when Rebecca arose.

"Thomas, I need to take a short walk. The night has made me stiff, and I need to move."

I roused George to keep watch, and we walked to the road together. The moonlight was still bright on the roadway, and it seemed to glisten. As we walked, the road began to sparkle more brightly. It came upon us that the glistening was not from the morning dew but from twenty-dollar gold coins. They were scattered along the roadway here and there. We began to gather them like picking strawberries. As the sun rose higher, it became evident there were more coins scattered at the edge of the woods. The coins went about twenty yards along the road and suddenly stopped. We picked up as much as we could and carried it back to the camp. We showed it to George and estimated there were around four hundred dollars in gold coins. Rebecca stayed at the camp, and George and I went back to the road. We found a few more pieces here and there, but the supply ran dry. We did find a paper that told us a lot about where the gold coins had come from. It was a counting slip from the Confederate treasury stating that there were one thousand dollars in coins in a bag. Through some strange twist of fortune, we were recipients of gold from the Confederate treasury. It must have been dropped by the riders that went through earlier. We temporarily piled the coins behind some rocks at the edge of the camp. After the harvest, a second conference was held to decide what to do with our captives.

"Mary was right about one thing," I said. "We are in Confederate territory and a long way from home. Getting them back to Galena as our prisoners to stand trial without a mishap would be a tall order. However, I don't relish my wife being kidnapped or me being shot at. If this guy is a mercenary that Mary hired, perhaps he could be bought. I suggest we use our newfound wealth to buy him out."

"I think it's worth a try, Thomas. What about you, George?"

"I don't know. Giving up all this gold to two nefarious characters? I would be more inclined to leave them here and take their horses. They would be a bother to no one for some time. And besides, we could split the gold between us."

"George, you know we can't do that. There is too much risk in their current state. If they find out about the gold, then they would be sure to come after us. The men who dropped it may also come looking for it. Besides, I think Mary would be inclined to leave us in peace if we paid her too."

"Well," George said. "Perhaps we can scare this mercenary enough he won't try anything. We all need to keep a cool head and be very aware when we address them."

I went back to our captives, freed Mary, and brought her to Rebecca. George took over guard duty.

"Mary," I said. "Every word of what I told you regarding James and your brother was true. To my knowledge, James is still alive. We did have a bond of having many of the same features. A passion for our causes drove us both to do what we did. In fact, I still have your stepbrother's uniform and have protected it from harm. God does not want us to kill each other as this is our own invention. I know times have been hard on you, and you have my condolences for the losses your family has endured. In case you are not aware, Richmond and Petersburg have fallen, and the Confederacy is in dire straits. You still have your life and the rest of your family to rely on. How many are in your family now?"

Her answer bore a softer tone.

"There are five left now," she said. "My mother, a younger brother, a sister, and two cousins have come to the farm."

I said, "Perhaps, now that you know the real story, you can find forgiveness in your heart."

There was a long pause, and she sat with her head down. When she lifted her head, her expression changed.

"It will take me a long time to get over this, but if what you say is true . . . then perhaps . . ."

"I believe I have a way to help you and your family. Would you be willing to return to Clarksville and your farm if I gave you enough in gold for a year's worth of crops plus some living expenses? I am willing to give you two hundred dollars in gold coins."

She looked at me skeptically. "Prove it," she said.

I took my bandana, went behind the rocks, returned with the coins, and dropped them at her feet. She opened the bandana and glanced back at us.

"Are you serious?" she exclaimed. You are willing to give me this, and the only stipulation is that I return to Clarksville? You must be crazy."

I looked at her, "No, Mary, we are not crazy, and it is yours. All you need to do is get on your horse and ride south and leave us in peace."

She paused for a moment.

"And you won't shoot me in the back when I leave?"

"As God is my witness, not one of us will harm you."

She got up slowly, shook off the effects of bondage, went to her horse, and prepared to leave. We followed her as she led her horse to the edge of the trees. She took one final look at us, stashed the coins in her saddlebag, mounted her horse, and rode off to the south.

I turned to Rebecca and said, "Well, we only have one left."

We waited an hour to be sure she was gone before returning to camp. There we found George waiting patiently.

"Did it work?" he said.

"Yes," I responded, "Now, let's see where we stand with this fellow."

I approached the man with some degree of trepidation. This was a hired assassin, and he might be harder to deal with. I untied him and took off his gag while George covered him.

"Can I ask you your name, sir?" I said.

"You can," he said. "But it will do you no good."

"Did you serve in the military?"

There was a long period where no one spoke. I thought it might be advantageous to check him for identification. What we found was an agreement to pay a Mr. Tollenger the sum of twenty dollars for taking care of certain business transactions and another twenty dollars when the job was completed. It was signed by Mary Blake.

"Well, Mr. Tollenger, I see you had some business that was not concluded. George came up behind him, holstered his pistol, and placed a knife to the prisoner's neck.

"Perhaps, Mr. Tollenger can be persuaded to tell us a bit more of what he knows," George said, "We can dispatch him the same way we did Mary, may she rest in peace."

"George," I said. "I am sure Mr. Tollenger is a reasonable man, and we will not need anything quite so violent . . . yet. Well, sir, again, I say to you, did you serve in the army?"

With the knife pressed against his throat and the thought planted that we dispatched Mary, he began to talk.

"I served with the 23rd Alabama Battalion Sharpshooters just for a month or so, and then I deserted. Military life didn't suit me."

"So, I assume Miss Blake didn't honor her portion of the contract, and you are out twenty dollars. It is too bad because now Miss Blake will never be able to pay you. That is tough, Mr. Tollenger . . . but I am willing to make up for Miss Blake. I am willing to pay you an additional sum in gold coins on the pledge you will ride away from here and never bother us again. Remember, if you take this offer, you must honor it. Otherwise, my friend here will have no qualms about dispatching you wherever you may be. Oh, and one more thing, you might be interested to know that both Petersburg and Richmond have fallen to Union forces."

There was a long silence while Mr. Tollenger thought this over.

"Show me what you got?" he said.

I took George's bandana, went behind the rocks, loaded it with the remaining coins, and returned, placing it at his feet.

"There you are, sir, nearly two hundred dollars in gold coins."

"Okay, it's a deal."

George relaxed his grip, Mr. Tollenger picked up the bandana and inserted it into the saddlebags on his horse. He never said another word; he just mounted his horse and rode away. It would be a while before he discovered Mary was still quite alive if indeed, he ever did. Chances are good there would be some betrayal somewhere along the line, so we made haste. We got our horses saddled and headed north, all the while knowing one or both of these people could double-cross us.

We retraced our steps and after three days made it across the Monongalia River before sunset. We stopped in Granville to get much-needed rest and a bite to eat. George went to the telegraph office and wired the scout network that we found Rebecca. Other telegrams would have to wait. We kept moving and rode in darkness with only the moon to guide us. We passed through Newtown and into Waynesburg. We felt a little better being back in Pennsylvania, so we began to look for a place to stay. All along the ride, George and I took turns doubling back a few miles to be sure we were not being followed. In Waynesburg, we came across the Bulls Head Tavern and thought it looked like suitable accommodations.

"Well, Colonel," George said. "I will take care of the horses. Get some rest, and I will see you in the morning."

Rebecca approached him and said, "Thank you, George, you are a true friend."

Rebecca soon laid her head on the pillow and fell fast asleep. I sat at the window of the tavern, watching the street for at least an hour. There was less and less movement on the street as people sought some shelter from the night. Shadowy figures dotted the boardwalk, but none seemed to be watching the tavern. I finally came down from the window, shed my clothes, and fell into bed. It was a long and harrowing journey so far and cost us in many ways, but I had my pregnant wife back, and that was worth all the gold in the world. I lay in the darkness, thanking God for the blessings bestowed on us.

I arose early the next morning, worrying the money was not enough to deter Mary or Mr. Tollenger. I wandered onto the porch as sun was beginning to peak over the horizon, and I could see a few farmers bringing their wares into town. I was alone with my thoughts about all that transpired. I was praying the money would be enough for Mary and her family to put their lives together again when I was joined by Rebecca. She took my arm, and we walked back into the tavern.

"Good morning," George said in a cheerful tone, "I hope you all got a good night's rest?" "Reasonable," I said. "You never cease to amaze me, my friend. You are almost always so cheerful."

"I believe we will make it," George said. "With the fall of Richmond and the Confederacy in its death throes, the gold will be worth more than Confederate paper."

We made it to Pittsburgh and purchased train tickets for home. I sent a wire to the scouts, thanking them for their service. I sent another to the judge telling him we were safe, on our way home, and according to the train schedule, would be there in two days. George posted a wire to his boss saying he would be gone a few more days and would accompany us to Galena. I sold the animals and gear back to the livery at a slight profit because we included the horse Rebecca was riding. It was early evening when we boarded the train and settled into our seats. I noticed the car had seen the worst of the war and troops. Most everything was worn down and uncomfortable. The dark green paint was peeling away from the walls, and there were scrapes and scratches everywhere. I purchased a pillow at a dry goods store before we left, and Rebecca adopted it. We held hands as the miles and stops clicked away. George sat across from us and occasionally engaged me in conversation.

"Well, Thomas," he said. "I suppose you will confine your activities to your wife and your lawyering."

"Yes," I said. "It would be a real pleasure for calm family life in Galena. With a baby on the way, we will really have our hands full. I can't imagine what fatherhood will be like, but I will certainly try to be the best father I can be."

"You will be a fine father, and you will have many, many stories to tell your child."

I turned away, pulling my hat down over my eyes and fell asleep.

We arrived in Galena, and the whole town was abuzz with the news that General Lee surrendered. There were celebrations in the streets, and some people were delirious with joy about the possible return of a loved one from the conflict. As the hired rig pulled around the corner onto Dodge Street, people lined the street to greet us. Jimmy was there with a few of the old boy's guard waving at us. We came into the house to a sumptuous meal. There was a roast turkey with stuffing, potatoes, and all the trimmings. We entertained a house full of people who dined with us, including the sheriff. He pulled me aside and said how grateful he was for my word about Nate Wilson.

"I think it's time for another toast," Judge Thatcher said. "Here is to the safe return of my daughter, my son-in-law, and their good friend. It is a true joy to have them return safely to the family. I wish to thank you all for your supporting us, praying for us, and aiding in the search. Without good friends and the help of our God, the strain would have been much worse. So, raise your glasses high and feel the joy."

# 18

## Riches

We awoke the next morning snug in our own little house. It was a lovely day, and I was getting dressed when Rebecca reminded me of losing to her at chess. She was indeed diabolical on some counts as the dishes from the party were still in the kitchen. I didn't mind because the mother of my child had a chance to really relax after several harrowing days. After washing and drying the dishes, I fixed her breakfast and took it up to her in the bedroom. Next, I fixed breakfast for George and me. The smell of bacon cooking must have roused him because he came sauntering down the stairs with a satisfied look on his face.

"Good morning Thomas, how are you feeling this fine morning?"

"Fine," I answered, "and how is George this morning?"

"Happier than a cat at a mouse convention," he replied, "Say, Thomas, I don't suppose you would be taking some time off."

"No," I responded, "Jimmy has been handling all my legal work, and I need to get back to the office. It has been great having you by my side through all of this. I can never repay you for your kindness."

"Don't mention it. It was the least I could do after all we have been through. Say . . . do you think Mary will ever come back after you?"

"No, I think not, she probably will return to her farm as it is all she has known. As for that assassin, he has been well paid. George . . . I promised Rebecca a real church wedding, and I intend for her to have it. Since I have no family here, I could think of no one better to stand with me than you. Would you be my second at the ceremony?"

"Most certainly, you let me know when and I will be there."

"Thank you, George. It would mean the world to me, and I believe Rebecca would approve."

After breakfast, George and I sat in the parlor and chatted for a bit.

"Thomas, I can remain here in Galena until tomorrow, but I need to get back to my job."

I heard Rebecca upstairs, and in a few minutes, she joined us in the parlor.

"I was just asking George if he would stand with me at our wedding ceremony, and he consented."

"That's wonderful, George," she said. "Thank you for the gesture. Thomas, I think we should plan the ceremony soon as I don't want the birth of our child to interfere. It need not be anything elaborate, but I do want it to be a church ceremony. I will inquire at First Presbyterian to see if there is a time available for us. I don't want Father to perform the ceremony as he has already married us once. He just needs to walk me down the aisle, sit with Mother, and enjoy the moment."

"Very well, dear," I responded. "Let's set a tentative date now so George will know. Today is April 10, and we could have a May wedding. What about Saturday, the 13th of May? That should give us enough time to plan the event. George, is this date good for you?"

"Yes, I believe I could make it work."

Rebecca and I grabbed our coats as the April air was still chilly, and we walked to the church.

"Thomas, while you were away, Reverend Addison Strong was called to the church and is now serving the congregation. I hope he will be amenable to our wanting to use the church for a service even though we are already married."

"He might even consent to perform the ceremony," I said.

We reached the church and found the Reverend was not available, but the secretary helped us check the Saturday date. She would speak to the Reverend about performing the ceremony but was sure he would go along. With that much of it done, I put forth the idea of us going shopping. We visited several stores and arranged for flowers to be delivered to the house the day before. When we reached home, I helped put some of the packages away, and in the process, I came across the one containing James Blake's uniform. I pulled it out of the closet.

"Rebecca, I would like to see Mary Blake get this uniform. Even after all she has done to us, I believe we should extend an olive branch. On my way to my office, I will stop by the post office and see if I can send it south. I still remember the address."

"Dear, I tried sending something to a store in Virginia, and it was rejected. There is still no established postal system in the South. Why don't you take it to the office, and when the time is right, you can send it to her?"

When I reached the office, I locked the package in the office closet. I found Jimmy hard at work. After briefing me on two major property cases he asked if he could head home. He put in long hours every day since my departure and deserved some time off. He left the office with a spring in his step and whistling a happy tune. I settled into my chair to review one of the property cases. After a few hours of work, I locked the office and started for home.

The evening was settling in over Galena as I picked up a newspaper and read that Joe Johnston could be nearing surrender to General Sherman. It was a relief to know most of the killing was ending. The sun departed, and there was a chill in the air, making me tighten my coat. When I reached the house, I found Judge Thatcher and Ida in the parlor with Rebecca.

"Thomas," Ida said. "We were hoping we could add something to the child's nursery, I crafted this quilt."

"Thank you so much, Ida. This is really beautiful."

"Yes," Rebecca chimed in, "I love it, and I think the baby will also."

"Thomas," the Judge said. "I have never told you this, but ever since you were a lad, I had dreams for you. I wanted you to be successful by becoming a lawyer or be in the military. You have fulfilled both of those prophecies with success, and I congratulate you. Now I have a new prophecy for your child. I wish the child to follow in your courageous footsteps and become the best lawyer in the United States, possibly a Judge on the federal bench."

"Thank you for your kind words, Judge," I said. "Our child will grow, with your acknowledgment of courage, into whatever it may choose to be. God will decide the path."

History will mark the end of the war with Lee's surrender but a greater event was to reverberate around the world. Headlines that should have been reserved for the nearing of an end to conflict were covered with the assassination of President Abraham Lincoln. Feelings as mixed as those caused by the war gave way to people morning or expressing joy. Black bunting draped the stores and houses. National mourning went on for days and there was no comforting some. This war seemed to have tentacles that stretched well beyond the battlefield.

Despite the solemn news, plans for our ceremony seemed to be going smoothly, but I was not at ease. I had Rebecca and the upcoming birth of our child to worry about. My law practice seemed to be doing well, and the war was winding down. I went to bed, asking for God to guide me through a peace that was elusive. I couldn't seem to finish a case, and Jimmy did it for me. Rebecca was also worried, though I tried to keep up a good front. Rebecca suggested I stay home for a few days and rest, so I took her advice.

On day two of my supposed repose, I took sick and began running a fever. The doctor came to visit regularly and was not having success with my illness. He advised that I be placed in a hospital to get round the clock treatment. Being a former Colonel in the military did have its advantages and despite my objection, room was made for me. Rebecca stayed by my side despite her discomfort with the baby. I lapsed in and out of consciousness all during the next day. During one of the conscious times, I told her to go home and get some rest. When I next awoke, she had taken my advice, and I was alone. I lay on the sweat-soaked sheet and closed my eyes. I was praying to God to deliver me from this illness when I heard a familiar voice.

"Say there, Colonel, Silas here, I has some water here if you want it."

My heart leaped.

"Silas you never cease to amaze me, how in the world?"

"We all made that journey, thanks to you. You got us here, and I is working here now. I found a safe place for my wife an children. That Judge fellow, he help us fine some land an a house with his bank. We is a free family because of you. I heard you was in this room, so I come to see you right off. You see Colonel, God was right with you all the time."

Two other staff came into the room, and Silas easily lifted me up while they changed the sheets on my bed. He gently placed me back on the bed and left the room with the other staff. I don't know if it was God that helped me get better, knowing Silas was around to see to it or a little of both. Regardless, I began to recover.

The next day Rebecca left my side for some lunch, and I asked to see Silas.

"Silas, I am going to have a wedding ceremony in about two weeks, and I was wondering if you would be so kind as to come. I would really like to have you at the ceremony."

"Colonel, I surely would, but you know how times is. There is some here in Galena don't take to kindly to me or my family."

"Silas . . . let me calm your fears. If there is anything to prevent you from coming, I will take care of it." He looked at me, and tears formed in his eyes.

"No one ever ask me nothing like that. I surely would like to if you can make it happen."

"Where is your family now?" I asked.

"We is just three miles up to the north on the Galena River."

"I will make arrangements for everything. The day is Saturday the 13th of May at 9:00 in the morning. It is at the First Presbyterian Church in Galena. I will send a carriage to pick up you and your family for the wedding."

Silas looked away for a moment and then spoke,

"We got nothing good to wear to a fancy weddin."

"I will take care of that too. I will have my partner Jimmy Miller call on you and take you and your family to get new clothes."

He smiled a big, warm, tender smile walked out of the room. I didn't want to forget to tell the judge how grateful I was for him helping Silas. I supposed it was his connection with the people of the Underground Railroad that brought them together.

I was to be discharged on the morrow, and Rebecca thought it best I should go to the judge's house to recuperate. This served a twofold purpose. It gave Rebecca a peaceful retreat on Dodge Street, and she didn't have to listen to me complain about not helping. The ceremony was now a little more than one week away. I was mentally running through all the things needing to be done while physically convalescing. My in-laws were a great help by bringing me things to do. Rebecca mailed two invitations, one to George and the other to General Halleck. I signed and put a personal note on each of them. I suggested all gifts be taken to the house on Dodge Street. We ended up sending out twenty-five invitations. Most would be hand-delivered by my bandana boys. This included a special invitation to the Grants. I helped sort and clean vases for the flowers. Gradually I regained my strength by eating lots of vegetable soup and praying.

"Judge, I need to confide in you. That black man named Silas, he saved my life twice, once on the battlefield, and again after being overtaken by bandits in Virginia. I owe Silas a great debt I can never repay.

I thank you for helping him and his family. Can you tell me about his family once they reached Galena?"

"It was a difficult time for them when they arrived. They had nowhere to go and knew no one. I found there situation most intolerable. When I met Silas, I saw something in him telling me he was an honest man who only needed someone to care. I authorized the bank to give him a loan for his house, and I found him a job at the hospital. He began paying back the loan and taking care of his family. He has borne out my original feelings toward him. Finding out you two had a relationship has only affirmed my decision. Thomas, I promise you Silas and his family won't have to worry about their house. I will authorize the bank to pay off their mortgage and assume the debt myself. I can easily pay it off."

By the end of the week, I was feeling much better and able to be up and around. Rebecca and I met with Reverend Strong to rehearse our vows. We decided to use our current rings as they were now part of us and our life together. Rebecca couldn't wear the traditional wedding dress belonging to her mother because of the baby. She wanted me to wear my army dress uniform as the army had taken up so much of my life to this date.

"My full-dress uniform?" I exclaimed.

"Yes," she said. "You look so dashing in your uniform, and it would be a shame to pack it away and not wear it again."

"But you wanted me out of the army many times. I thought it might have painful memories for you."

"No, it is meaningful because you respect the army, have fought for your country, and risked your life for it. You need to wear it as a symbol to me, our guests, and our child."

"Okay, I will wear it on one condition."

"What's that?"

"That you don't go into labor during the service."

It felt good to be back in our little house on Dodge Street. We prayed together that evening, and I asked God to forgive my sins and help me be a good father to our baby. Rebecca prayed our baby would be healthy, and God would grant the child His favor.

I awoke at about three in the morning with a start. Slipping out of bed so as not to disturb Rebecca, I went to the window seat. The moon shown gloriously, and the clouds drifted as gray shadows across its face. I could have died that day at Bull Run, and none of the rest of my life would have taken place. I sat in the window seat, closed my eyes, and asked God why? The moonlight was bright enough to cause shadows under my eyelids. These shadows seemed to become characters . . . like the characters in my life. Perhaps it was God trying to tell me something, so I sat quietly and listened. I heard nothing but Rebecca's soft breathing. I tried harder and fell deep into a state of meditation. It was not long before something came to me from within.

"Thomas . . . the war was of man, and your part was well lived. Rejoice in your being."

It was not long before morning light was pouring through the windows. I was wondering if it was all a dream. I confided in Rebecca, and she responded, "Thomas, God was speaking to you, and you needed to listen. It is not for us to wonder why, but to take on the responsibility God has for us. You need to rejoice. You are here for me, and for our child."

"You know, you are right. It is a chance to take stalk of what life has given me. I feel the baby move in your body, and God gives life anew. It is a great joy to be able to know there is life inside that would soon become our child. I have the feeling Bull Run will haunt me no more."

I kept going to the office on occasion to get caught up on work. I would need to pay Jimmy more for covering my absence as my time was occupied in many directions. One morning I was busy looking over some land grants, and a stranger came into the office. At first glance, he seemed to be of an ordinary sort. He was tall, in his mid-40s, with dark black hair, a beard, and moustache, brown suit, and well-worn black boots.

"Sur, I assume I have the pleasure of addressin' Mista Sawyer?" he said

"Yes, I am Mr. Sawyer, and who might you be?"

"Dexter Andrew Jackson the third, Attorney," he replied, "I have tracked you down, sir, at the request of one Mary Blake. You see, sur, she asked me to deliver this letter to you in the hopes you would better understand her situation."

*April 18, 1865*
*Dear Mr. Sawyer:*

*I have engaged Mr. Jackson to let you know of the passing of a certain Mr. T. who expired on our property and was buried on April 10th nearby. As a consequence of his death, I have come into a small sum of additional funds. I was wondering if you would*

*be so kind as to return my stepbrother's uniform. Mr. Jackson will see it is delivered here. James has returned to the plantation, and we have discussed your visit in our home while James was held in Union prisons. He has told me of your actions and regards these as a consequence of war. He does not bear any hard feelings against you after the reading of Father's will. I have copied the most important part for you.*

*"I Jesse Blake do hereby give all lands and property I own to be divided amongst my children. This would include my twin sons from my first wife, Millie Toliver Blake, who were separated at birth and the rest of my children born to Martha Moyer Blake. This property will be divided as follows."*

*Jesse goes on in the will, but you can see from this statement it is likely you are the other twin born to Millie Toliver, and you are his lost son. With times as hard as they are, there will be no money to share with you, only gratitude for saving James.*

*Mary Blake*

I sat for a moment, stunned at what I just read. I didn't really know how to take this. We lived completely separate lives, and I had no knowledge he even existed. I was raised by my aunt, but she never said anything about my mother having twins. I quickly pulled the package containing James' uniform out and gave it to Mr. Jackson.

"Please," I said, struggling for words. "See that this package is returned to her with haste and protection. I trust you will do so?"

"I will, indeed, sir." He smiled.

I sat for a long time and just thought about the possibilities. After regaining my composure, I locked the office and rushed home to show Rebecca the letter. We stood holding each other in stunned silence.

"How are you feeling now?" she said.

"I will pray about the situation and place it in God's capable hands. That is all I know to do for now."

The evening settled down, and Rebecca kept exclaiming that the baby kicked her.

"I think we know where the additional funds in the letter came from, but I can't speculate on how it happened. It probably involved killing, and I didn't want to be part of any more killing. It was enough to know James was back at his home, his uniform was on its way back to the family, and one hired assassin was no longer around."

The night before the ceremony, I was somewhat nervous. Perhaps it was because we were to perform this ceremony in front of family and friends. Perhaps it was the telegram from George saying he was delayed. The gifts began to arrive and ranged from new kettles and dishes to baby diapers. We laughed at the diapers, and both of us agreed it was the thought that counts. Rebecca recorded everything in our gift registry.

"Rebecca, are you feeling all right?"

"Yes, Judge, thank you for asking."

"We need to go upstairs and make some adjustments to the dress," Ida said. "It looks like you have grown another half inch since we last fitted you."

It was a beautiful pale blue dress that Ida and some members of the church made for her. It had a high lace collar with a full silk skirt and lace veil with a coronet of flowers. She was, in a word, beautiful. While the adjustments were being made to her gown, I went upstairs and pulled out my dress uniform and tried it on. Everything seemed to be in order, so I quickly changed back into my clothes. We retired that night as we always did by saying our prayers and asking God's blessing on us and our family.

When the night gave way to morning, there was a flurry of activity at our house. I made breakfast, and Rebecca came downstairs, not feeling so well. She drank just a glass of water and ate an apple. I put her dress in the carriage the Thatcher's provided and went back to make sure she was able to continue. We climbed aboard the carriage and headed for the church. On the way, I spotted George coming down the street.

"George, I don't know if I should hug you or smack you in the head. You made it here just in time."

"Sorry, Colonel, I had a rough time. The train I was aboard suffered an engine break down and I was delayed until a replacement was brought in. Besides, I knew you wouldn't get married without me."

"Oh, you did, did you? Well, what makes you think we wouldn't," I said.

"We have been through too much together. Besides, you will need someone to prop you up during the ceremony."

We laughed all the way to the church. It was only an hour now until the ceremony. Flowers adorned the entrance to the sanctuary and the chancel area. My trusted partner Jimmy and two of his friends were seating the guests. Rebecca and I entered through the back of the church, and she went to change into her gown. Ida was there to help her with this grand experiment in dressing. I just hoped the baby had not grown any since last night. Just then, Jimmy came into my room.

"All the guests are in place, Colonel."

I asked, "All the guests?"

"Yes, Colonel, all the guests."

The church was festooned with spring flowers on both sides of the center aisle. Reverend Strong gave me one of those warm, pastoral, similes. Silas, his wife, and their two children sat in the third row. Then the music changed to the wedding march, and Rebecca and her father came down the aisle. She looked lovely in her gown, and I was so proud to take her again as my wife. As a surprise for us, Ida arranged for the church choir to be there and sing one of our favorite hymns, "Abide with Me." All too soon, the hymn was over, and the minister's pronouncement was concluded. We kissed, and it seemed as though everyone else just disappeared for a glorious moment. God truly blessed the ceremony. The guests stood, and we walked but a few steps when I halted Rebecca and turned to Silas. Loudly enough for those in attendance to hear, I made a proclamation.

"Mrs. Sawyer, George, I would like you to meet Silas. This man single-handedly rescued me from death, twice, and nursed me back to health. He is someone truly to be admired as a man of good character and a servant of God."

Some in the congregation were taken aback, but both George and Rebecca greeted him and his family warmly. We turned to exit the church, and I whispered to Jimmy,

"Get Silas and his family out of the church and be sure they are safe, will you?"

"Yes, sir, I certainly will."

We went to the front of the church and greeted our guests. George waited faithfully by my side until the last guests departed. Our house was filled with well-wishers when we arrived. We celebrated with punch, cookies, and a persimmon wedding cake. It was Rebecca's idea because her grandmother always loved the persimmon trees in their back yard. Rebecca only lasted another hour until she had to lie down and rest. By 3:00 in the afternoon, the party wound down, and only George and I remained.

"Well, George, I want to thank you for taking the time out of your schedule to return to Galena for our ceremony."

"It was indeed a pleasure. Besides, I like Galena. I imagine General Grant will come back here now that his war days are closing down. Miss Henry has turned down my proposal. If railroading gets to be too much, I will move to Galena. I can't think of better company than Rebecca and yourself."

"Say, George, what is your real name?"

"It's George, he said calmly . . . it's George Francis McElhenney."

There was a short silence, and we both laughed.

"No," George said. "That's me God-given name. You don't know how long it took for me to lose the accent."

"Well, it has been quite a specular day. George, I think of you as family now, and I would be remiss if I didn't say you may stay with us for as long as you like."

"Thank you, Thomas. I do feel exhausted from the trip. I believe I will turn in. No special fuss for me."

Breakfast was served, and this time, it was Rebecca who was famished. We all sat down together to talk and enjoy the pleasantries.

"I want you to know, Thomas," George began, "I really have come to think of you both as family. However, I don't want to overstay my welcome, so I will be leaving tomorrow. I need to get back to my railroad job and earn a living."

"I believe the feeling is mutual George, would you not agree, Rebecca?"

"Absolutely," she said. "You kept my husband alive, and he kept you alive. I don't think there can be a much tighter bond. But we will be sorry to see you leave so soon."

"I know my stay has been short, but I promise you I will be back in the fall of the year to stay. I have asked Judge Thatcher to look for some property for me near Galena. I have enough saved that I can retire here."

George and I played chess, and Rebecca continued reading the latest book on raising children. Every so often, she would chuckle and make comments under her breath like "nonsense" or "ridiculous." As it got on toward evening, we all bid each other good night. "What time will you be leaving in the morning?" I asked.

"I have a ticket for an 8:00 train to Indianapolis."

"Very good, I will see you to the station."

As we turned in, I said to Rebecca, "You know I finally found out what George's real name was and it only took five years."

She smiled and said, "Oh, you mean George Francis McElhenny? He told me when he was here looking for you."

"I love you," I said.

Steam billowed from the locomotive as we arrived at the train station.

"I will return," he said. "I promise."

With hugs from Rebecca and me, he boarded the train. Rebecca and I began a leisurely walk back to our house. It was a lovely day with a slight breeze wafting through the trees, making it seem like angel's wings were rustling them. We reached the house and sat down in the parlor to recount the ceremony. Rebecca pulled out the gift book and went over the record of each gift.

"Thomas, I noticed something here," she said.

"What's that?"

"There is a gift here from each of our wedding guests, but nothing from George."

"That's odd," I said. "I would have thought . . . well, maybe he just didn't have time to pick something up. I am sure we will hear from him later."

I went on to the office to get some work done and found Jimmy already there. I began to apologize when he interrupted me,

"It's okay, Colonel, I don't mind doing it. Besides, I did the accounting, and we are becoming a very successful firm. Our profits have doubled from our re-opening, and we have several new clients. I expect it will continue to grow. Here is the latest list of cases I have filed at the courthouse. You can take this one at 2:00 this afternoon. Our client has sued the government to get claims for beef cattle as they were furnished to the Union troops without consent. He has evidence the cattle were taken by Union troops, but the government refuses to pay."

As Jimmy and I walked to the courthouse, I thought about how perfect my life was now. I was about to become a father and Rebecca, a wonderful mother. After the bench heard the evidence we presented, the judge sided with us and proceeded to award our client his fair dues. Jimmy and I made our way out of the courthouse. When I walked in the door of our house on Dodge Street, Rebecca was there to greet me.

"Well," she said. "It seems George didn't forget us after all."

"What do you mean?"

"Just take a look on the mantle."

There was a small black box with a note attached. It read;

Colonel Tom's a mighty man
His wife's a strong woman, too
Death was cheated as they ran
Now their days are never blue

When the baby child is born
The fireside hearth will exclaim
True tales to have only sworn
If you have an honest aim

I opened the box, and inside was a frame with a background of black velvet. A small note in one corner read: "Much love, George." Mounted on it were two objects, a crushed button from a Confederate officer's uniform and a twenty-dollar gold piece.